RETURN TO
THE SCENE

Carmella Gates

ISBN 978-1-937862-87-9

Library of Congress Control Number 2015931968

This book was published by BookCrafters, Parker, Colorado.
http://bookcrafters.net
bookcrafters@comcast.net

This book may be ordered from
www.bookcrafters.net and other online bookstores.

This book is dedicated to the two most important people in my world—my husband Randy and my daughter Meghan. Thanks for your support. I love you.

Remembrance of things past is not necessarily remembrance of things as they were . . .

— Marcel Proust

CHAPTER ONE
OUR RETURN

Nostalgia: n. A bittersweet longing for things, persons, places or situations of the past
—*The American Heritage College Dictionary*

Nostalgia: n. Wistfulness; sentimental recollection
—*Word Dictionary*

Nostalgia is highly overrated! And the older we get, as the serotonin levels in our brains decrease, the more we forget the bitter memories and remember the sweet times. Even the most horrendous events can be blocked from our minds. This phenomenon has probably evolved in human beings for our self-preservation. We don't need a bunch of angry old people running around crazy or filling up mental wards. But at the same time, when those painful memories do come to the surface of our consciousness, they can really knock our socks off.

For several months, I had been planning a trip with my husband Dan from our home in Colorado to the old vegetable farm in central Massachusetts where I grew up. Remembering a few happy moments of childhood, which fostered warm Crayola-colored scenes, presented in Technicolor and slow motion and surrounded by a light golden haze; I had totally blocked the bitter memories that came flooding back with a vengeance as soon as we turned onto the dirt-packed driveway of the farm. I could practically feel the synapses going off in my brain, crackling like lightning as they zapped from one to another, and it was overwhelming, to say the least.

Had I really been nostalgic about this place? Had I actually been looking forward to coming back here? What the hell was I thinking? I was returning to the place I fervently hated when I was a kid! Farming was most assuredly not a lifestyle I remembered fondly. And in my mind, I had downplayed the pain that could come from this trip. The main reason we were here was to clear out all the bric-a-brac of my family's three generations on the old homestead and prepare the place to be sold. As if that could be a fun, joyous event!

After my mother died a year ago, and months of legal haggling and rigmarole, sort of by process of elimination, I had inherited the farm. By process of elimination, I mean my brothers didn't want it either! Go figure. I loved my mother dearly; she was my major solace growing up. And after a year, I was reaching a plateau in my mourning, having gone from full body, overwhelming pain to more of an ongoing dull ache. I still thought of her every day, but now the difficult times occurred mostly when certain things reminded me of her, and the pain was brief and not as sharp. If I went to antique stores and saw utensils like she had used for cooking, or maybe smelled fresh donuts like she used to make in the fall, or especially when I make her homemade Italian pasta sauce, the best in the whole world, then I would feel the ache, and sometimes a few tears would moisten my eyes.

I guess I knew that getting the contents of the house and other buildings, including farm equipment and paraphernalia and yes, lots of junk, sorted and the property ready to sell would dredge up old memories. I thought it might even be kind of a catharsis, and give some closure to that period of my life. Now returning to this place where everywhere I looked, everything I touched, brought back memories of my family and the farm, filled me with dread and a sense of fatigue that encompassed my whole being. I wasn't sure I was going to be able to do this without constantly falling apart or worse, being filled with unresolved and probably unresolvable anger.

Most of the buildings and their contents that we needed to sort through dated back even before my grandparents bought the farm in 1931. The additional accumulation from our three generations had resulted in all the buildings being full, literally to the rafters. Nothing was ever thrown away, nothing. If something ever left the farm, it was probably organic and rotted away, but its removal or demise was not intentional on the part of my family. Living through the Great Depression as my parents and grandparents did meant you kept everything. You couldn't take the chance of getting rid of something because you might need it again someday. Perhaps things got outdated or broken but might still be good for parts, or no one else wanted them, so they just got stored and eventually forgotten, as more stuff was put on top of more stuff.

Believe me, a farm has lots of places to store things—barns, garages, greenhouses, and the huge old farmhouse, as well as 100 acres of land. I knew it was going to be a monumental, backbreaking task, but my nostalgic state of mind had me believing we would discover family heirlooms and antique treasures. So many times when I engage in my passion of prowling antique stores and estate sales, I see things that I remember seeing on the farm when I was a kid. It might be butter churns, milk cans, old farm machine parts, metal toys, baby carriages or highchairs, or other items from my parents' younger years. As I get older, the furniture, dishes, appliances and toys that I grew with in the late 50s are becoming very popular in the vintage market, reminding me not only of my childhood, but that I'm becoming an antique myself! If I see an old pedal car, I practically salivate with longing for the red racer convertible we had as kids.

I had hoped this trip would be a nice, leisurely adventure, and I thought I was emotionally ready for it, but as we arrived at the farm, I had my doubts. At least there was no deadline to accomplish this task. I had recently retired from teaching kids with special needs, and Dan had all but retired from his website design business. We weren't rich, but we had planned well financially, and the money from the sale of the 100-acre farm and its contents would take care of us quite nicely. It would allow us to travel extensively and live quite comfortably, while still leaving an inheritance for our kids. That was the big plan. Believe me, the thought of keeping the old place had never, ever in a zillion eons crossed my mind! We would do the work and leave in a cloud of dust.

"Are you all right, Lily? You look pretty tense." Dan was always aware to the slightest change in my feelings. He always said he could "read me like a book," which irritated the hell out of me but was very true. I liked to imagine I was somewhat mysterious.

"I'll be fine. I guess the sight of the old place just hit me with all kinds of memories there for a minute. Just thinking of all we have to do to get this place ready to sell! We have a lot of hard work ahead of us, old man."

"Who are you calling old man? You know, the homestead doesn't look so bad. The caretaker did a great job fixing up the buildings and painting them like you asked. It sure looks a lot less decrepit than the last time we were here."

Mom had a hard time keeping up with everything after Dad died. Ten years without repairs and basic upkeep were hard on these already tired buildings. I think the place has been getting progressively more rundown for as long as I remember. Lack of money, time, or incentive; I'm not sure which, but when things other than farm equipment broke or fell apart, they just never got fixed. If a barn board fell off, it stayed off. If a window broke anywhere but the house, it stayed broken. It was practically a way of life. I'm not sure why Mom even tried to keep this place going. She could have sold it and had a comfortable last few years.

I guess it's not easy giving up something that has consumed almost every minute of your entire life. Especially when you've put your blood, sweat and tears into it. They held on through the Depression, World War II, while their kids were growing up; most of their lives went into this farm. Or maybe she just wanted to leave all the hard work of cleaning out and selling the place to me! Mom was never good about getting rid of stuff, and she could be very passive aggressive about emotional issues or any tasks she didn't want to deal with. She would just ignore them.

"Paint covers up lots of flaws, doesn't it?" I responded. "I bet you will be amazed at all the stuff we find, some nice things, but also lots and lots of junk--including all of our old school stuff. You cannot look at my elementary school pictures. They are gross! On the other hand, whoever finds my first grade report card gets to choose pizza toppings for two months, okay?"

"Deal. I'm anxious to look at all your dad's tools. He must have had two of every woodworking and machine tool ever made! He always told me you could build anything if you had the right tool. And I'm sure your mom kept all of them. I picture myself building all kinds of things in my retirement years, just like your dad did. Hey, do you remember that little red wagon he built for Meghan when she was little? It was amazing! She made us save it for when she has kids someday."

"Remember trying to package it and get it shipped back to Colorado? Meghan was determined to take it home with us. There was no way she would leave it at the farm to play with when we visited. But it was well worth the effort. She got hours and hours of enjoyment out of that wagon! That was a very special gift.

"Despite the lack of repairs around here, Dad was a gifted carpenter. He was great at designing and building all kinds of things, but fixing them was not his idea of fun. I didn't realize until I married you that car radios, latches, cabinets, screen doors, whatever, could actually be repaired; they didn't have to be left broken."

My father had actually studied to be a master carpenter at the old Worcester Trade School, but he had to quit school and take care of this place and my grandmother after my grandfather died. Not long after my grandparents bought the property, my grandfather contracted tetanus from stepping on a rusted spike that went right through his foot. He got blood poisoning, and he passed away in less than a week. They had bought the property because of the huge house that would be a perfect size for them and their eight children. My grandfather had also been a carpenter, but the Depression made finding work difficult. No one could afford to build or remodel. My grandparents hoped to eventually build houses on the land and sell them, providing work for him and income to take care of their large family. Grandpa's death put an end to that plan.

Of course everyone in our large Italian family contributed ideas for what was the best thing to do for Grammy and the land, many of which were impossible because of the Depression, or because they were dumb ideas to begin with. My two uncles were the ones who decided the place should be turned into a farm. They argued that the property wouldn't sell at that time, so they might as well work the land and at least provide the family with food. My uncles were long on bluster but short on the brainpower and the brawn needed to run a produce farm. The popular stereotype of the dumb, lazy farmer is far from the truth. Farming requires a great deal of knowledge and constant physical work. So my uncles tried farming and bungled the job, and after two years of minimal crops and no profit, it fell to my father, the youngest, to fix the situation.

Dad never wanted to be a farmer, but he had to take over from my uncles because someone needed to help the family survive the Depression. Italians felt that filing bankruptcy was the ultimate failure, and my father was determined not to bring that shame on the family. He had worked on another uncle's farm for several summers, so he quit school and became a farmer, just like that.

"I suppose everyone has to deal with doing things they should do instead of what they want to do at times, but I can't imagine having to do something you never intended or wanted to do for your entire adult life," I thought out loud.

"So woodworking became a hobby, or maybe a practicality, instead of a profession? Well, he certainly was a good farmer and a good carpenter. I always admired your dad. He was a smart, hard-working man. He worked hard to take care of this place and his family and never complained," said Dan.

"Oh, he sure could get angry and yell sometimes, though! Especially when we didn't work as hard or as fast as he thought we should. I guess now I can see why he resented us kids complaining about farm work. He had to give up all his dreams, so he probably felt we damn well better appreciate it and do our part. Well, shall we go in? The journey begins!"

We unloaded our suitcases and entered the 250-year-old home of my childhood, and believe me, it creaked and groaned with every one of those years! When I tell people I grew up in a farmhouse that dates back to mid-1700s, they are shocked. First of all, no one has ever heard of a farm in densely populated, industrial Massachusetts. Then they picture a majestic manor house, sort of like the ones at nearby Sturbridge Village, with wide floorboards and lots of rooms built for every little purpose, sweeping staircases, huge high-ceilinged guest rooms and a long forgotten attic bursting at the seams with trunks and chests of drawers crammed with all sorts of wonders, antique furniture and other treasures.

Well, our house had a lot of those things, but they had never been properly maintained, so the wide floorboards were nicked and scratched and had spaces between them where the wood had worn, allowing dust to rise up from the old coal furnace in the basement. We used to dust and vacuum every single day, but dust and dirt from the furnace and soil tracked in from the farm made it a losing battle. Once Grammy's immediate family had married and moved out, my father renovated the home, if I can use that euphemism, into three apartments, one for my grandmother, one for my newly-married parents, and one to rent out to bring in much-needed income.

After my grandmother died, in a fit of remodeling, my parents removed all the brass and a few crystal chandeliers and replaced them with ugly 1950s lighting fixtures. They covered up the fireplaces with cheap, faux wood paneling and replaced all the glass doorknobs with modern metal ones. Even the claw-foot tub was shown no mercy. Out it went, replaced by a plastic tub and shower insert. My mother loved how modern it all looked. I thought it was pretty awful, but my mom firmly believed that having old things in your house meant you were poor. She hated antiques or anything old! On the other hand, her Depression mentality would never allow her to throw things away, so she either covered them up or moved them someplace for storage. The fun part would be finding all those treasures!

My parents never had enough money to remodel everything, so our house was eclectic before eclectic was chic. The ancient Oriental rug in the living room was so threadbare you could see the floor through it in spots. And here and there were old pieces of furniture that had belonged to Grandma, so in good conscience, or because no one dared, they just couldn't be removed to the outer buildings. So by and large, it was probably the attic, garage and the barn where we would find and sort the detritus of my family's lives.

We unpacked our stuff in the "guest" room, formerly my childhood room. It still had the once bright yellow wallpaper with white flowers, now faded with age to a dusty pastel color. The room held a hand-me-down double bed and dresser, and a kidney-shaped vanity table and mirror bordered with a layered organza skirt with fluffy ruffles on the top and bottom. My aunt had made the skirt and given the vanity to me when I turned twelve. It was one of my favorite possessions. I can remember my mother starching and ironing those layers of fabric. It was not only my make-up table, it was my desk to do homework, and especially the place where I could look in the mirror and imagine a world away from the farm. Now the skirt was dusty and had lost its crispness, but I still loved this very personal piece of furniture. It was probably the most feminine thing I had ever owned.

We chose to sleep in this room because I wasn't quite ready to sleep in my parents' larger bedroom; somehow that just didn't seem appropriate. So we stuffed our clothes into the tiny closet and dresser drawers that had a few missing handles and no drawer stops, causing everything to fall out as soon as we filled them. Another problem of old houses is that there is very little closet space. We kept bumping into each other as we unpacked, and saying, "Excuse me," "Sorry," until we felt we were in a slapstick comedy. We finally just laughed about the whole thing. We were used to a huge walk-in closet and built-in drawers back home.

"Hey, Lily, I'm really beat after traveling a few days just to get here. How about you finish unpacking while I run to the Clam Shack and get us some of their great fried clams for dinner? Then we can take it easy for the evening and get a fresh start on all this tomorrow."

"Dan, dear husband and love of my life, that is the best idea you have had in a very long time! When you return, the room will be in order, your darling wife will be refreshed, and the wine that sweet caretaker kindly left us along with some groceries will be served in a fancy goblet . . . and thank you."

"For what? A few fried clams? In my day, we would have called that a cheap date."

"Well, you haven't seen the current price of clams, but I mean much more than that. Thank you for putting up with all my moods over the last year, and for making me feel we are in this together."

"We are in this together. You and me, kid! And I do want those tools. I'm out of here. Be back shortly."

Dan kissed me quickly and flew out the door. That man had more energy than a jackrabbit! I knew he had enough energy to clear out a whole building, even after traveling all day, but in times of stress, he was always sensitive to my needs. Dan could be obtuse like most men a lot of the time, but he was good at picking up on nuances. He not only figured out what I was feeling, often before I did, but he would suggest a solution in a way that made it sound as if it was meeting both of our needs without putting me down or telling me what to do. He would never make me feel uncomfortable or beholding. This was one of the many reasons I had loved him for over thirty years, and I hoped I would live long enough to love him for thirty more.

When Dan returned, everything was in order, and we sat down to wine and moist, tender, mouthwatering fried clams that you can only get in New England. My spirits were greatly improved. A good night's sleep and I would be ready to take on everything! Later, as we contentedly lay in bed, we started making plans.

"I think we should tackle one building at a time. Sort everything into trash, things to sell, and things to keep," said Dan, the organizer.

"Well, there won't be much in that last pile. Maybe some of my mom's jewelry, her recipe box, and stuff like that, but everything else can go to the dump or the flea market."

"What, Liliana, the Archduchess of Antiques, the Viscountess of Vintage, the Princess of Primitives, doesn't want to keep any of the truly tantalizing treasure trove we find? I don't believe it! If we do find some really cool pieces though, we might want to get an antique dealer in here to appraise or maybe buy them."

"Your alliteration is more like a tongue twister. Besides, I doubt there will be much of value. But who knows. What building should we start with? I think the house. That way we can get out all the junk, fix stuff and get it staged to sell."

"Lily, dear, why did you ask me what I thought if you had already made up your mind?"

"I guess I hadn't really decided until the very second I asked. Do you think it's a good plan?"

"That I do. Now let's get a good night's sleep so we can be fresh and ready for a full day of work tomorrow. Good night, Hon. Love you."

"Love you, too. Good night, Dan."

CHAPTER TWO
THE ATTIC

I awoke the next morning to the heavenly aroma of fresh-brewed coffee. Had they finally gotten a Starbucks in this god-forsaken town? I washed my face, brushed my teeth and hair, threw on old clothes suitable for cleaning out ancient ruins, and headed to the kitchen to find Dan waiting with two enormous cups of coffee and a pastry bag.

"Good morning, Sunshine! While you were sleeping in, I went out and got us breakfast, and before you ask, no I couldn't find a Starbucks. But remember, this is Massachusetts, the state with a Dunkin' Donuts on every street corner, sometimes directly across the street from each other, so I went to one of those."

All this chattering came from Dan, my bright-eyed and so very obnoxious morning person. It took all I could manage not to scream that I was still half-sleep, so hush up!

"At this point, I will drink anything labeled coffee. What's in the bag?"

"Why, world famous Dunkin' Donuts, of course. I got you the chocolate glazed you adore, and chocolate frosted for me. I do love their donuts."

"Me, too," I responded with my mouth full. "I hope you got me two. We need lots of nourishment for all the work ahead of us."

"At your service, my lady, although nourishment is questionable when one is speaking of donuts. Hey, I was looking at the house as I pulled back into the driveway, and I really paid attention to the architecture for the first time. The two-story central portion of the place reminds me of a New England saltbox. And the one-story east side, where we are staying, and the ell on the other side both look like additions to the original."

"I think you're right. This place used to be an inn a long, long time ago. The ell part was the tavern. Supposedly a man was shot to death in the tavern in the late 1800s."

"Seriously? You never told me that before," exclaimed Dan. "Why was he shot?"

"Who knows? Probably one of the usual things men fought about—land, love, or the Lord. But I'm betting it was about a woman."

"When did all this happen?"

"I'm not totally sure. You have to remember that I learned most of the history of this place from elderly people who stopped at the vegetable stand in the summer. One man told me that the saltbox part of the house was built around 1760, and was originally the single-family home and farm of a family named Wilcox. Then in the mid-1800s, after several generations, the only Wilcox heirs still living were a lawyer brother and a sickly sister who had no interest in operating the farm. They sold the place to a family by the name of Harrington who built on the additions and turned it into an inn. They also added a wide wraparound porch that surrounded the front and ell side of the house. My grandmother called it the piazza because it was so big and had columns. One of my earliest memories is of running back and forth on that porch from one end to the other when I was a little kid. It seemed to me like a massive racetrack."

"That must have added a lot of character to the house. It would have looked much more stately and elegant. What happened to it?" asked Dan.

"Like everything else around here, it wasn't properly maintained. The wood rotted away in places. My father and his workers removed it so no one could get hurt. They tore down my grandma's pantry at the same time and made that god-awful concrete slab they called a porch. The place went from charming to downright ugly!

"This property is right on the old Boston Post Road, which back in the 1800s was the main east-west route from Boston to Springfield and on to New York. Stagecoaches passed here almost daily, as well as the postal service. It was a great location for an inn at that time. A small portion of the land was used for crops and some livestock for the inn. The rest of the land became a golf course."

"A golf course? Really?"

"At least that's what I was told. We used to find lots of old golf balls in the fields when my dad plowed each spring, so I think there was truth in that."

"So what happened to the inn?"

"Well, from what my vegetable stand historians told me, in the early 1900s, as cars became more popular and the use of stage coaches died out, as well as new roads were built, there were fewer overnight guests who stayed at the inn. The Harrington family had to depend more and more on the income from the tavern. Then Prohibition came along in the 20s, and they struggled to just hold on."

Dan pondered this tidbit of history and then asked, "Why didn't they just make hooch way back in the woods? I can't believe a few federal laws would keep my hearty Irish countrymen from getting their liquor! They could have set up a big still and made enough liquor for themselves, the tavern, and probably a few other nearby establishments! Just think. Your house could have once been a speakeasy!"

"Don't laugh. You may be close to the truth. My dad told me stories he had heard about The Harrington Inn during Prohibition. They got whisky from Canada, smuggled in in the middle of the night by bootleggers. They supposedly also made some of their own liquor and mixed it with the Canadian whisky to increase their profits."

"Can you picture huge bouncers wearing baggy suits with wide lapels and black shirts and ties? And white spats; they surely had white spats! I bet they wore fedoras low on their foreheads so their faces were partially hidden. And they would have had shoulder holsters with pearl-handled pistols under their jackets, just in case the police showed up, or worse--the Revenue Man!"

"Dan, I think you've watched "The Untouchables" too many times.

This is still the country here, not Chicago. However, there is an old tale about a Revenue Man. But we have work to do; maybe I should tell you later."

"Spill it, woman, or I'll eat your second donut! You can't leave this story hanging!"

"Oh okay, I always knew you were a sap for a good story! But then we have to get to work. From what my dad said, the powers that be did periodically check out the place, but the Harringtons were able to buy them off. Corruption was common back then, as you know from the movies. Anyway, there was one Revenue Man named Roy Abernathy who could not be bribed. He would show up at all times of the day and night, trying to find liquor on the premises. He even scoured the fields and woods for a still or storage place for whisky barrels, but he could never find anything. He was said to have the determination and drive of an Eliot Ness, but the demeanor of a Casper Milquetoast."

"You know, you are quite a gifted storyteller, Lily!"

"Thank you, but that won't get you out of work. Anyway, Abernathy drove the Harringtons crazy. They had to be ready to hide everything at a moment's notice. He would sometimes show up at noon, have lunch at the inn, check things out and then leave. They would think they were done with him for a while, but then he would show up again that same night to start searching all over again. Well, one night, he had been hiding, staking out the place, when the bootleggers arrived. He had no back up, but he decided to take on these huge gorilla-like delivery guys, who were armed to the teeth with rifles and Tommy Guns, while he was all by himself with his little pistol. There was a gun battle, and that was the last of the Revenue Man."

"Are you serious? They killed him! Is that what really happened?"

"Well, that's the part of the story that is unknown to this day. Dad told me that the following morning the yard smelled like booze, and the Harringtons were busy cleaning up lots of glass and probably bullet casings on their driveway. But no one dared talk about anything that had happened. The Feds came and questioned the owners and their neighbors. They scoured the premises, but no evidence was ever found. The FBI finally gave up after a few months. After that, business continued as usual. As for Roy Abernathy, no one ever heard of him again. Neither he nor his body has ever been found. His fate, as they say, remains a mystery."

"That is amazing! Do you think it's all true?"

"Most of it anyway, because Dad was not one to spin a yarn, but he was pretty young when all of this happened, and I'm sure the story has been embellished over time. When we were kids, we would try to find the still they used and Roy Abernathy's grave. Along with 'Cowboys and Indians,' 'Finding the Revenue Man' was our favorite game. Our property includes the woods at the end of the fields up to the railroad tracks. We would spend hours in the woods looking for areas that seemed suspiciously like a grave, or parts of a still, not that we really knew what a still was or what one looked like. Then we would dig and dig to find evidence."

"Did you ever find anything?"

"No, just the residue of some old hobo campfires, tin cans, and the like. So we played hobo, too, making believe we were riding the rails."

"I'm surprised your parents let you play there. You could have gotten hurt handling that old rusty stuff, or going too close to the train tracks."

"I never said they let us play there. There were Boundary Rules. The woods were Boundary Rule Number 1—Do not go in the woods! But the trees and ferns grew so thick, we didn't have to go very far before we were totally hidden. With that and 100 acres of cultivated fields, the chances of getting caught were pretty slim. If we had gotten caught, I still wouldn't be able to sit down from the spanking I would have gotten!"

"And you would have deserved it. So how did your grandparents come to buy this place anyway?"

"From what I understand, the Harringtons held on to the business during the Prohibition years, but then came the Stock Market Crash of 1929, resulting in the Great Depression. Business dropped to nothing, and they just couldn't operate the inn or tavern any longer. They ended up selling out to my grandparents for a portion of what the property would have been worth before the Depression. A place with all these rooms was perfect for a family with eight kids, and that's how the Martelli family came to own it. Now, time to work."

I threw the paper cups and bag in the trash and wiped the table while Dan collected cardboard boxes, packaging tape, trash bags and a dolly.

"Shall we start in the attic and work down from there?" he asked.

"Sounds good to me. Put on this breath mask; it's sure to be dusty. Let's go for it!"

We climbed the stairs to the second floor apartment and looked around. There was an old chrome table and cushioned kitchen chairs from the 1950s, a little scratched up but serviceable, and a really old gas cook stove, but most of the place was empty. I opened the door to the attic, causing layers of dust to start swirling around. As we climbed a short flight of stairs, more dust blew about, and its scent was a combination of the musty smell of yellowed, aging paper, old clothes, mothballs and a slight mildew aroma. The air was hot and heavy with age and stagnant from disuse. Dan had to carefully walk in the dark to turn the switch on the one light bulb dangling from an early, insulated electrical wire in the center of the room. It threw off very little light, whether from low wattage or dust, I wasn't sure. But it was enough to see several cardboard boxes bursting at the seams. In the dim light I could also make out a few trunks, a coat rack, some small tables and chairs, an antique croquet set and who knew what else. Dan crossed the room to open the dormer window to let in some fresh air.

"We have to be very careful walking around up here. My parents said the floor wasn't very safe. That was Boundary Rule Number 2—Don't go in the attic."

"Now you tell me. The floor must be pretty strong to hold up all this stuff. This place is packed. We may be working up here for a week! Maybe we should wait until the kids get here this weekend to tackle this place and get all this stuff sorted."

"We're going to need the kids for the heavy lifting in the garage and barn. Besides the obvious stuff we can see, most of the boxes hold old ledgers and guest books from the Inn. We can sort those pretty quickly. But those trunks and boxes of old clothes and stuff are what I'm looking forward to going through."

"How do you know what's up here if you've never been in the attic?"

"I said I wasn't supposed to come up here, not that I didn't. After all, I had to make sure the Revenue Man's corpse wasn't hidden in this mess, didn't I? Most of the stuff up here was either from the inn or my grandparents. I never understood why they didn't get rid of the inn records before they piled their own things in the attic, but they didn't. I suggest we pull a few things at a time down the attic stairs to the apartment below and check them out there. The larger bedroom with more light and cleaner air will be a good place to sort."

"Good idea. Let's grab that old headboard over there and place it on the stairs. Then we can slide things down on it. That will be much easier than lifting everything, and will probably cause less damage to these already dilapidated boxes."

We angled the wooden headboard on a slant down the length of the stairs to serve as a ramp. Dan slid the boxes down as I caught them at the bottom of the stairs and moved them on the dolly to the old bedroom. The system worked well. It was faster than carrying them down the stairs and saved our backs as well as the boxes. After moving about fifteen of them, he joined me in the apartment.

"These are most of the old boxes filled with papers. Let's check them out."

"Remember, the name of the game is 'Trash Disposal.' We are getting rid of all this old stuff."

We each opened a box, and as I thought, they were filled with old ledgers from the Harrington Inn. They contained accounts of lumber, seed, tools, linens, and anything else bought for the operation of the inn, as well as accounts of income. Some boxes were mildewed, probably from a leak at one time in the old roof, and others were falling apart. The majority were yellowed and the paper brittle, but in decent condition.

"These are really interesting. Listen to this: 'Purchased: 5 lb. bag of corn seed, 1/8 lb. tomato seed, 2 hoes, 1 spade and a gallon crock of molasses . . . $2.00,'" Dan read.

"Here's one for a work horse, with saddle and feed for $5.00. And a hand plow for $2.45. Gotta love these prices. We can't read all of these, or we will never get done. How about if we find any from the Wilcox farm days, we keep one from the late 1700s or early 1800s, and an early one from the inn, probably around 1870 or so, and the latest one we find from the farm and the inn. We can read them as we hang out in the evenings. If we find anything interesting, we can give them to the Public Library or Historical Society."

"That sounds like a good idea, as long as we can keep all the inn's guest registers. Maybe George Washington slept here!" Dan agreed.

"If George Washington slept in every place that claimed he had slept there, he would have had to live to be 108 just to have enough nights to do all that sleeping," I retorted. "But I agree, it will be fun to look through the guest registers. Who knows, maybe we will at least find a few famous signatures to frame. Oh look, this is the register from 1862-64. That must be one of the earliest ones from the inn."

"I have one from 1868-1870. Let's put them in this new cardboard box."

It was difficult to stop ourselves from reading everything in every old box, but then again, we could only look at so many accounts of cows and chickens bought, costs for butchering hogs, and glasses and dishes bought for the tavern before but we finally got better at perusing and sorting.

"I didn't find anything that looked like a second set of books about bootlegging. Did you, Dan?"

"Not yet, but let's get the rest of the boxes."

Continuing our ramp system, we brought down five more boxes. The last two were made of cheap wood, and the papers were in such bad shape that they practically disintegrated on touch.

"It looks like the stuff in the wood crates goes back to the time when the Wilcox's farmed the property. I will try to save a few of the best, but these are so old they will probably fall apart on touch. If not, you could probably rub two pages together and start a bonfire."

"Dan, I think I've found something in this box. This ledger goes from 1922-25, and this one is 1926 and doesn't have an end date. I already have found inn ledgers for those years. The entries in these seem coded or something. Listen to this: DLM 5b at 24ca, 22c at 18ca. 6 b at 38ca, 30c at 16ca. I bet that the c means cases and b means barrels of whisky from this DLM. That might be a person or a company. The ca must mean cash. This stuff goes on and on with similar entries for purchases from several different initials. I think I found the second set of dirty books!"

"Fantastic! Those books deserve further scrutiny. Definitely add them to our special box. I think I'll read them tonight while I sip a nice, cold drink by the fireplace."

"There is no fireplace, remember; my parents covered them all with cheap paneling. I found a few other references to purchases of liquor, and one other book with inn expenses, which was also written in some kind of shorthand. To think these historical records were right above my head all those years I lived here, and I never knew it!"

Next we lowered several old trunks. Two of them had been a feast and nest for mice and were worthless, but we did find a few that were interesting. One in particular seemed to be the steamer trunk my grandmother must have used when she came over from Italy. After they got engaged in 1902, my grandfather came to America, and worked as a carpenter. Then he sent for my grandmother. When she arrived, they were married in America. I almost wept when we found what must have been her wedding gown. It had been carefully folded between layers and layers of tissue paper. The satin had yellowed, but the fine lace and seed pearls sewn to the bodice were still intact. It was a fairly simple design, with long sleeves, a fitted bodice and a full skirt, which made it all the more beautiful. The veil had not fared as well; much of the netting had disintegrated, but the headpiece, a seed pearl tiara was still in great shape. It was hard to picture that dear old lady, hunched over with age, as I remember her so well from my childhood, as a young, hopeful bride.

"Your grandmother must have been a big lady. Usually dresses from that time are diminutive."

"She was a big lady, not fat, but tall and big-boned. I remember her hands were huge. At least they seemed so to a little kid. She was pretty strong, too. In old pictures of her at the weddings of her numerous kids, she was as tall if not taller than the other ladies, and even some of the men."

"What else is in that trunk?"

"Some old embroidered linens, doilies and such. I wonder if this was part of her trousseau. And this framed picture . . . Oh my God! Look! It's their wedding picture. I have never, ever seen a picture of my grandfather before. I didn't think any existed. My family had very few photos taken back then. I guess they were too expensive. This is amazing!"

"Wow, he was a handsome dude, wasn't he? Even by today's standards. He looked a lot like your father, or rather your father looked like him. Same Martelli curly hair."

"He was nice-looking, wasn't he? And she looks so pretty, young and happy; so different than she did when I knew her. I have to keep this. This is my heritage."

"Of course you have to keep it. The kids will be thrilled to see it, too. We'll keep anything you want, Hon."

"Look Dan, here's their wedding license! 'Nicola Antonio Martelli wed Giana Isabella Noccia, June 23, 1904, St. Michael the Archangel Church, Worcester, Massachusetts.' I have goosebumps! This wedding picture and license are like evidence of their lives that I had been told about, but just sort of took for granted or couldn't really relate to, you know, but these make it so real. It makes them real. It's kind of a validation of their life before me. And look, this is Aunt Michelina's birth certificate, and here's Aunt Philomena's and . . . here's my dad's. It's my dad's birth certificate, Dan! Now I am going to cry. Gianni Nicola Martelli, January 27, 1916."

"Honey, that is amazing. That paper looks like parchment and look at the calligraphy. You have to keep all of these things. So your grandparents lived in this area even before they bought the farm?"

"Yes, when my grandparents were first married, they lived in the old brick house across the street. My dad told me he and his brother and eight sisters were all born in that house. There were no hospitals around here back then."

"I thought there were eight kids."

"There were ten all together, but two little girls, Mary and Rose, died in 1918 from the Spanish Flu. They were three and five years old. My dad was only two, so he was sent to stay with his newly married sister Luciana for three or four weeks, which kept him from catching it. I can't imagine losing two children, especially at the same time. And my poor dad was so young to be sent away from his mother and father. I'm sure he couldn't understand what was going on."

"It probably saved his life. People did what they had to do back then to survive, and they didn't have time to think about the emotional impact. I can't imagine losing a child, but they endured such things fairly often. Hardly a family didn't lose at least one child to illness or accident. Just think. If he had died, there would never have been a Liliana Caterina Martelli Delaney."

"You're right, and lucky for you there is. What did you find in that trunk?"

"A few old photos, some kid's clothes and a few toys. I say we take these trunks downstairs with us and look at the rest of their contents tonight when we have clean hands and more time."

We put those trunks aside and continued clearing the attic. Some of the furniture looked primitive and others were antiques, probably from the Wilcox farm days and the Harrington Inn. We stored those in the living room of the upstairs apartment, what we used to call the parlor, until we could sell them to an antique dealer or at a garage sale. I was only interested in keeping a few pieces, particularly those that belonged to my grandparents. The last two trunks held little of value, but the trunks themselves could be cleaned up and sold. We put the croquet set in the garage sale area, along with some old decrepit fishing gear. A beautiful birdcage of delicate wire twisted into ornate designs went in the antique pile, as did the coat rack and a crystal decanter with eight glasses. Most of the remaining clothes were moth or mouse-eaten and were put in trash bags. We found a couple of boxes of books; one box was moldy, but the other had some possibilities, so we put that aside for further study. By 3:00, we were filthy, exhausted and starving. We hadn't even stopped for lunch, but most of the attic was cleared.

Dan could see my energy was fading. "We've made a lot of progress. Let's say we quit for the day. If I don't eat something soon, I might take a bite out of your arm," he threatened.

"I'm sure a ham and cheese sandwich would taste much better than my arm. All the crud on it might also give you the plague. Let's go."

"If we wash our faces and hands, do you think we can eat before we shower?"

"My mother always said you have to eat a peck of dirt before you die, so we should be fine. Of course, she was referring to wiping dirt off a carrot or strawberry in the field and eating it without washing it first. I don't know how that applies to disintegrated mouse and probably other varmint poop."

Dan's mouth dropped open. "I think I just lost my appetite."

"Sorry, I'm sure we'll be fine if we wash up well. If I shower before we eat, I will fall and die in the bathtub due to exhaustion and starvation."

As I made the sandwiches and cut up some fresh fruit, Dan pulled my parents' vacuum out of a closet. "This thing is old enough to be an antique! I'm surprised it still works. Wow, it sure is heavy."

"That ugly thing will go on working forever. I can remember vacuuming was my job when I was a kid, and I had to use that clunky thing. I called it Godzilla Vac. It's not self-propelled at all, so it about tore my arms off, and it's pretty loud, too. I hated it! I'll tell you a little secret: when no one was around, I would just push it around the carpet without turning it on. It was so heavy, it would make tracks in the carpet, and so it looked like I'd vacuumed even though I hadn't. I thought I was so smart."

"You sneaky, little rascal, you! Didn't your mom ever notice the carpet was still dirty?"

"Not really. Or if she did, she didn't say so. She would comment sometimes that I didn't do a very good job and to do better tomorrow. Then I felt guilty, so the next day I worked doubly hard to get it clean."

"So you didn't really gain anything by being devious, did you? And guilt got you in the end."

"I guess you're right, but sometimes it feels good to be sneaky and devious. Especially when you feel you have been unjustly overworked. Where are you going with that thing, anyway?"

"If I can carry it upstairs without getting a hernia, I thought after lunch I would take it to the attic and finish clearing the few things left, and then vacuum out the attic. That will be one less thing we have to do to get it ready to sell."

"Do you really think someone would actually buy this place to live in rather than just bulldoze it down? Or at the very least, gut it?"

"This house still has lots of possibility, Lil. Its age alone makes it worth something. And it is still pretty sturdy. If someone wanted to sink quite a bit of money into the place, it could be a fabulous house once it was restored. Remember, 'One man's trash is another man's treasure.' Some famous person said that. And besides, there is only one shower, so I'll vacuum while you get cleaned up."

"Thank you, Dan, my sweet husband."

"Just try not to clog the drain with that half inch of dirt covering your body!"

CHAPTER THREE
MOUNTING EVIDENCE

I made Dan's all-time favorite food: baked penne with Italian sausage for dinner. Good thing our caretaker is Italian. He had stocked the refrigerator not only with staples, but with all the ingredients I needed—pasta, his wife's homemade marinara, ricotta, Parmesan, and fresh Italian sausage. Mangia!

It felt good to smell the aroma of Italian food in this kitchen again, even if it wasn't my grandmother and mother's amazing spaghetti sauce. I can remember when I was little, my older brother and I would be outside playing when we would catch a whiff of something delicious cooking. We would sneak in here to visit my grandmother—Boundary Rule Number 3: Don't go into Grammy's house unless invited—we knocked and she invited. She made everything herself—all kinds of pasta, ricotta, sausage, zuppa, cannolis, and so many other wonderful things. Store-bought could never be as good as Grammy's ricotta, warm and creamy; it practically melted in your mouth. She would give us each a bowl of it, sprinkled with a little sugar and cinnamon. Heaven! If caught by my mother, my brother Tony and I always said Grammy had invited us in, and that we were helping her. She always covered for us, but we really were there to sample the food.

Two of my aunts even gave Grammy a goat so she could have the fresh goat milk needed to make real Italian ricotta. I don't remember the goat, but I guess he was an ornery cuss, always nipping or charging at people. Mom told me that he tried to charge me one day when I was playing in the backyard. My grandmother saw him revving up to attack, and she ran over and swooped me up with one hand while she slapped the goat in the face with the other. Mom said both the goat and I were pretty stunned, and if it had been a cartoon, that goat's tongue would have been hanging out and stars would have been revolving around his head! Well, that was it for the goat; Grammy made my father stop work in the field and immediately take the goat to another farm that didn't have young children. She was a tough person, my grandmother, especially when it came to her family.

My father was second generation Italian, and my mother was second generation Irish. But thanks to my grandmother and aunts, my mother learned to be a fantastic Italian cook. I remember watching some of my aunts and my mother making ravioli as Grammy ordered them about. Ravioli takes a great deal of preparation, and my grandmother felt that if you were going to go to all that work, you might as well make enough for all her kids' families for several meals. My mother and aunts prepared a number of different fillings under my grandmother's watchful eye, while she, and only she, made the pasta dough. When everything was ready, my grandmother would almost reverently take down the special rolling pin from a shelf in the pantry. This heavy wooden rolling pin was long enough to extend from one side of the table to the other. Grammy would put a big glob of dough on the table. Then one woman stood on each side of the table and held a handle of the rolling pin. They would start at one end and slowly walk the length of the table, rolling out the dough until it covered the entire surface. Of course it came out perfectly and evenly rolled every time; Grammy's dough wouldn't dare do any less. This layer of dough was delicately folded and set aside while another glob of dough was rolled out the same way.

Then the women would spoon lumps of filling, probably about a tablespoon or so, on top of the dough, a couple of inches apart. They made rows and rows of these lumps across the whole surface of the dough. Next, the rolled dough that had been set aside was very carefully laid on top of the filling, so as not to smear it around. Finally, Grammy would use a cutting tool to cut the little mounds of dough into ravioli squares, while the aunts and Mom followed behind and lightly pressed and sealed the layers. Cooking fresh dough takes very little time, so that was the easy step. Those were the best ravioli I have ever eaten, including when I was in Italy. Maybe I'm biased, but I still remember them well. I hoped I would find that old rolling pin, but I was pretty sure one of my aunts had taken it.

After dinner, Dan and I settled in the living room to look through some of the trunks and boxes we had brought downstairs. He concentrated on the guest registers while I concentrated on my grandmother's trunks. In the same trunk that held her wedding license and the birth certificates, I found a tissue-wrapped packet and opened it very gently. It was a long christening gown made of silk and hand-tatted lace. The fabric was very thin and somewhat yellow with age. With it was a bonnet of similar lace, so delicate and aged, it was almost falling apart.

"Dan, look at this! This christening gown must have been used for my dad and his brother and sisters. It's handmade, even the lace. Isn't it beautiful? Be careful when you touch it; it is very old and some of the lace is beginning to disintegrate. We have to keep this, and preserve it. I would love to get it properly framed."

"I think that's an excellent idea. Here, let me get some more tissue paper, and we can lay it flat between layers of tissue, and then put cardboard on the top and bottom. That should keep it safe till we get it to a framer."

"I've always found it difficult to conceive of my parents having a life before us kids—you know, that they were once children, and teenagers, and such. Seeing these things makes their lives so much more real, so much fuller. Sort of like when we found Grammy's wedding picture. Too bad it took becoming an adult to fully appreciate my heritage," I mused.

"I think all kids are that way, maybe a little out of selfishness or conceit, but mostly because they are too young to cognitively understand time and aging. Be thankful you have this opportunity to learn and appreciate them now."

"You're right. Thanks. Let's put this away somewhere where it won't get jostled around. Did you find anything interesting?"

"I think so. I have been looked through a few of the guest registers from the Inn, and I found a few very interesting names in the 1880s. Did you know Susan B. Anthony stayed here? I also found an old flyer tucked in the book, advertising a speech given by her and a Lucy Stone at the Redmen's Hall. Pretty amazing, huh?"

"I know Lucy Stone was from West Brookfield, not far from here. She wasn't as famous as Susan B. Anthony, but she was a suffragette and women's rights activist also. Maybe that's how they ended up speaking here. Save that signature. Anyone else?"

"I found Clara Barton in the early 1900s. Didn't she start the Red Cross? And listen to this: in 1912, George M. Cohan stayed here! Well I'll be a Yankee Doodle Dandy!"

"Ha ha. Clara Barton was from Oxford. I went to a camp near her home when I was a kid. George M. Cohan had a house at a lake nearby and came here most summers. My vegetable stand historians told me he was very friendly. There is a place near here called Podunk, an old Indian word, I think. He loved Podunk, and used the name in his act, calling any small, nothing-happening town Podunk. The real place is quite lovely, lots of old homes and woods."

"I have heard people say Podunk my whole life and never realized it's a real place. I will definitely make sure we keep those signatures. I haven't found any other names that I know yet. There sure are a lot of people named Howe in these registers."

"There were a lot of Howe's in early Massachusetts. One of them owned the Wayside Inn in Sudbury for a while and was a Colonel or General or something in the Revolutionary War. You know 'The Tales of the Wayside Inn,' which includes the famous poem, 'Paul Revere's Ride'? Longfellow wrote that book with the Wayside Inn as the setting. And Elias Howe lived in Spencer. He invented the lockstitch, aka the first useful sewing machine. He supposedly also invented the zipper, but he never patented it, so some other guy got credit. There is even a Howe State Park near here."

"Well look at you, so full of all these old historic stories. You could be the town historian."

"Please, I just want to clean out and sell this place and move on! I didn't find much else in these trunks. Most of the stuff is falling apart. I did find a pair of very old pierced earrings that I think I will keep. They look like garnets, and I bet they were my grandmother's. Now I think I will switch to the bootlegging ledgers—if that is what they are."

"Still trying to find the Revenue Man, huh?"

"I always did enjoy a good mystery."

The 1922-25 ledger that I had already looked through contained more of the same semi-coded purchases. I also found some sales to places that sounded like other taverns. I'm sure they weren't selling vegetables to them. Then I picked up the 1926 register that did not have an end date. At first I found similar entries of debits and credits. Near the middle of the book, I found a section of names and payments made to them—John Turro, $100. James Conlin, $200. Sam Johnson, $100. Each entry was for a large amount of money for those days, and always in even hundreds. The pages continued with payments every three months or so. A name might be entered several times in a row, and then there would be another name for a few entries.

"Hey Dan, look at this! I think I found a record of payoffs to Revenue Men. The amounts, the repetition of names, and the timing of the payments sure make it look that way."

"Are you sure it couldn't be repairmen or loan payments or something?"

"I doubt it. This goes from the early 20s, and this one is 1926. This must be bribe money to keep them quiet about the bootlegging."

I turned the page.

"Look here. It's kind of scratched out, but tell me that doesn't say Roy Abernathy. He was real, Dan!"

"Lily, are you sure you aren't trying to make those ink marks into what you want to see?"

"Dan, look. That is a capital R, then a short name. And that's a capital A, and you can see the TH and the Y at the end very clearly. It definitely says Roy Abernathy. And there is no record of money paid to him. He probably wouldn't accept a payoff, so they crossed his name out. Then, they snuffed out his life!"

"Snuffed out his life? Snuffed out his life? Now who sounds like Eliot

Ness? But I will agree that you seem to be finding evidence to support those old stories. What a history this place has had! I can't wait until tomorrow to see what else we find. Right now, I am exhausted. Shall we pack up this stuff and call it a night?"

"Sure. I'm tired, too. We should sleep very soundly after all that hard work!"

CHAPTER FOUR
CONFLICTED DREAMS

I was sitting in the kitchen about 5:30 the next morning, drinking my first cup of coffee and watching the sunrise. I had tossed and turned all night, and I was trying to reweave the fabric of my dreams when Dan entered the kitchen.

"What are you doing up so early?"

"I kept having weird dreams, so I decided to just get up. Want a cup of coffee?"

"Sure, thanks. What were you dreaming about? Ghosts of revenue men?"

"No, just crazy dreams about the farm. Things that happened, but exaggerated. I was in the house trying to cook dinner for my family at the same time that I was keeping watch out the windows for customers at the vegetable stand. I was supposed to cook the meal, but also run out to the stand if there was a customer. Then more and more cars kept stopping at the stand, so I would have to shut off the stove and run out there, wait on them and run back, over and over and over again. The cars kept coming and blowing their horns, louder and louder. Then the food started burning and smoking. I was practically running in circles. I was getting more and more frustrated and so angry, I started to scream. I guess the screaming was not out loud since I didn't wake you up. It was insane! And it was exhausting … so since I wasn't getting any rest anyway, I decided I might as well get up. Lovely sunrise, isn't it?"

"Lil, you've been having dreams about the farm ever since I've known you, but this one seems more intense than those in the past. From all the stories I'm hearing you tell, there were lots of good times here, and you loved your family. Why all these negative feelings about the farm?"

How could I explain this to Dan or anyone when I didn't totally understand it myself? Any mention of growing up in this place filled me with all kinds of anxiety and anger. I can honestly say I hated the farm! All my parents, brothers and I did was work. It often seemed our home life was more like a business than a family. Every spring, summer and fall from the time I was nine or ten years old until I graduated from college, I worked on the farm from sunrise to sunset and beyond. It was hard, it was dirty, it was not fun, and it was my childhood. No vacations, no birthday parties, no to so many things because we always had work to do. After college, I taught summer school every year just so I had an excuse not to go home to help on the farm. And yet I still feel guilty about that. Even after I moved as far away as Denver, summer would arrive and I would feel that I should be here helping on the farm.

I know lots of people who think growing up in the country, close to the earth is wholesome and healthy. They picture riding horses around green fields full of wildflowers and clean, fresh air. Or bountiful harvests with everyone happy and smiling. Remember the hippie movement, and their thing about living simply and returning to the earth? It had to be all those drugs those people took that made them so oblivious to reality. Believe me, farming has its good points, but it is not an easy life. It is ongoing physical labor, day in and day out, at all hours of the day and night and with constant uncertainty since farmers are at the mercy of Mother Nature.

When the Earth Mother was in a good mood, crops and harvests were plentiful, and though never wealthy, we got by. But a few bad storms, droughts, hurricanes or whatever else she could think of to throw at us could totally destroy a growing season and leave us with little or no income to make it through the winter months, until it started all over again the next spring. As a child, seeing my parents whispering about money and looking so worried was very frightening. I still get overly anxious about money issues to this day, usually for no realistic reason. The thought of having none or being heavily in debt can give me a burning sensation in the pit of my stomach, and I forget to breathe.

And did I mention the hard work? Working in the hot fields every day, planting, weeding, watering, picking, and selling crops. Or working in the vegetable stand from eight o'clock in the morning until nine at night. When I think of all the school events and opportunities for a social life I missed because of the farm! Or staying up late into the night to do homework because we were also expected to be excellent students. Some people might call farming a noble profession and say that I had a familial duty, but as a kid, it was not easy to understand what was important or necessary and be altruistic about it. I think I was probably the only kid in school who dreaded summer vacation!

My feelings about the farm really affected my relationship with my parents, especially my father, and things got worse when I started high school. Mom would try to find ways for me to get off work to do things with my friends, even though it usually meant that she had to work in the stand at night after running the stand in Worcester all day. She was a buffer between my and my father's tempers. Italians raise boys very differently from girls, whose role is to be subservient and stay home and take care of the cooking and cleaning. So in addition to the farm issues, Dad and I were always butting heads over my going out with friends, driving the car, having boyfriends. Each new milestone was a battle I fought with him. Mom would try to ease the way by talking to him and softening him up. Sometimes it worked, and sometimes it didn't. I had to fight every step of the way to be my own independent person.

"I really hated the farm! I hated all the hard work, getting dirty, being hot, dealing with bitchy customers, never having a birthday party, missing out on stuff because I had to work while all my friends were having fun. I would get a stain on my thumb and index finger from opening so many husks on ears of corn, probably sixty to a hundred dozen ears of corn a day to check that they were good enough to sell to customers. The stain would not come off with soap or a brush. I had to use straight bleach to get it off. A kid, putting her hands in full strength bleach to clean them! It would burn and hurt. Then the next day, I had to open the husks again and the stain would be back, over and over again . . . I sound like a selfish brat, don't I?"

"I think you sound like a normal kid. Give yourself a break, woman! You weren't asking to be a princess, just a regular kid. We know life isn't fair, and yes, you didn't get dealt the deck you would have liked, but don't get down on yourself for hating it! I think the main reason the farm upsets you so much, and the reason you keep dreaming about it is because you still feel guilty—guilty for being so angry with your parents, guilty for wanting other things, and guilty for leaving the farm to build your own life."

"Guilt is a big part of it for all those reasons you mentioned. I think I felt even guiltier as I got older, and I guess a little wiser, or at least now that I understand more about life. My dad had to give up his dreams to run this farm and take care of my grandmother and his family. He did it because it was necessary. He never asked for this job, and I don't even know if he liked it or hated it. I never even cared enough to ask. I didn't have to give up my whole life, just a little of my time, and I didn't care that it was necessary for my family. I only cared about me and what I wanted. No wonder he would get so angry with me. I wasn't willing to give up one dance, or basketball game or one opportunity to hang out with my friends, when he had given up everything, all of his hopes and dreams. And I was so self-righteous about all of it! Add to that, I was always told that girls weren't supposed to do such things, and you have a perfect recipe for anger and guilt."

"Lily, guilt is a worthless, wasted emotion. It accomplishes nothing, but it sure can mess you up. It has messed you up! You dream about the farm, you work at a job or other parts of your life as if you are driven, and you never have learned to relax. You've got to let it go, Hon. I want you to think about something. You've always told me your parents were adamant about your going to college. Why would they want you to go to college if they expected you to come back and work on the farm? They didn't expect or want you to have this life forever."

Close to tears, I replied, "I never thought about that. Dan, you should have been a shrink. And in my heart of hearts, I know you're right. I hope being here will help me sort some of this out. I thought getting rid of this old place would be kind of a catharsis, you know. As I was sitting here drinking my coffee, I was thinking about all the things we had found already, and all the good times they have helped me remember. Maybe that's what I need—more of the pleasant memories to show me my childhood wasn't totally awful and to help me let go of this guilt."

"Well then, what do you say I grab a piece of toast and then let's find some more memories? How about we clear the upstairs apartment next? And bring along that coffee pot, too!"

"I love you, Dan. Thanks for helping me try to figure this out; to figure me out."

"I wouldn't have you any other way, Hon! You're my love, and that includes your strengths and quirks. And Lily, I also promise I will never ever ask you to plant or weed the flower garden again."

CHAPTER FIVE
THE APARTMENTS

The upstairs apartment didn't require a lot of work because it was already mostly empty, or at least it was before we added the items from the attic. We dusted and Godzilla Vacced the rooms, moved yesterday's trash outside to the porch and organized the boxes we had moved down from the attic. I found some old cleaning supplies and canned goods that went straight to the trash. Who knows how long they'd been there! We didn't need our own toxic waste dump.

"Did you say you used to live up here when you were a kid? You didn't always live in the downstairs apartment?"

"We lived up here until I was five years old or so. When my grandmother got really sick and more and more frail, we moved downstairs so my parents could take care of her. I'm surprised how much I remember about this apartment. The room where we put all the boxes was my parents' room. Tony, Domenic and I shared the other bedroom. We had three twin beds and all our toys in there. I can picture our rocking horse, a white metal child's table and chairs covered in red vinyl, my dolls, my brothers' cars and trucks, puzzles, crayons."

"You're kidding me. Three of you shared that room. It's so small."

"When we were only two or three feet high, it seemed huge. I can remember playing house a lot. I cooked little cakes in my Easy Bake Oven. My Aunt Kay gave me a set of little metal dishes and pots and pans, and I would play with them for hours. One time I cut an apple into tiny pieces and put them in one of the saucepans. Then I put the pan on that radiator over there to make applesauce, but all I got were brown apples. My brothers ate them anyway. Have you looked at all the old radiators in this house? Some of them are very ornate with scrollwork or fancy casting designs. This one is absolutely beautiful. I'm glad they never changed to floor ducts. These radiators have much more character! The one in the parlor is really nice, too."

I remembered that room well. There was a red cut velvet couch and chair, and one blue cut velvet armchair and ottoman, but we called it a hassock back then. We had coffee and end tables with blue glass in them. Quite chic! And our first TV went right over there between the two windows. We watched "Howdy Doody," and all the cowboys— "Roy Rogers, Gene Autry, the Cisco Kid, The Lone Ranger," but our favorite was "Hopalong Cassidy." He was always dressed all in black, with a white bandana and a black hat, even though he was a good guy. He had a gorgeous white horse named Topper, and a fancy studded gun belt. And he always drank sarsaparilla.

One time while my mother was busy changing Dom, Tony and I sat on the coffee table as if it was our horse. Tony made himself Hopalong Cassidy, and I had to be his sidekick, Gabby Hayes. Tony put this glass magazine rack, shaped kind of like a swan on his head for a cowboy hat, and we bounced up and down, as if our horse was trotting along. Well, we got going a little too fast, and Tony's "cowboy hat" fell off his head, hit the glass coffee table and smashed it to smithereens. My mother came running in and practically choked. Tony and I started crying. I'm not sure how much of that was fear for our safety and how much was fear of getting in trouble for what we did.

Whichever, she had to save us from all the glass first. She picked us up one at a time and carried us to our room. It is amazing that we only had a few superficial cuts on our legs. Then she punished us. We had to stay in our rooms all afternoon, on our beds. No toys; no talking. And we couldn't watch Hopalong and our other TV shows for a week. That was a pretty heavy punishment for a four and five year old! But worst of all, we had to confess to my father what we did.

I wasn't really a mischievous child; I prefer adventurous. I also remember getting in trouble because I often played in the crawl space in the kitchen. My mother always said that the crawl space floor wasn't safe, just like the attic floor—Boundary Rule Number 2a. She stored all of her canned jars of tomatoes, corn, pickles and such in there. It was a great place to play hide and seek or to get away from pesky little brothers. One day when my brother Dom was about two, and I was about four, he told on me for playing in the crawl space. I was so angry, I called him a little pukehead four-eyed bastard! It just slipped out. I don't think I even knew what bastard meant, but I had heard some of my Dad's field workers say it and other words I probably shouldn't have repeated either. On that day, I found out mothers really do wash kids' mouths out with soap for saying bad words. My mother sat me on the counter on the side of the sink, wet and lathered up a bar of good old 99 and 44/100% pure Ivory soap, and stuck it in my poor little four-year-old mouth. Then she made me bite down on it—three times. It tasted awful! I thought I was going to vomit! I could actually taste it any time I ate for several days. I'm surprised bubbles didn't come out of my mouth when I opened it.

I remember this event even though I was pretty little. Research shows that children can remember traumatizing events that happened to them when they were as young as two or three years old. And I was traumatized! I made sure I didn't say any more of those bad words in front of my mother, that's for sure.

Dan started checking out the kitchen. "Hey, that old gas stove looks to be 1930s or 40s. Do you think it still works?"

"Last I knew it did. These old stoves are really popular again. People are buying them and refurbishing them. Same with that chrome table and chairs. I remember when my parents bought that set. My mother loved it because it was so 'modern.' I hated the 'cush' sound when you sat on the chairs. Everyone would look at you whenever you sat down. And in the summer when you had shorts on, the plastic would make you sweat and then you'd stick to the seat. I think that's probably why they went out of style. God knows why they're coming back. It is in pretty good shape though. A little elbow grease, slap a retro sign on it, and it will sell in a heartbeat for $300 or more. Well, shall we move on to the other apartment?"

The apartment in the ell portion of the house looked exactly what it was—one large room that originally had been the tavern and was later sectioned off with walls to make a kitchen, living room, bath and two bedrooms. In my mind, I could picture a long bar against one wall, with a bartender swishing a white towel around the inside of a glass. Barstools were probably in front of the bar where patrons could sit and rest their feet on a brass rail. Wooden tables and chairs would have filled the rest of the room. It was quite a large place for its time. Maybe there were backroom storage areas for supplies of bootlegged whisky. There was still an old sink and pantry off the kitchen. I had a great imagination, but other than another old stove and one of those old refrigerators with the motor on the top, the place was empty.

"You know Lil, the attic we cleared didn't cover this part of the house. I wonder if it has its own attic or crawlspace. This roof is quite pitched, and the ceilings aren't very high, so it's likely there's some storage space above."

"I have no idea. This apartment was always rented out, so I never spent very much time in here. Let's look for an attic entrance."

We split up and checked the ceiling in each room. I even checked the walls and ceilings of each closet. I found nothing except a pair of worn out high heels way back on a closet shelf, and I was about to give up when Dan called to me.

"Lily, come to the pantry. I found an attic cover."

The cover was about two feet by two feet, and held in place by some plain wooden molding. There were handprints on the cover and molding from who knows when, probably as a result of someone touching the dust that must have constantly leaked from the attic above, due to the poor fit.

"I'll go get a stepladder so we can open it up and see what's in there," Dan offered.

"Maybe the Revenue Man was hidden up there. I can't wait to see!"

"I would think people in the tavern would have been able to smell it, if a dead body was decomposing up there."

38

"Not if they covered it in lime. That would make it decompose faster and lessen the smell."

"Did you learn that on TV?"

"No, Charles Dickens--'The Mystery of Edwin Drood.'"

"Well, we'll soon find out. Could you get flashlights while I get the ladder?"

"I'll get breath masks, too. Just in case of disintegrated varmint poop."

"Good point," Dan agreed.

We placed the ladder under the attic cover, and Dan climbed up and carefully lifted the cover. Dust fell all over him! Despite the mask, he started sneezing so hard I had to hold the ladder to keep him from falling. Finally he recovered enough to turn the attic cover so he could get it out of the hole and pass it down to me.

"Aren't you glad I got you a mask? At least that stuff isn't inside you. I'll get you something to brush yourself off."

"Don't bother. I've come this far; I'll just keep going. Pass me a flashlight, please."

Dan slowly flashed the light around the room, stopping and leaning forward a few times to see better. The anticipation was killing me!

"Tell me, tell me! What do you see?"

"It's a lot smaller than the other attic, and it looks like there are some crates and boxes of bottles and dishes, probably from the tavern. There's an old desk and office chair, but your friendly varmints ate the cushion. There's other stuff, but it's too dark to make it out. I don't see an overhead light at all. I wouldn't be surprised if no one has been up here since the tavern was in business."

"Okay, my turn! Get out of the way so I can get up there."

"Wait a minute, Hon. I'm going to check the floor first before you come up. There are some things I can't see from here. But I don't want either of us falling through the ceiling."

"Okay, but be careful—and hurry. I think I hear Roy Abernathy calling me!"

A few long minutes later, Dan proclaimed the attic floor to be safe. I climbed the ladder, and he gave me his hand to help me climb into the attic. There were several different areas of stuff, as if someone had sorted the items into piles as they were put up here. One section held crates of empty liquor bottles and another the dishes Dan had already mentioned. The desk and chair were in another section along with three broken, but fixable chairs and their parts. I opened the desk and found a couple of ornate bottles of dried up ink, some fountain pens and nibs. There were a few old pads of paper and some 1-cent postage stamps, but no interesting papers or files.

That left three more areas. One consisted of crates of large pots and pans, and a big copper teakettle, all in good condition, probably also from the tavern days. The next pile had boxes of tablecloths, once white, but now yellowed with age and stained and rotten from vermin nests. They were going straight to the trash. The last area was the most intriguing. There were some old canvas tarps that had been thrown over something, probably to obscure it from view. I could feel my heart beating faster.

"Dan, could those rusty-looking spots on the canvas be dried blood?"

"Don't jump to conclusions, Liliana."

He brushed his hands over a couple of the spots, and tiny bits of rust fell away.

"It looks like regular old rust to me."

We carefully removed the tarp, resulting in squeaking and the pitter-patter of lots of tiny feet. I was so anxious I screamed a little, and Dan laughed at me.

"It's just a few little mice."

"It's a lot of mice, and how can you be sure they're not rats?"

"I can't, but they're gone now. Your scream scared them away."

"Good! If I hear them again, I will scream even louder."

With the tarps removed and thrown aside, we found what looked like a primitive wooden blanket chest, about six feet long, two feet wide and two feet high. It had a hasp locking mechanism, but no padlock, so we were able to open it.

"Dan, I'm so nervous! What if we find a dead body?"

"It would probably be a skeleton by now."

"Don't be technical at a time like this. I'm talking about solving a mystery here."

"Lily, let's not get ahead of ourselves. Help me lift this cover; this thing is made of solid planks of wood and is really heavy."

It was like a scene in a horror movie. The hinges creaked—of course—as we slowly lifted the lid. We pushed the top up and back until gravity took hold of it and made it fall and crash against the back of the chest, making an extremely loud noise in this otherwise still and quiet room. And the ever-present dust rose and formed a cloud around us. I jumped just a little at that, too. I grasped my flashlight tightly in my hand, shone the light into the depths of the chest, took a deep breath, looked inside, and found . . . absolutely nothing. The box was totally empty. There was hardly even any dust.

"Well, that sure was a bust!"

"Sorry you are so disappointed, Dear. I, for one, am glad there was no body, dead or otherwise, in that box. Let's close it back up. Hey, you know what I'm wondering? How did they get some of this stuff up here?"

"Good question. That desk and office chair and this chest could never have fit through that attic entrance."

Dan shone his light around the room, looking for clues. "Wait, look over here. Doesn't it look like there used to be doors on that wall? You know, like the ones upstairs in the barn for getting hay bales up to and down from the haylofts?"

"You're right. It looks like it was two doors with an opening between them. And look, there are two hinges on the side of each door. How come I never noticed this from outside?"

"I'm sure if you had, you would have found a way to get in here."

"You're probably right, but I wonder why it was built in the first place. I'm sure this was never a hayloft."

"No, but it would explain how they got those big things up here, and it sure would have been a quick way to unload and hide a shipment of bootleg whisky. I bet your parents or grandparents had it covered over when they put new siding on the house and never thought a thing about it."

"I bet that's true, even though I have no idea why they would do that. Or why they never cleared out the old stuff from the previous owners. This entire place has so many odd little quirks. If only the walls could talk! Well, this was interesting, and we have some more things for a garage sale or antique dealer, even if we didn't find Roy. Let's get out of here and get cleaned up. We're so dusty, we could scare someone."

CHAPTER SIX
THE CELLAR

The basement, or as we called it, the cellar in our house was for me, the scariest place I remember from childhood, and it's probably why I still don't like basements, even finished ones. Our cellar was ancient. The walls were made of old New England rocks, layered stone on stone with little mortar left holding them in place, and what was there was broken and falling off. The floor was dirt, not concrete, and it was uneven, as if it was dug by hand. The cellar extended under the whole house, winding and turning from one dark scary section to the next. The few small windows at ground level were so encrusted with dirt that light had to fight its way through. There were only a few old insulated wires with dangling light bulbs placed far apart, so you had to walk forever in the dark until you reached the next one. They barely lit a small circular area around them. Such light only accentuated the dark, dreary corners, full of old stuff that cast strange shadows all around. There were spider webs and numerous holes from mice, and who knows what other varmints. It was dark; it was dirty, and as a kid, it frightened me to death! I avoided going down there whenever I could.

Dan and I entered the cellar from the kitchen of the first floor apartment. There were deep shelves all around the stairway full of old boots, lanterns, an ancient cooler, waders and stuff further back that couldn't be seen with the naked eye.

"Let us proceed to the bowels of the earth!"

"How disgustingly graphic, Lil."

I pulled the chain on the dangling light bulb to project a dull ray of light downward as we descended the stairs made of rough planks. The steps were steep and open in the back, which always made me nervous, and the wood groaned with each step.

"Are these stairs safe?" Dan asked.

"I guess we'll find out. Seriously, I'm sure they're fine. They groan and are worn, but they are built of stout planks of wood. Hold on to your flashlight; you're going to need it. The few lights that are down here have to be individually turned on by a pull chain or a turn switch above the bulb. So without the flashlight, you'll have to walk in the dark from one bulb to the next one, which you hopefully can find. Spooky, huh?"

"I'm beginning to understand why this place freaked you out as a kid."

"It still does. We probably should have worn breath masks down here, too. Okay, this area on the right with the floor-to-ceiling cupboard was where my mother and grandmother kept the jars of food they canned every year. This was the farthest I would go into the basement alone."

The wooden turn latch on the cupboard was wedged tight against the door, so when I finally got it turned, the door came flying open, just for dramatic effect. I moved back to allow any vermin that might be hiding in there to escape. Nothing jumped out. Inside were still some jars of canned tomatoes and corn, peaches and what looked like bread and butter pickles.

"These still look good, don't they? Shall we take them upstairs? Uh, except for that one. Look at the mold growing in that thing! We may have discovered some new form of penicillin here." Dan exclaimed.

"I say we take them straight to the dump with the rest of the botulism-infected toxic waste we find. Who knows how old these jars are. I do not want us dying of poison. Those big bins over there were for potatoes and onions. Luckily, they are empty. The freezer adjacent to the bins belonged to my parents, so Roy couldn't be in there, but I bet there is old food in that, too."

We opened the freezer, and it was about a third full. Mostly meat, covered with aging butcher paper and frost. There were packages of pork chops, sausage, pork roasts, and bacon. This stuff was from years ago when my parents used to fatten a pig and have it slaughtered each year. The pork chops and roasts were always frozen. Then they would have the bacon and hams cured, and make pounds and pounds of Italian sausage. And the fat was rendered into lard, back when lard was not considered a bad thing. Dad died almost ten years ago, so this stuff was really old. I bet my mother hadn't been down here since he died.

"We better find out what day is trash day and get rid of all this old food." Dan said.

"I don't even know if there is a trash pickup. We took trash to the dump ourselves when I was a kid. I always volunteered to go to the dump with my father. I loved to check out all the old stuff people threw out like furniture and toys and stuff. Dad thought they were junk and that I was just weird. He used to tell people he found me in a junkyard because I was so interested in looking at old stuff."

We continued on to the oil furnace my parents had installed when I was in college, and next to it was the huge old coal furnace that I remember from childhood. My brother had to come down here and fill the furnace with coal every winter night, and then use a big tong thingy to take out any clinkers, the pieces of fused coal residue. And coal smoke smells! The smell and the oily dust would get into the house and make everything dirty. I'm surprised we didn't get miner's lung. The grate on the front was enormous. When that old thing was stoked, big roaring flames could be seen through the grate. I used to think that was the door to hell! The furnace was so huge and heavy that they just left it here when they got the new oil one. Kind of par for the course around here. And next to the coal furnace was the coal bin. A big truck full of coal would pull up outside, open the cellar doors, and then dump a ton of coal in the bin. There was still some coal in the bottom of the bin. No surprise there.

"Did your family ever suspect there were any ghosts in the cellar or house?"

"Not that I know of. I imagined some whenever I was alone in the house for an evening, but no confirmed sightings or events. If the Revenue Man is here somewhere, he is very quiet. I used to ask my vegetable stand historians, but they'd never heard stories of ghosts in the old place, though I bet a lot of people died here over the years. Maybe they were too afraid of this basement to stay around and haunt us."

"This turn seems to lead to the section below the ell part of the house. It looks like they stored stuff down here. I see some old picks and shovels, and few hoes and saws. Over there—do you think that was the old bar from the tavern?"

"Maybe so. It about the right size and has a brass rail. Cool! Shine your flashlight over here with mine. Hopefully the rodents haven't ruined it."

"There are a few damaged places, on the top and side, but they can be easily repaired, said Dan. "I think it's made of cherry wood. And look at this hand-carved scrollwork on the front. It must have been quite nice in its day."

"Here are a few wooden boxes, some with old metal stuff in them; one with more canning jars. No whisky bottles or human bones anywhere, huh? Another bust!"

"Look at it this way, it won't take long to clean this place out. Let's get all the small stuff out of here today. Then we can wait to clean out the cellar until we find out when trash day is, if there is one. We also need to have a place cleared in the barn or garage for the good stuff, as well as people to help move and clean up that bar. I'm anxious to see it in daylight."

"I'm anxious for me to see daylight. I'll take the tools if you take the boxes, deal?"

"Deal."

We made quick work of cleaning out the cellar and finished in about an hour. The tools were old, but serviceable. I thought buyers might be more interested in them as vintage tools than for gardening. Lots of people like to display tools or paint decorations on old saws. One box held gears for an early seed-sowing machine. I'd seen lots of similar gears in antique stores; people like their cutout patterns, and hang them on walls. I put them in the sale area, which was getting quite large.

"I think we should call it quits for the day, don't you? I want to go into town and get more trash bags and heavy cardboard boxes so we can get a lot done when the kids get here," said Dan.

"I agree. I think after I scour off all this dirt and grime, I'll go to the grocery store to pick up food for the weekend. I may stop and put flowers on my parent's grave, too. I feel a need to visit."

After I showered, I put on a flowered summer dress. I thought it might take my mind off grime and grossness for a little while. I stocked up on all kinds of food, knowing how my son and son-in-law love to eat, and that they would be especially hungry after all the hard work I had planned for everyone to do.

Next I stopped at a greenhouse and bought a lovely planter of mixed flowers, hoping they would last for a while with minimal watering. As I approached my parents' graves, I was pleased to see that the dates of my mother's death had been added to the stone. This was the first time I'd been here since her burial, and I was immediately filled with sadness. Becoming an orphan, even a middle-aged adult orphan, made me feel as if pieces of me had become detached from my body. My anchor was gone, and I felt untethered and ungrounded. I really missed my parents, especially my mom.

"Hi, Mom and Dad. I know you've moved on, but I feel close to you here since it was the last place I saw you, and I kind of feel a need to talk to you. So... how's heaven? Are you getting to see your old friends and relatives? I hope you haven't run into that grouchy old crab Mrs. Martin who used to live across the street. Or is it true, everyone is nice in heaven—if she even made it up there! I've always tried to imagine how that works, especially if you didn't like some of the people when you knew them on earth. And what about people who had multiple marriages or feuding families? Now that has got to be weird! Well, I'm sure God has it all figured out and makes it all work somehow. It must be one of those things we have to believe on faith since we can't conceive of it in our little minds.

"I wanted to tell you that Dan and I are at the house, cleaning out the old homestead. You sure had a lot of stuff! All those years of accumulation, I guess. Oh Dad, I think I found some of the old ledgers from the bootlegging days. Maybe I'll track down the Revenue Man yet. And yes Mom, I am going to keep your china and crystal. I would never let anything happen to them. So anyway, what I came here to tell you is that I'm going to sell the property. I hope that's okay with both of you. You know I was never the farming type, and neither are Tony and Dom. We all feel it's best to pass it on to someone else. But we will make sure some good people buy it--people you'd like who appreciate the history of the place and will take good care of it, as a farm or whatever they do with it.

"I love you both. I really miss you, and I think of you every day. So, keep that light shining down on me okay, and I'll be back to visit again soon. Oh Mom, I brought you some flowers because I know you always loved flowers. Enjoy them, okay? Bye for now."

CHAPTER SEVEN
THE LINEN CLOSET

I'm not sure at what point my body turned into an automaton. All it took to activate the clean-and-sort mode was the opening of a cabinet or closet door, at which point my arms became robotic and would immediately start clearing out items and sorting them into keep, trash, or sell. Once all items were removed, the next stage was activated, and the shelves were washed or dusted and the floors cleaned, followed by organized replacement or removal to suitable locations. Only then did the automaton rest, and the real me could do whatever I intended to do in that space in the first place. It wasn't even 10:00 a.m., and I had already cleaned the refrigerator and five of the kitchen cabinets. It took me forever to get breakfast ready.

Now it was the linen closet. The closet had two doors that opened in the center to reveal several shelves, each about four feet wide, and I thought, about two feet deep. My original intent in this instance was to make sure there were enough fresh, clean towels and sheets for when the kids arrived today, but like a woman possessed, I was taken over by my inner Cleaning Robot and started in on the linen closet. I kept the good towels for our use, and put some of the tattered ones in piles to use as rags. Same with the sheets. Various bric-a-brac like old bathroom candles, macramé towel hangers, and other worn-out and dated bathroom décor went straight to the trash. I thought I was about done when I realized that the closet shelves were much deeper than I realized. I didn't know that they continued further until I had moved out the front items. I grabbed a flashlight, and shone it into the top shelf space. There was about four more feet of shelf and closet space behind what I had already cleaned out. And the shelf was filled with stuff. Using the light, I checked the other shelves and noted they were as deep as the top. Only in this house would one find a linen closet big enough for Buckingham Palace! And how had I lived here all those years and not known that this space was here? I have to say I was intrigued to see what lay on the back of the shelves.

"Dan, look what I found."

Carrying his coffee cup, Dan came into the bathroom.

"I thought you were getting linens for the kids' beds."

"I was, but then I discovered that the shelves in this closet are five or six feet deep, and they looked packed with stuff. Should we check them out?"

"Sure. Let me get a couple of hook lights so we can see what we're doing."

He got a stepladder, a hammer and nails, and the lights. He hammered the nails in the sides of the closet, and we hooked the lights on them. Now we could see what there was stuffed in there that hadn't been touched for years. A layer of dust about a quarter inch thick sat on top of everything. We decided we better put on the breath masks again.

I climbed a few steps on the ladder, which gave me the extra height I needed to reach into the depths of the top shelf. I pulled out a pile of old bath towels that were so threadbare they couldn't have dried a teaspoon. I continued pulling piles of old linens. As I neared the back of the shelf, I touched something hard. I felt around and found there were actually three rounded shapes, about seven or eight inches high and about ten inches in diameter. When I tapped one of them a few times, it made a sound like a lid being fit on a piece of china.

"Dan, did you hear that? Hold the ladder steady, I'm going in!"

"Be careful! You're practically lying on the shelf. Who knows how strong it is."

As I started pulling one of the objects forward, I realized there were

50

handles and used those to slide it toward me. Handles? Big bowl with a cover? My first thought was soup tureens. As I got one into the light, I saw there was no slit in the top for a ladle. The bowl and lid were made of creamy white porcelain with tiny pink rosebuds strewn all over the surface. I turned it over, and I couldn't read the manufacturer, but I could read "England." I climbed down the ladder and carefully passed it to Dan.

"It's a chamber pot. A very nice chamber pot in beautiful condition. Look at the lovely rose design. There are two more. I'm going to get them."

I climbed the ladder again, carefully crawled onto the shelf, and got the other two chamber pots. They were the same design. All three were in perfect condition with no chips or cracks.

"I wonder if these were from the inn. They wouldn't have had indoor plumbing in the early days."

"I'll put them in the sell pile, right?" asked Dan.

"Well, maybe we should keep one. They are very nice and historic."

"I thought you might say that. I think I can do most of the reaching on the second shelf without the ladder."

The second shelf contained more of the same old linens, one with a mouse nest with a few squeaky babies, which gave me the heebie-jeebies, but we did find twelve of the original crystal doorknobs that used to be on the doors in this house. I was ecstatic to see that, as I predicted, my mother had not thrown them away. There were also five wall sconces for candles, and a pair of old kerosene lamps with cut glass bowls. And then on the third and fourth shelves, we found four of the brass chandeliers that I remember from when I was a little kid. They were badly tarnished and two of them needed lots of repair work, but they were still a treasure.

"These are really nice—simple but elegant," said Dan. "I think I can fix them, and if we use a little elbow grease, they'll shine like new. I am beginning to get a picture of what this place must have looked like as an inn. I wish I could see what was behind those paneled walls."

"I wish I could see what was behind those walls before my father made this place into apartments. There have been several fireplaces, old wallpaper, and who knows what else."

"Maybe a few secret passageways, you think? I'm game for knocking down a few walls if you are."

"We are selling, remember. If they don't gut the place or bulldoze it down, I think the new owners would not appreciate holes in their walls, despite our curiosity. I'll help take out the treasures. Then if you will take out the trash, I will finish cleaning these shelves and sweep up. Oh, and I'll put the linens on the beds in the kids' rooms, which is what I was supposed to be doing in the first place."

My mother's intuition told me that Meghan and Nick, our daughter and her husband would arrive around lunchtime, so I had prepared homemade beef barley soup and enough ham and cheese sandwiches for the four of us, even allowing for Nick's hardy appetite. Sure enough, as soon as I had finished setting the table, they pulled into the driveway in their Toyota Rav4. Dan and I went out to meet them. I wrapped Meghan in a huge hug, practically bouncing up and down with joy. Meg and I were very close, and now that they lived in Chicago, I didn't get to see her as often as I would like. We talked on the phone several times a week, but that wasn't quite like being with her, looking at her beautiful face and warm smile. Dan had shaken hands with Nick with just a tiny bit of reserve that said, "You are cool, but no man is quite good enough for my only daughter." I adored Nick, and hugged him tight as Dan hugged his Meghan.

Our daughter is an artistic person through and through. She majored in theatre and art in college and was excellent at both. She also has a beautiful singing voice. I remember when she went away to college, I missed her dreadfully, and I especially missed her singing around the house. She currently taught theatre and art to disadvantaged kids part-time and was making a name for herself acting in community theatre. She was also a scenic painter, designing and painting sets for various theatres around Chicago, so she stayed very busy.

Nick, on the other hand, was an architectural engineer for some kind of building conglomerate. He worked very hard and made good money, so they lived comfortably. To some, they seemed like very different people, but for them it worked. They each respected and appreciated the other's interests and had lots of interests they shared like hiking and other outdoor activities, music and building things. They had done an amazing job customizing their home. Nick sometimes helped build sets for Meghan's plays, too. Few couples were as comfortable with each other as Meghan and Nick. I thought they were perfect for each other, and so did Dan, even though he might not admit it.

We were so excited to see each other that they were barely out of the car before we all started talking at once.

"How are you?"

"How was your drive?"

"Look at this place. Have you gotten a lot done?"

"Are you hungry? Lunch is ready."

We helped them with their bags, and Meghan and I got drinks ready as Nick put the bags in the bedroom, and Dan served the soup. As we ate, we filled them in on what we had accomplished, and we made plans for the weekend.

"After lunch, if you two aren't too tired, I thought we would start in the garage. There's a lot of stuff up in the rafters, and Nick's height would be really helpful in getting it down."

"We're ready and raring to go. After all that sitting in the car, I'm looking forward to some exercise," responded Meghan. "And I can't wait to see what else we find. It's kind of like a treasure hunt."

"I'll just change into old clothes, and I'll be ready. I'm looking forward to this, too," added Nick. "I've never explored the farm before."

"I lived here my whole childhood, and I'm finding things I've never seen before, so it's an adventure for all of us."

"What time do you think Lucas and Emily will be getting here?" Meghan asked while we all cleaned up the table.

"Dear girl, you know that is a silly question. Remember your brother's mantra—'I'll be there when I get there,' so maybe by dinnertime. He tends to arrive when food is on the table."

CHAPTER EIGHT
THE GARAGE

In our oldest clothes, and armed with gloves and water bottles, the four of us advanced on the six-bay garage. We opened the six sets of double wooden doors to let in as much light as we possibly could. The building was made of wood, painted white on the outside and unpainted on the inside with no insulation or ceiling, just rafters that led to a shingled roof. The floor was made of rough concrete. The building was long enough and wide enough to fit six big trucks or farm machines. When I was a kid, this place was always full of tractors, trucks, plows, or such.

Now, only one lonely orange tractor sat in the third bay and a golf cart that had seen better days was parked in the fourth. The tractor wasn't shaped like most others; the engine was in the back, and the front had wide-set metal pieces hanging down that kind of reminded one of spider legs. One set of legs led to the small front tires and others had holes near their ends to allow farming machines to be attached to them. This tractor was used mostly for sowing seeds, cultivating, and digging up rows of root vegetables like carrots, depending on which attachment you used.

"All the rest of the trucks, tractors and machines were sold except for this one, a pick-up truck and the golf cart. The pickup must be in the barn."

"How come Grandpa kept this tractor, Mom? It looks kind of like a spider."

"He said he bought this tractor brand new the year I was born, and so he wanted to keep it."

"How sweet!"

"Yeah, despite Grandpa's rough exterior, he had a sentimental heart."

"What's with the golf cart?" asked Nick.

"As my dad got older, he had a harder time walking around the fields. He always kind of thought of the pickup truck as his dress-up, go-to-town vehicle, and he didn't want to get it dirty in the fields, so he bought the golf cart. He built a little trailer for it and used it to get back and forth and to carry a few baskets of vegetables or bags of corn as they were needed for the vegetable stand.

"He loved this little thing. I can remember coming home from college one year during strawberry season. There was a big sign out front saying 'Pick Your Own Strawberries.' The fields were full of people, and there was my father, sitting on the back of this golf cart with a rainbow umbrella over his head, and a moneybox next to him. He was having a great time just sitting there and collecting money from the people. I thought it was hilarious. I have a picture of that somewhere."

"I learned to drive on that golf cart. Remember, Dad?" asked Meghan.

"I sure do; I thought we were both going to die! You hit every rut in the fields, scared a poor dog so badly he wet himself, and finally stopped in a cornfield."

"Oh come on, Dad! It wasn't that bad."

"Actually, once you got the hang of it, you drove that thing all over the place."

"If it still works, I'll take you for a spin later, Nick. Where's Grandma's car, Mom?"

"I guess she must have sold it when she quit driving. When she turned eighty, she decided she had driven long enough and gave up her license. I thought that was so funny, especially since the first time she got a license was when she was seventy-seven! She knew how to drive; she drove vehicles around the farm all the time, but if she ever had to go anywhere else, my dad or my aunt would drive her around. She was always a timid driver. But after my father died, she took lessons secretly, so no one would make fun of an old lady, and she got her license. I loved that she did that all by herself."

"What a great lady Grandma was! She always did have spirit. It seems weird to be here without her, doesn't it? Well, where should we start?"

"I think we should do one bay at a time. Let's start with this first one so once its cleaned out, we can store stuff we want to keep or sell in here," said Dan.

"Sounds like a plan. I'll start with that old corner cupboard in the back, Meghan offered."

"I'll sort out all the stuff in the crevasses between the studs and that pile of stuff near the back wall," I added.

"I guess that leaves you and me with the rafters, Nick," said Dan.

"I'll climb the ladder and pass stuff down to you, okay, Dad?" offered Nick.

We all set about our tasks. I found lots of pieces of metal, probably broken parts of old machines with no apparent use, as well as jars and cans of rusted spikes and screws, and a few glass milk bottles and oilcans. I placed the milk bottles and oilcans in a box.

"Why are you saving those old used oil cans?" asked Dan.

"These oilcans have become collectibles. People are paying $15 or $20 for these small cans, and the big ones, depending on age and how rare they are, can go upwards of $75," I informed him.

"Yeah, Dad. Haven't you been watching 'American Pickers?' They're always buying and selling these oilcans and signs. Do we have any signs?" asked Meg.

"We haven't found any yet, but we probably will." I responded. "What do you have there, Meghan?"

"I found a few old bottles and a small milk or cream can. I'm not sure what these two things are," she answered.

"That glass jar with the paddle inside and a crank is a small butter churn. Save that to sell. And that metal thing with the handle is a bottle capper. You would set it on a table, put the filled bottle between the machine's legs, load the press on the top with a bottle cap, then lower the handle, and the cap would be pressed onto the bottle. Neat, huh?" I explained.

"The caps must be the metal discs I found in a box in the cupboard. They are flat with crinkled edges. There were small round pieces of cork, too."

"That's exactly what they are!" I answered. "Before they started using plastic under the caps on bottles, they used to use cork to seal them. I don't know how old this machine is, but I remember my father finding this bottle capper and a bunch of old green bottles in that cupboard when I was a kid. He went out and bought extract and made root beer."

"Ooh, I bet that tasted great! Homemade root beer!" mused Nick.

"It was god awful! So strong it could make your hair curl. I can still taste it! Bitter! And it smelled like an old rotten potato. That's why the bottles, caps, and capper ended up back in the closet. We can put those in the sell pile also."

"Lily, maybe the bottle capper was originally used to bottle liquor during prohibition. You think?"

"Oh come on. Are you serious, Dad?"

"I certainly am. Wait till tonight when everyone's here, and your mother will tell you all about it. This old place has a mysterious past!"

"I can't wait! I love old historical stories, especially if there are skeletons in the closet," said Nick, warming to the subject.

"No skeletons yet, but we have found some interesting items and possible evidence of shady dealings," Dan replied.

"Mom, look at these," Nick said as he handed two huge black enamel pots with white spots and wire baskets inside down to Dan.

"Those are my grandmother's old canning kettles. We used to can about 100 quarts of tomatoes a year, plus corn, beans, pears, peaches, pickles, anything that could be canned. The baskets are pretty rusted, but someone might want the pots as planters or something."

"Look at this old baby rocker. Careful, Dad. It's solid oak and heavy." Nick said as he passed it down to Dan. There was a child-size seat in the middle of the rockers and a string of old wooden beads attached in front to play with. "This thing must be ancient."

"Watch what you're calling ancient, son-in-law!" I admonished. "I can remember my brother Dom rocking in that thing, which means Tony and I probably did, too. I think it's quite cool. Sale pile, gentlemen."

"All that's left up here are old storm windows. One or two have broken panes, but most are in good shape," Nick informed us.

"I've seen lots of old windows in antique stores the past few years. People are making them into tables, and all kinds of stuff. We can save those to sell, too," said Meghan.

Meghan and I started on the pile of old asphalt shingles in the back of the garage. Some were falling apart. They looked like they had been there since the garage was first built who knows way back when.

"These can all go in the trash. I can't imagine there being any use for them. I doubt anyone is interested in old broken shingles."

"Look, Mom, there are two big wooden boxes under these things. They're full of slate roofing tiles. They must have been removed from one of the buildings to put on asphalt shingles. Some of them are broken, but most are still in great shape. Can I sort them? I would like to keep the good ones to paint on. And maybe some of the storm windows, too? I've seen painted windows in craft shows, and they are really popular."

"Sure, let's get a box for the good ones. And put your name on it so it doesn't get thrown away. That looks about it for this section of the garage. Let's sweep it out and move on to the next one."

"Mom, why is there a section of the back wall of the next bay that juts out about two feet farther than the rest of the wall?" asked Nick.

"Who knows? Probably a truck or tractor wouldn't fit in so they just cut out the back wall, put up a few boards and extended the garage. The roof of that little alcove, for lack of a better word, is even shingled on the outside. I can remember we used to climb up the rough boards to the top of that thing when we were kids and then onto the roof of the garage. That sure seems scarier now than it did then."

"What Boundary Rule was that, Liliana?"

"We didn't have a Boundary Rule for roof climbing because it never dawned on my parents that we would be dumb enough to climb up there—and because we were never caught."

"I've learned a lot about your mother since we've been here, kids. Wait until you hear the stories. Your mother was a hellion and a daredevil."

"Mom, have you been holding out on us?" Meghan joined in. "This alcove, as you call it, is full of stuff. We can use these old crates to store stuff, and there are two more milk cans in pristine condition to sell. Oh wait a minute, look at this. At first I thought it was just some old shelves, but look, it's a dollhouse! Nick, help me pull it out."

The dollhouse was about four and a half feet high to the tip of the dark green roof and about three and a half feet wide. It had been divided with partitions into three floors to make six "rooms" of equal size. It was painted white on the outside and on some of the walls, and a little red chimney straddled the roof. Some rooms had painted floors, a few had linoleum, and one had a worn and tattered rug attached to the bottom. There were windows with green shutters but no glass, and a doorway with no door, but there were small staircases between each floor. Any dolls or furniture were long gone.

"This is amazing! What a treasure for a child. I just love it," Meghan exclaimed.

"This dollhouse was handmade," Dan said. "Those linoleum pieces match some of those in the upstairs apartments, don't they, Lily?"

They all looked at me and realized I was standing there in shock with tears rolling down my face. Meghan rushed to my side and held me.

"Mom, what's wrong?"

"My dad made that dollhouse for me for Christmas when I was about five or six years old. He made tables and chairs and beds, too, and my mother made curtains and linens, and that rug. Grammy made a family of little cloth dolls to live in the house. I played and played with that thing for hours on end. I never knew what happened to it. I wanted it for you, Meghan, when you were little, but no one could find it. I thought it must have fallen apart or gotten thrown in the dump."

"What a wonderful gift, Mom! A dollhouse built with love for a special little girl."

Dan put his arm around my shoulder and kissed my hair. "I guess your parents didn't just think of you as a worker, huh Lil?" he remarked.

"I guess not. Can we just put this aside for a little while. Maybe we will find some of the things that went inside. I'm sure the dolls have rotted away, but maybe some of the furniture survived. I'm not ready to make decisions about what to do with my dollhouse yet."

We carefully moved the dollhouse to the back of the first bay. I continued to examine and dust it for several minutes before I returned to work. So many memories came flooding back. Not just of playing with the house, but the love I felt for my parents for making it for me. This was the best treasure we'd found yet!

The rafters in this section contained more storm windows and a few tractor parts. The old tractor seat would sell. We pushed the orange spider tractor outside and started on the third bay. There wasn't much around the walls except a well-used pick, axe, and sledgehammer that got added to the pile. The rafters were a different story.

"Whoa ho ho, will you look at this?" Nick exclaimed as he passed a long, thin, object loosely wrapped in a dirty chamois down to Dan. "Handle that very carefully."

Dan peeled away the chamois to find an old shotgun. The double barrels were dark metal, but the triggers, trigger guards and the circular site were silver-colored metal. The stock of the gun was a dark walnut with scrollwork on it, but it was hard to see the design very well because of the darkening of the wood due to age and the poor lighting. Dan carefully opened the shotgun to make sure it wasn't loaded. When he deemed it safe, we all moved closer to check it out.

"Do you think this goes back to the bootlegging days, Hon?"

"No, I don't think so, because I remember my Dad telling me a shotgun was up here somewhere. It does have quite an interesting story, though."

"Oh, I can't wait to hear this one!"

"Well, remember I told you my father was the youngest in a family of eight, at one time ten kids, which means that he had lots of older siblings. The oldest was Aunt Luciana who was thirteen years old when Dad was born. When Luciana was about fourteen or fifteen, she started sneaking around with this guy Paolo, who was working at a nearby farm. Paolo had recently emigrated here from Italy, and he was quite a bit older than Luciana—like in his late 20s, at least. They apparently fell in love, and knowing that my grandparents would not allow her to get married so young, especially to someone so much older, they decided to elope. One night while everyone was sleeping, they ran off together.

"The next morning, when my grandfather realized what had happened, he went out and bought this shotgun and went after them. According to my aunts, Grandpa wasn't really going to shoot Paolo; he hadn't even bought bullets. He planned to just scare the bejesus out of the poor fellow and drag Luciana back home with him. He caught up with them at a little inn in a nearby town. I guess Luciana got hysterical, professing her love for her new husband, and begging Grandpa to give them his blessing. Her tears softened old Grandpa's heart. But then they told him they had been married by a judge and not a Catholic priest, and he went ballistic again. When he finally calmed down, he brought them back to the house, and over espresso and cannolis, they discussed the situation with Grammy. Whenever solving any problem, Italians must have food.

"Paolo told them how much he loved Luciana and promised her a good life. He was saving his money and planned to buy his own farm very soon where they would live and make beautiful babies. Grandpa almost choked over the idea of his Luciana engaging in the behaviors necessary to make beautiful babies, but Grammy, realizing they would just run off again, and that she and Grandpa might lose their first child forever, finally convinced my grandfather to give his blessing to the marriage, as long as they were remarried by a priest.

"Grammy made Grandpa put the shotgun up here so he would never do anything so foolish again, and so the kids wouldn't find it. As for my aunt and uncle, they had a great marriage with eight kids and a successful farm. So that's the story of that shotgun. It's been up there since about 1917 or so. We better keep it wrapped up and put it some place safe till we decide what to do with it."

"Talk about skeletons in the closet! How could you look them in the face once you knew the story, Mom?" Meg asked.

"My father didn't tell me about it until I was an adult, and by then my aunt and uncle were both dead, so I never had to face them."

"You know, antiques are so much more interesting when you know the story behind them, aren't they?" asked Nick.

"That's one of the things I love about antiquing. An object means so much more when someone tells you its history. It goes from being a junky piece of nothing to an heirloom with its own story. It might be full of nicks and scratches that maybe were put there by someone using it hundreds of years ago! It could have traveled from another country by boat and then out west on a covered wagon, like some of our antiques in Denver. It's even more interesting when the items are from your own family."

While Dan and I pushed the little orange tractor back into the garage, Nick and Meghan argued about who was going to drive the golf cart outside, only to find the battery was dead, so we all ended up pushing it out. The fourth bay contained more of the same types of things, used tools, windows, and such, but we did find a wooden ice cream maker with a metal crank. It would have to be cleaned before we could determine if it was too rusty or worn to be salvageable. Nick was ready to try it out right then!

The fifth and sixth garage bays had been turned into my father's workshop after he retired. Dad had insulated the area and put up walls to make a huge workspace. Dan was right, just about any tool every invented was in that workshop. He had them all neatly displayed on hooks on the wall or stored on shelves. There were two huge workbenches with attached vises and a metal cabinet full of nuts and bolts, nails, screws, hinges and other woodworking needs.

"Ah, this is the place I've been waiting to explore. I can't wait to use some of these things!" exclaimed Dan.

"This place is better than a man cave. Look at all these tools, and they look like they have barely been used," said Nick.

"I'm sure lots of them haven't. When he retired, my Dad decided to build the carpenter's workshop he'd always wanted. My mom used to say that he had duplicates of lots of things, but he assured her each hammer, drill, or whatever served a different purpose. He did build some tables and Adirondack chairs as well as Meghan's red wagon, but he died before he got full use of the workshop. It certainly made him happy, though."

"It's like a hardware store!" said Meghan. "Are all these tools just for woodworking, or are there tools for fixing cars and trucks and stuff, too?"

"These tools are mostly just for woodworking, believe it or not. The machine tools have their own place in the barn. We haven't even gotten there yet. But I think we should call it a day. We got a lot done this afternoon. Thank you both for helping."

"I really enjoyed it! Dibs on first shower!" shouted Meghan.

"You go ahead, Meg. I think I'll stay here with Dad awhile and check out this workshop a little more. It's a pretty amazing place!"

"We'll be lucky to see them before dinner time." Meghan said to me. "Come on, Mom. Let's go get cleaned up."

CHAPTER NINE
FAMILY TIME

Meghan and I showered and got dressed in clean, comfy clothes. I was beginning to worry if this old plumbing system could handle all this dust and dirt we were forcing down it. I hadn't even done any laundry yet.

"Mom, it feels wonderful to be clean again. I think I just lost five pounds!"

"Really. That old dust is so fine, it sticks like glue, especially when you sweat."

"I think we are all too tired to cook, so tonight we should go out to dinner. I would love some fresh clams or fish, or there's that really good Italian restaurant near here. How about we take a vote when the guys come in?"

Dan and Nick finally finished playing with all the tools and came in to get cleaned up. Dan was carrying a large cardboard box with a cover, like a file box. "Lily, look what we found. I think it's some of the furniture from your dollhouse. The box was in a cabinet in your father's workshop. He must have been repairing them."

Each piece was wrapped in paper towels to protect it. The first item was a dining room table. It was in fine shape and looked as if it had a new coat of paint. Next were the four chairs that went with the table. Two looked like they had repairs done on the legs, but they were now solid and lovely. I set each piece on the kitchen table as I finished looking at it. I then found one "double" bed, and two "twin" beds. I used to place the large one in the parents' room and the smaller two in the children's rooms. The mattresses were dirty and lumpy and would need to be thrown away. Next came dressers for the bedrooms, each with tiny gold knobs on drawers that opened. One had a leg broken off, but it was taped to the back so it could be glued back on. The stove, which looked a lot like the one in the upstairs apartment, had been painted to look like metal. I hoped the little pots and pans and dishes were in the box, too. I found the kitchen table and chairs, which needed a lot of repair, if they could be fixed at all. The doll family was not in the box. Being made of cloth, they probably hadn't survived as well as the furniture. My father had been working on repairing these pieces before he died. My eyes welled up with tears.

"Everyone, I've decided I want to keep my dollhouse. I am going to clean it and repaint it, and finish fixing the furniture. I think I remember what the doll family looked like, and I am going to remake them, too. Then Meghan, when you or your brother have a child, it will go to one of your kids."

"Mom, that is so sweet! And we can tell everyone that our grandfather made this dollhouse and furniture for our mom. I hope I have a kid first."

"Well, this should be fun to ship! But I totally agree we have to keep the dollhouse and its contents in the family, Hon. I love it and its story. Maybe with your dad's tools, I can make a few more pieces of furniture for it."

That decided, I wiped my eyes, and pulled myself together. One can only handle so much nostalgia, and tears, in one day.

"Okay, you two hurry and get cleaned up. Meghan and I decided we're going out to dinner. Fried Clams or Italian?"

Suddenly the door opened, and a voice was heard saying, "Oh, definitely fried clams. And lots of them. We can bring in the luggage later."

"Lucas, Emily, you made it! I told you he would show up just about dinnertime."

We all greeted each other and hugged, excited to have the whole family together again. We all felt festive, even if it wasn't a holiday.

"You two bring your stuff in and get settled why Nick and Dad get cleaned up. And then we'll go," I ordered. Your dad and I had clams the other night, but no one can have too much fresh seafood."

"And hurry it up, you two, we're starving!" said Lucas.

"You haven't even done any work yet; you're lucky they let you eat at all," responded Meghan."

Lucas and Emily lived in Pennsylvania. Lucas was an Associate Professor of Applied Mathematics at the University of Pennsylvania. He was licensed as a CPA, but after a few years, he gave it up for academia. Lucas was easy going and always joking, but he was a real nerd at heart. The university life seemed a better fit for him. What Meghan was to the arts, Lucas was to math and science. Things that were way above my head were a piece of cake for him. He was gifted both theoretically and practically. Lucas could look at a problem, on paper or in reality, and immediately see a solution. Dan and I weren't sure where he got his abilities because we certainly weren't gifted that way. Some of it may have come from my father. Dad was always inventing machines or farm equipment when he saw a need for something that wasn't available. Soon other farmers or manufacturers were copying his ideas. Dad was undereducated, but he was extremely intelligent.

Emily was a pediatric nurse at the renowned Children's Hospital of Philadelphia. She worked in oncology and loved her job. I really admired her ability to be so effective with very sick children. Emily was somewhat quieter and more laid back than the rest of our family, but not uncomfortably so, and she enjoyed our times together. Poor woman probably couldn't get a word in edgewise! Her personality was a nice balance to Lucas' boisterousness, and they adored each other. Dan and I felt blessed that our kids had married people that suited them so well and were enjoying happy lives.

Dinner was wonderful, both the food and the company. I loved having my whole family together. Luckily we are all very close, and even a minor event becomes a major happening because we enjoy each other so much. I loved the bantering that went on between my kids. There was lots of teasing, and they could be mildly sarcastic, but it was always done with humor and love. I was looking forward to a fun weekend, full of work, but also full of laughter.

After our delicious seafood dinner, we headed home. When everyone was comfortably seated in the living room, we shared with Lucas and Emily what we had accomplished so far. They were impressed by how much we'd gotten done and the things we'd found. I could see they were already getting into the excitement of the hunt, which made the physical work more tolerable.

"And you wouldn't believe all the things I've been learning about your mother. She was a pretty awful kid, always disobeying, breaking rules, and a total risk taker! She used to do things that she would never have allowed you kids to do," tattled Dan.

"Mom, our dear, sweet, level-headed mom?" asked Lucas. "Are you sure we are talking about the same woman?"

"Please Dad, tell us more!"

"Now, in my own defense, times were different then. The world was a much safer place. My parents didn't have to worry about us being kidnapped or harmed or sued like we do now-a-days. And yes, a farm is a place where there are lots of things you can get hurt on or doing, but people weren't as protective back then, even if they should have been. So we were allowed to play unsupervised a lot, and yes I did, on a few occasions do a few things against the rules, but I think it taught me to be a more creative, independent person, and I only broke rules when it was absolutely necessary!"

"Oh hogwash, the world might have been safer, but the things you did were far from safe, or things your parents would have approved of, like prowling in the woods around old hobo camps, sneaking into an attic with a floor that wasn't solid, even faking vacuuming, and searching for the Revenue Man..."

"You don't know the half of it! If you paint me in a bad light in front of my kids, Dan Delaney, I may not tell you anymore of my stories. And believe me, I've just begun to warm up!"

"Mom, I am shocked! You faked vacuuming? You horrible child! Dad, please share everything you know with us," joked Meghan.

"Really. You never know when this knowledge may come in handy," slyly responded Lucas.

Dan told them some of my childhood misbehaviors, but the story of the Revenue Man he turned over to me. I repeated what my dad had shared and showed them the ledgers we'd found in the attic. By the time I had finished, everyone was hooked and ready to find poor Roy Abernathy.

"Nick, where's your laptop? I'm going to see if I can find out anything about this guy or a shooting incident at the inn during Prohibition," said Meghan. "Mom, what's the name of the newspaper around here?"

"Now it's the *Worcester Telegram and Gazette*. But back then, there were two, I think, and they eventually joined together. Do you think you can find news reports from back then?"

"It can't hurt to try. Here we are: *Worcester Telegram and Gazette*. Let's see . . . I'll try archives. What year did you say it was?"

"I think it was 1926, and the place was called the Harrington Inn."

"Meghan, try entering 'Gunshots at Harrington Inn,' maybe in 1926 or 27. That should work if anything was written about it."

Meghan entered the information, and even though the results were almost instantaneous, I was holding my breath. I sort of felt that finding any mention of the incident would validate my childhood and be vindication for my disobedience and misadventures while trying to find the Revenue Man. This was probably rationalization, but it worked for me.

"I found one article dated September 8, 1926. It's kind of sketchy.

> '*Police investigated reports of a shooting outside the tavern of the Harrington Inn. Neighbors reported hearing several gunshots and possibly a Gatling gun about midnight last night, coming from the area of the tavern. Police found at least forty bullet casings and some damage to the siding of the tavern. When questioned, the tavern owners said three or four men had started a fistfight in the tavern. When they were asked to leave, they continued their battle outside, which escalated to a gunfight. No one was reported hurt.*'"

"Interesting, but it seems there is more that they didn't say than they did. And nothing about our Revenue Man. Try looking a few days later and see if there are any other reports," said Lucas.

"I don't find anything else about the incident. Let me try something— Missing Revenue Man. Well, will you look at that! There's an article dated about two weeks after the other one entitled, if you can believe it, 'Missing Revenue Man.'

> 'Roy Abernathy, who worked for the Internal Revenue Service investigating Prohibition violations throughout the county has been declared missing. The Internal Revenue Service reports that they have not heard from or been able to contact Mr. Abernathy since early September. His last report stated he was closing in on serious bootlegging violations in the area. Anyone with information as to his whereabouts is asked to contact the IRS immediately.'

"That's it. I can't find any other references to him, what happened, or if he was ever found."

"I knew it. I knew it. I knew it! He was real. And he was here."

"That's proof he was in the area, but not proof positive that he was here or died here," Dan said. "It does add to the information we have— we know he was in the area, we know there was a gunfight, and we know he disappeared around that same time. But without a body, we can't be sure he was shot and died here. Sorry, Lil."

"Don't burst my bubble, Dan! We may just find him yet. And if not, it was a valiant effort and is making all this work much more interesting."

"Mom, I thought you hated the farm," said Meghan. "You would never tell us much about it, and if you did, it was never positive. But it sounds to me like you had a great childhood full of exciting adventures."

"Well, I must admit, being here is bringing back some very pleasant memories that I'd forgotten or blocked because of my dislike for farming. I still hate farm work, and all the anxiety that goes with it, but I am seeing that lots of good things happened, too, even if I was an 'awful kid.'"

"Maybe awful wasn't a good choice of words. Maybe I should have said misguided, or impulsive," said Dan.

"Or devious," added Meghan.

"How about sneaky or bratty?" added Lucas.

"How about persistent and adventurous! Enough, let's talk about something else," I demanded.

"Okay everyone, I have something to share, and Meghan and I wanted all of us together before I told you."

"Meghan, you're pregnant!"

"No! Shut up, Lucas. This is serious."

Nick began again. "Well, it seems I've lost my job. With all the new computer advancements in architectural engineering and a lagging economy, my company doesn't need more than one of us, and since the other guy had seniority, I was let go."

"Oh Nick, I am so sorry! You are so good at your job, and they loved your work. I can't believe this!" I replied in shock.

"Sorry, Nick. What are your plans, son?" asked Dan.

"Well, because they loved me, they gave me excellent references and a phenomenal severance package, so Meghan and I don't have to worry for a year at least, and I have plenty of time to look for something else. I'm thinking I might want to explore some new ventures for a change of pace. We're just starting to consider the possibilities. But the good part of all this is that we have some free time. Meghan is between shows right now, so we thought if you would have us, we would like to stay here and help you out with the sorting and selling of everything."

"If we would have you—of course we would have you. We would love your company and your help!" I replied excitedly.

"We decided it's kind of the cloud and silver lining thing, you know," said Meghan. "This way we get to spend time with you that we wouldn't have had otherwise, and we have time to figure out our next steps."

"And so," Nick said, "In light of the fact Meg and I will be here for a while to help, I propose we all work real hard tomorrow, and then we make Sunday a day of rest and fun . . . and search for the Revenue Man!"

We all agreed that was a wonderful idea! We decided to scour the woods again, and any other place that looked promising. And even if we found nothing, we would share the adventure.

CHAPTER TEN
THE BARN

The next morning dawned sunny and bright, and the air felt warm but also chilly, typical of a crisp New England fall day. Everyone was up early, in great spirits, and ready to get to work.

"Lily, I think you should take the brains and get started on the barn, while I take the brawn and move all the items we found in the apartments to the garage," suggested Dan.

"I think there is something sexist in that comment somewhere, but it sounds like a very good idea," I responded. "Ladies, grab your gloves, and let's be off. I'll take some breath masks in case we need them. See you guys later."

We headed out the door and up the hill to the barn. The poor old building looked ancient. The caretaker had fixed any rotting or missing siding and repainted it white with red trim, but it still showed its age. I suspected we would have to replace the roof before we sold the property. The barn had two and a half levels above ground, in addition to a full underground cellar dug out of the hill. It had a gambrel roof, which allowed for more headroom in the haylofts in the second story, and an extra half level for an additional loft.

"You know, your land must be the only flat acres in New England!" mused Emily. Why do you think they built the barn on the only hill?"

"Careful what you are calling a hill, woman! We would consider this barely an incline in Colorado," quipped Meghan.

"Our land really is pretty flat, and the soil is very fertile. I don't know if it once was full of rocks, but you're right, it is not typical New England land. As for the barn, I think they put it there so they could easily build cold storage cellars underground. I do know that hill came in handy when a truck or tractor wouldn't start. You could push it down the incline and then pop the clutch and get it started. I also remember my father teaching me to ride a two-wheeler bike by pushing me down that hill! You know what's weird—the barn sure seemed a lot further away from the house when I was a kid!"

"I bet this 'incline' seemed steeper, too, when you were riding that bike down the hill."

Walking into the barn felt like coming home to an old friend. I always loved the smell of old hay whenever we played in this building. There was a family of barn swallows who came back to their nest in the rafters every year. I used to watch them with their wide, forked tails, swooping in and out of the barn to bring food to their babies. The nest was still there. I wonder if their subsequent generations still came here to lay and hatch their eggs. Suddenly, Meghan began belting out "Defying Gravity" from "Wicked."

"The acoustics in this place are amazing! Mom, this would make a fantastic community theatre or a dinner theatre. Can't you see it?"

"I suppose it could be with some very serious renovation. But I don't want to think about anything like that. Whomever we sell it to can do that or anything else they desire with it."

"Look at the size of those beams. They must be twelve or fifteen inches thick. Can you imagine what they had to do to build this place?" said Emily.

"They probably took a whole tree and just cut off the bark and squared the sides for each beam. They must have been really heavy. I wonder how they got them way up there. The haylofts must be about twelve feet above the concrete floor," guessed Meghan.

"It is twelve feet to the lofts. And the half-loft is about ten or twelve feet higher up than the second floor lofts. Originally the haylofts ran all along both sides of the wide central area, which was left open to the half loft. But since we didn't raise farm animals, we didn't need all those lofts for hay storage, so my Dad and some workers removed the second floor over two-thirds of the right side. It made it easier to store irrigation pipe in the winter because they could just slide them across the beams. My brothers and I used to walk the beams from one hayloft to another. I don't think I have that kind of balance anymore."

"You walked those beams? Twelve feet above a concrete floor? Was that allowed or did you break another Boundary Rule there, Mom?"

"I can't remember if it was Boundary Rule 4 or 5 that said 'No going into the haylofts.' Some of the floorboards were rotten and there were holes, and my mother was afraid there would be rats. But it was fine as long as you watched for the holes."

"So you broke that rule, too. You really were a daredevil, but a horrible child, Mom! What rule was it that said you couldn't walk on the beams?"

"There wasn't one. Again, they didn't think we would be stupid enough to do that. I would have killed you and your brother for a stunt like that! But I have to admit, it was exciting!"

"If your parents only knew."

"Really. Well, where should we begin?" asked Emily.

"Why don't we scope out the place a little and then decide what to do first," I suggested.

"Then we can choose the fun stuff to do and leave the dirty stuff for the guys," quipped Meghan.

"Great idea," agreed Emily.

On the left side we had the stairs, which were more like an expanded ladder to the loft, followed by lots of machine parts and broken things that were left here as their finally resting place. Some of those parts might be serviceable or could be used for yard art, but I bet we would be better off selling most of them for scrap metal. I noticed an old wheelbarrow that as kids we used to give each other rides in. We must have been pretty little to fit in that thing. I was so thankful my father had sold most of the farm equipment when he retired. I couldn't imagine trying to sell all of that stuff, too! Plus this place would have been totally packed to the rafters.

"At the end of this side, we find a workbench and tools."

"More tools? And another workbench? Why did they need all this stuff?" asked Emily.

"The tools here are older ones and mostly machine tools, used to work on metal. The tools in the garage are for woodworking. Most of those tools were bought when my father retired and built his dream workshop. And no one else was allowed to use them. He waited many, many years to get his carpentry shop, and it was his personal space.

"The majority of the tools here in the barn have been here for as long as I can remember. They have been added to over the years, like the welder and some of the saws, but most are pretty old. They have fixed many tractors, trucks, harrows, cultivators, bikes, and who knows what else, and many of those machines had to be fixed several times. Farm machinery breaks a lot, if you hit a rock or something, or parts wear out, and being able to fix them saves the farmer a lot of money."

"Look at this sledge hammer. The edges are worn down and rounded from use. It's hard to believe you could wear down a solid piece of metal like that. Yuck, these tools are pretty greasy, too."

"Working on machines does get tools very dirty. That's how my parents always knew if we were in here using the tools to build stuff without permission. We would have grease all over us when we went into the house."

"So using the tools was a no-no, too?"

"I think it was Rule 6 that said, "Do not use any tools, wood, metal, nails, nuts, bolts, screws or any other building materials without checking with Dad first." My dad encouraged us to be creative and build stuff, but to use scrap wood or metal, not good lumber or parts needed for farm stuff. Plus we weren't always good about replacing tools where we found them, and nothing irked my dad more than not being able to find a tool when he needed it. I often used his hacksaw as a jigsaw and sometimes broke the blade, or we forgot to pick up bent nails, or made a mess of the workbench, or left things outside where they'd get rusty. So Rule 6a was to put everything back when you were finished, and 6b was to clean up your mess. There were very good reasons for the rules."

"What kinds of things did you kids build?" asked Emily.

"Oh, all kinds of things, like birdhouses, soap box cars, stuff for school or scout projects. We even tried to build a tree house one time. We weren't very good at carpentry, so my Dad would often end up helping us, after he yelled at us."

"So, you obviously broke those rules quite often, Mother. What were the consequences when you did?"

"It seemed the punishment was in direct proportion to how valuable my father considered the materials we had used, or how long he had to search for the tool he needed. Minor infractions included getting yelled at and a promise of extreme repercussions that involved not being able to sit for at least a week if the behavior occurred again. More serious violations included spanking and/or being grounded until the millennium, which in the 1950s seemed a very long time away."

Spanking was not a big issue like it is now. When I was a kid, my parents only used a hand, never a paddle or belt or anything. It was one swat, and the point was made, and it didn't happen very often--only for major screw-ups. The infrequency confirmed the severity of the infraction. My father had huge hands, and that one swat could tingle a little, but it was mostly my pride that was hurt. I was never sure if that was because I got caught or because I had disappointed him. But I don't think spanking hurt my self-esteem, and I never felt abused. Maybe because most kids I grew up with were spanked. It was commonplace.

"I understand the arguments against spanking, and I never spanked Meghan or Lucas, but I don't believe it left me with any lasting scars."

"Plus, we were perfect children! So you never needed to."

"That's not quite how I remember it. Okay, it looks like the right side under the loft contains more machine parts, and even more machine parts, and a few tools that we kids probably never put away."

"What's that way back against the wall? It looks like a big cabinet," asked Emily.

"Oh my Lord, it can't be! It's an old icebox. You know, they used to put ice in these to keep the food cold, before they had electric refrigerators. I remember we had this one in the vegetable stand when I was little. I can't believe it's here. It must have been concealed behind all the farm equipment, and I never noticed it there."

"And luckily, it is empty. The doors were left open a little to keep it from smelling bad. The wood is in great shape and there's hardly any rust on the metal inside. It's really nice, Mom."

"I've never seen one this big. It must be six feet long and four and a half feet high," Emily exclaimed."

"I think my dad said they found it in the tavern of the inn when they moved here. But I never knew what happened to it after they moved it out of the vegetable stand. This should be worth something to someone. Wouldn't it look great holding beer or wine in some steampunk or antique-decorated bar?"

"Where did those pieces of marble come from, Mom?"

"My father and brother Dom salvaged those when they closed the old railway station in Worcester a long time ago. These were once the stairs and counter tops in the station. My dad got an old-fashioned baggage cart with big wooden wheels, too. He would fill it with pumpkins and melons each year and put it by the vegetable stand. It attracted lots of business."

"And in this open area is Grandpa's pickup truck. Do you think it runs?" Meghan asked.

"I'm sure Nick and Lucas can get it running in no time, said Emily. It will come in handy to move stuff around."

"This small trailer to the golf cart will also be helpful to move stuff to the garage. The rest of this side looks like it has, can you believe it, more metal parts and the stairs to the storage cellars below. I say we wait to sort the stuff on this floor until we have the brawn, as your father called it, to help us decide what to keep and what to sell for scrap metal."

"Yea! Let's tackle the haylofts!" Meghan yelled as she raced to the stairs.

"Meghan, remember to be careful where you step. Looking at this ceiling, which is also the floor of the loft. It looks like the caretaker replaced some of the rotten boards, but maybe not all, and the floor is liable to be very uneven."

"Mom, you can stay down here while Emily and I go up, if you want."

"Not on your life! I'm not missing a chance to relive my youth."

We carefully climbed the stairs and paced the floor for weak spots with no mishaps. In the first section of the loft, there were three shelves and a built-in corner cabinet with a door held closed by a wooden latch. The items on the shelf were covered with light dust, a quarter inch or more thick. These things had been here for a very long time!

"Time for breath masks and gloves, ladies. I claim the cabinet," said Meghan.

"Then we'll take the shelves," answered Emily.

On the top shelf, Emily and I found some old gauges and air hoses. What they were for, I had no idea. I found a large thermometer mounted on a piece of metal with the words International Harvester and a picture of one of their tractors printed on it. It was colorful and looked intact, but I doubted it would work. Emily found a Farm Bureau sign, a couple of No Trespassing signs, and a small Orange Crush sign, all in good shape. The second shelf contained more old metal parts, an ancient car horn, and a wooden radio that made me think of a family sitting around to listen to "Little Orphan Annie" or "Amos and Andy," which were before my time. The third shelf held a couple of old wooden clocks, one a mantle clock and one a school-type regulator clock.

"I wonder how these got up here. It's seems a weird place for clocks and radios and such. Maybe Dan can fix them. Meghan, did you find anything?"

"A few empty canning jars full of nails and hinges and stuff, some mousetraps—empty, thank goodness, and an Eight O'clock coffee can with coins in it."

"Oh my, I hid that money up here! I had a dream one night that we were robbed, and I wanted a safe place for my fortune where no one would find it. I guess it was a good hiding place."

"Mom, there is only $4.48 in various coins in here. Hardly a fortune."

"It was to me way back then. What's that wrapped in paper at the bottom?"

I gently lifted out the faded, crumbled tissue paper packet and carefully opened it. Inside was a tiny baby doll, not more than an inch and a half tall, dressed in a tiny, white and pink crocheted dress and bonnet. It had a safety pin on the back, so it could be worn on clothing as costume jewelry.

"I always wondered what happened to this little doll. I won this in a spelling bee in second grade. I was so proud of myself that I wore it all the time. I must have stuck it in with the money for safekeeping."

"What kind of words did you have to spell, c-a-t, l-o-o-k, b-a-l-l?"

"Meghan, you have a smart mouth! And you shouldn't make fun of a sentimental old lady. I'll just take that coffee can with my doll pin and my $4.48, and proceed to the next part of the loft."

The rest of the big hayloft contained a few forkfuls of very dry hay and a couple of birdhouses, obviously made by us kids, but not much else. We could see from this vantage point that the half loft above was empty, so we thankfully didn't have to climb way up there. Dan, Lucas, and Nick came into the barn just as we finished this side of the lofts, so we started passing the things we had found down to them.

"We moved all the trash and the things we are going to sell into the garage," Dan reported. "Except the stoves, and the blanket chest, desk, and a few other objects from the smaller attic. Since Nick and Meg are staying for a while, Nick and I decided we would wait for some other day to take off the siding and get those items out those doors we found. Don't worry; we'll be putting the siding back on as good as new. We wanted to get up here to the barn to help you."

"That sounds great. Thank you."

"Watch how you handle that old coffee can," cracked Meghan. "It contains Mom's life savings."

Dan looked inside the can, shaking it a little to better see the coins. He looked at me amused. "The can is probably worth more than the money inside it."

"This is where my daughter gets her smart mouth! How about you guys start sorting through all the parts and stuff on this floor while we check the smaller hayloft on the right side of the barn. And remember, ladies, walk carefully in case of holes or rotten boards."

The narrow stairs and floor of this smaller loft were in better shape, probably because it was used less than the larger one. In the center was a big pile of stuff of all different heights and shapes covered with a canvas tarp that was torn in several places and must have had close to a half-inch layer of dust on it.

"Let's see what's under this tarp, but be careful lifting it so as not to rouse too much dust, and in case some varmints have made it their home."

We lifted the tarp off the top of the pile to find old baby furniture—a wooden highchair, a white wicker bassinet, an old-fashioned child's swing, and a walker. They looked dirty, and the bassinet mattress looked stained and worn, but otherwise they were in good shape. When we removed the tarp totally off the pile, we found a child's table and chairs, a little ironing board and iron, and a large, handmade toy chest. My father had made that chest for us when we were little. Meghan opened the lid until the chain became taut and held it up. It was filled with old dolls, a small case of doll clothes, metal trucks and tractors, baseball gloves and all different kinds of balls, child-size pots and pans and dishes, and games.

"Ladies, what you see before you are the remnants of my youth. All these things belonged to my brothers and me. They certainly bring back many, many memories. One Christmas, my mother gave me that doll, and the clothes in that little plaid suitcase. She had made all the clothes. Look, there are dresses, skirts, blouses, coats, hats, and even little hand-knit sweaters. I wasn't one who played with dolls very often, so I'm not sure I appreciated them then as much as I do now that I see how much work and love went into making all those things. If I had, I would have been a more grateful, thankful child. Well, there are a lot of things here to sort, that's for sure."

"Mom, if it's okay with you, I would like the keep the doll and doll clothes. Maybe I'll have a kid someday who will play with them. And if not, I would still like to have them."

"I'm sure Lucas will want to keep something, too, if that's all right," said Emily.

"Of course! All of you can have anything you want. It makes me feel good that you would want a piece of my history. I'm just surprised to find that my parents kept all this stuff all these years. I wonder why they didn't mention it when Meghan and Lucas or your cousins were little."

"Maybe they thought you wouldn't want it, or to deal with shipping it."

"Or most likely they forgot it was here like so much of the stuff we are finding. Hey, guys," I yelled down to them, "Can we pass this stuff down to you? We found lots of toys to play with!"

Once we had everything down to the first floor, Nick drove the golf cart with its new battery up to the barn, and we attached its small trailer. We loaded it with hayloft finds. Nick and Lucas drove everything to the garage while the rest of us followed on foot to help unload. I had ordered pizzas, and when the pizza delivery guy arrived, we decided to break for lunch before sorting the things on the first floor of the barn. The pizza guy could not believe the stack of stuff in the garage.

"Are you starting an antique store or something? I've never seen so much old stuff in one place before!"

"An antique store; now that's a novel idea," said Dan.

"We are selling everything." I retorted. "Do you see anything you would be interested in?"

"My wife would sure like one of those old milk cans over there. And I would love to have one of those metal dump trucks. How much would you sell them for?"

"Well, since the pizza arrived nice and hot, and because you are our very first customer, how about $25 for both of them."

"That's a deal! And thank you."

I took the money and stuffed it in my coffee can while Lucas helped the pizza guy load up the milk can and toy truck. I was quite pleased with myself.

"Mom, you do realize those things could have sold for two or three times that much, don't you?" Meghan asked.

"Of course I do, but look how happy he is, and we have plenty more to sell. Maybe he'll tell others, and we'll get lots of customers. Dearest ones, my coffee can is now our official money bank."

We ate a leisurely lunch, just enjoying each other's company. Dan and I loved having our whole family with us. I wished we all lived closer to each other, but like so many families, our kids had moved for more lucrative work situations. When we were together, there was always lots of bantering and laughter, coupled with caring and love. It was always so hard to say goodbye when everyone went home, but at least

Meghan and Nick would be staying for a while and that made me very happy. Having the kids there made all the work seem like fun, and it certainly made it easier to have all those strong bodies.

After lunch we sorted all the things on the first floor of the barn into items to sell, which included all tools, signs, mechanical parts and whatever else seemed collectible or serviceable. Dan took the old clocks and the radio to Dad's workshop to fix. Nick drove the golf cart with the trailer, while racing Lucas who was pushing an old wheelbarrow full of rusty tools. Boys will be boys!

The icebox would have to wait until we had piano dollies to move it. That thing was heavy! The rest of the metal things were put in a pile. Dan called a scrap metal business that was willing to come pick up everything in their truck. They had a scale to weigh the metal and would pay us cash. More money for my coffee can!

"What about downstairs in the barn cellar, Lily? Is there anything still down there?" asked Dan.

"There are two big storage rooms and a place to wash and bag vegetables, and I hope little else. Let's look down there and see what needs to be done. But we can save any work down there for another day."

"Sounds good to me. Everyone, we're going to check out downstairs. We'll need flashlights. Lucas, run to the house and grab those big flashlights, will you?" Dan asked.

The rest of us proceeded down the stairs. We turned on the few dangling lights, but it was still pretty dark. This cellar was stone on stone with a dirt floor, just like the one in the house. At the bottom of the stairs was a long room the length of the barn, and one-half its width. It was used as a washroom for vegetables.

On one side of the room was a large bin about three and a half feet high, five feet wide and ten feet long, but only about a foot deep. The bottom of the bin was covered with chicken wire. It was on wheels that rolled on a track that ran across the room to and under the vegetable washer on the opposite side. Crops, mostly carrots, were loaded from bushel baskets into the door of the washer, which was a large wooden barrel, about twice the size of a typical barrel, with separations between the staves. Water was piped into the washer, and a motor turned the barrel over and over until the vegetables were clean.

When the washer door was opened, the carrots dropped into the bin. Any remaining water dropped through the chicken wire. The bin was then rolled back on the track to its original position, and workers proceeded to fill cellophane bags with one pound of carrots. This was one of my dad's inventions, and a very effective one it was!

One person at the end of the bin twisted the bag shut and put the twisted part through the taping machine to seal it. Sealed bags were packed in crates, and my father would transport them to Worcester or Boston to produce wholesalers who would sell them to grocery stores and restaurants. They were one of our major crops, and I certainly had bagged a lot of carrots in my day. I bet I could still accurately put a pound of carrots in a bag within an ounce without weighing them! I could probably do the same with apples, tomatoes and potatoes.

I didn't like this basement either, but my father had built a wood burning stove out of an old metal barrel which kept the place warm, even in late fall. The workers were usually men and women, nice people who joked around a lot, so it wasn't too bad. If my father was in a good mood, we might even have music, and someone always brought something delicious for coffee breaks. One time someone even brought travel posters of places in Italy to "decorate." But as a kid, I hated to go into other parts of the cellar—the storerooms alone. Without other people and the warm stove, those dark and dank rooms were scary!

The other half of the cellar was divided into three parts. The first and third parts were cold storerooms for vegetables, and the middle area was a driveway for vehicles full of baskets of vegetables to be driven under the barn and right up to the washer or off loaded into the storage areas.

"There are no lights in the storerooms, just a small window, so we will definitely need those flashlights. I have no idea what we will find. Watch out for rats."

Each storeroom had stonewalls and a central door about four-feet wide made of heavy wooden planks. Of course the rusty hinges creaked when we opened the first door, just to spook us a little. We shone our lights around, and all we saw were a few empty bushel baskets and covers and a torn and dilapidated cardboard box. We took them outside to add them to our storage area. Bushel baskets were quite popular these days, especially when they still had their colorful labels on them. Inside the box were cellophane bags with a picture of a tractor and the words "Martelli Farms. Fresh Produce. One pound."

"Mom, you had your own specially-printed carrot bags? How awesome!" said Lucas.

"Pretty cool, huh? We were a classy operation back in the day."

"Let's keep some of those," said Dan. "They are a piece of history. Or we can at least use them to store stuff."

We moved on to the second storeroom. It was empty, too, except for something in the back corner, covered with a canvas tarp.

"Maybe it's a body!" sad Meghan.

"Not funny, Meghan, and it's too big for a body anyway."

Nick and Lucas carefully pulled off the tarp. Luckily, no squeaking critters came rushing out, although there was evidence of a few ancient nests. What we found was a stacked pile of broken crates.

"Why would someone go to the bother of covering a bunch of empty, broken crates with a tarp?" asked Lucas.

"Maybe they aren't all empty, or they are covering up something else . . . oooo!" replied Nick with a spooky voice.

"Well, we'll just have to see, I guess."

They carefully removed each crate from the pile, checking to be certain they were really empty. At the bottom of the pile, they found the dirt floor—no bodies, no treasures, nothing.

"I guess a pile of crates covered with a canvas tarp is sometimes just a pile of crates," said Lucas philosophically.

"Well I, for one, am glad we didn't find the Revenue Man in these storerooms." quipped Nick. "If we had, we wouldn't have an excuse for a day off tomorrow."

"He's not in there unless he's buried several feet under the ground. We looked in here and dug around quite a bit in our searches. Look over there. That's where Tony and I pulled out part of the rock wall that we thought looked promising, but no Revenue Man. My father wasn't very pleased about that either."

"What did he do to the two of you?"

"We were grounded for that little escapade for a month. But at nine or ten years old, where did we have to go anyway? And we still had a hundred acres to roam. Besides, by the second or third week, my parents usually forgot we were grounded. We did have to shovel all the dirt back and fix the wall. I did always believe natural consequences taught the best lessons."

"Lil, it is amazing you ever grew into a responsible, law-biding adult."

"Oh pooh! I was just a curious child. Okay everyone, that's it for today. Let's go get cleaned up and enjoy the evening."

"I think we've accomplished a great deal today, and frankly, I'm tired. I can't wait for a nice shower, a home-cooked dinner and a few games of cards. I'll beat you at Hearts, Lucas ... as usual," teased Meghan.

"Sound wonderful to me," said Dan. "Let's do it."

CHAPTER ELEVEN
A DAY OF ADVENTURE

I awoke the next morning to the mouthwatering smell of frying bacon and freshly brewed coffee. I had planned to sleep in a little, but when I could no longer resist those delicious scents, I got up and headed to the kitchen to find the four young adults bustling about.

"What are you all doing up so early in the morning? I thought this was a day of rest."

"Well," said Meghan, I am preparing breakfast—bacon, scrambled eggs, homemade blueberry muffins, and coffee. Emily made the muffins."

"I'm packing a picnic lunch to take with us on our explorations today," replied Emily.

"And I am preparing the juice and helping Meghan," said Nick.

"That leaves you, Lucas, what is your contribution?"

"I'll have you know that I made the grocery store run for supplies at 6:00 a.m., and now I am in charge of toast."

"Why, this is absolutely wonderful! Thank you. What can I do to help?"

"You, sweet Mother, can sip this delicious coffee and let us wait on you. But first, you better go wake up Dad. Breakfast is just about ready. Nick and Lucas, please set the table."

"You know, Mom, you have a very bossy daughter!" complained Lucas.

"Well, someone needs to keep you organized and working," quipped Meghan.

Dan joined us, and we all sat down to a fantastic breakfast. Maybe it was the wonderful service, or that I didn't have to cook, or the excellent company, but for whatever reason, it seemed to me that everything we ate that morning was especially delicious.

"Emily, these are the best blueberry muffins I have ever had! May I get your recipe?"

"Sure, it's my mother's. She gave me some great recipes for muffins, scones, and coffee cakes that are to die for. Back home she is the queen of every bake sale."

"I am so full that you might have to roll me down the field road today. That is, if my pants will even fit. Thank you, kids; this breakfast was amazing." said Dan.

"And thoughtful. I thank you, too. Dan, we need the exercise to wear off some of the calories from this breakfast. How about we clean up the kitchen while the rest of you get ready. Shall we leave in say, forty-five minutes?"

The kids had done a great job of cleaning up as they cooked, so it didn't take long to get the kitchen back in order. They had learned a lot about cleaning since the days they lived with us. We threw everything in the dishwasher and started it, and were dressed and ready with five minutes to spare.

"So, does anyone have an idea of a route?" asked Emily.

"I've never been in the fields before. Actually, I don't think I've ever been past the yard before now," said Nick.

"Mom, I think you should take point and decide the route. We can explore the farmland and look for possible hiding or burial plots for the Revenue Man at the same time," said Lucas.

"Lucas, you occasionally, though very infrequently, astound me with an excellent suggestion," confessed Meghan. "I think that is a great idea."

"Okay then, shall we be off? I say we take the field road by the barn and head in the direction of the woods and the railroad tracks. We can take turns carrying the picnic basket."

We headed off, full of good cheer and full of food. It was a beautiful

Indian summer day, as only New England seems to have. The leaves were starting to turn bright red, Halloween orange, and brilliant yellow. It was the kind of day that lifted your spirits and made it impossible to be a curmudgeon. We thoroughly enjoyed the weather and the camaraderie.

"Mom, do you remember what was planted in each of the different fields?" asked Lucas.

"It actually varied from year to year to keep the soil fertile. Plants like corn use a lot of the soil's nutrients, so crops would be rotated. We grew all kinds of vegetables—corn and carrots were our biggest crops, but we also grew tomatoes, both in the greenhouse and outside, lettuce, cabbage, radishes, several kinds of peppers, potatoes, onions, beets, wax, green and shell beans, cucumbers, broccoli, cauliflower, watermelon, cantaloupe, pumpkins, gourds, strawberries, and probably others I'm forgetting," I said, practically out of breath after that long recitation.

"Stop! It sounds exhausting just to hear the list. No wonder you hated all that work. But how lucky you were to have all that fresh food," said Meghan.

"That's true. I remember one year my Dad even tried growing popcorn. It had to be planted way down in a corner of the field, far away from the sweet corn plants, or they would cross-pollinate, and we would end up with acres of popcorn and no sweet corn. It was fun to get the popcorn kernels directly from the ear instead of a bag. You know, you may still see a few vegetable plants that sprouted from stray or late germinating seeds as we walk along."

"Do you think you can tell us what kind of plants they are?" asked Emily.

"Honey, I can pick out a pepper plant at fifty yards. Even further for tomatoes and beans. And the length of a football field for corn. I was no slouch of a farmer's daughter!"

"Well, all right, Momma! You go, girl."

"Seriously, look over there. That is a pepper plant. That sprawling plant on this side of the road is a cucumber, and even you city slickers will be able to tell that over there is a cornstalk. Picture rows and rows of five or six-foot stalks going on for acres. We used to play hide and seek in the cornfields at night."

"That is awesome! I bet you loved that!" exclaimed Nick.

"Actually, it kind of spooked me. On a humid summer night, the plants would cling to our sweaty bodies. The little tiny projections on the sides of the leaves would prick us, and the leaves were sticky with sap. It felt like something was grabbing at me as I ran. And it was so easy to get lost! Everything looked the same for acres and acres, and in the dark, you could easily change direction without even realizing it and then you didn't know which way to go to get out ... or if you ever would. Sometimes someone would make spooky noises, but it was almost scarier when the only noise was the wind and our shoulders brushing the leaves of the cornstalks. The swishing noise as we touched the leaves made it hard to hear anyone coming. And then someone would sneak up and jump in front of you, or even worse, grab you from behind! It gives me the heebie-jeebies just to think about it."

"I still think it sounds totally, absolutely awesome!" said Nick. "I wish there were still cornstalks here so we could play tonight!"

"Hey, what's that small crater in the soil over there? It looks like the land is sinking. Is that a piece of metal sticking out? Come on, let's go check it out," said Dan.

We walked over to the area Dan had spotted. The soil was really sandy here, and it did look like the soil was sinking, but it also appeared that something was buried underneath.

"It is a big piece of metal," reported Dan. I can't find an edge and it's stuck too deep for me to pull it out."

"Look over here. This looks like a big piece of rotting leather. What could be buried here?" asked Nick.

"I think I know what it is! I remember my father telling me that he and my uncles had to put in landfill to level off this area a long time ago. He said they threw in old junk, too, including a Model A Ford."

"A Model A Ford! Let's dig it up!" Nick exclaimed. "It could be worth some money."

"That was exactly my thought when he told me about it, but he said it would be all rusted and worthless."

"Not anymore. It could be rusty gold," Lucas said, equally excited. "We have to at least try to get it out before you sell the property. Maybe we can do it when Emily and I come back for Thanksgiving."

"The soil level is lot lower than it was back then, and it is more sandy here than the rest of the farm, but it still could be a difficult job."

"We can rent a small tractor with a scoop for a day or so," said Dan, getting into the spirit of the discussion. "Can you imagine if we could get it out? Even if part of it is rusted away, it would be great just to see such an important piece of history!"

"Well, I guess we will be digging up the Model A! I have to admit, I always kind of wanted to see it myself."

"Wait, maybe they buried the Revenue Man down there! We better dig it up now."

"Roy Abernathy would have been buried during the Harrington's ownership, and the car was buried when my family owned the farm. If he had been buried under there, they would have seen the bones or something. Sorry, Nick, the car will have to wait a little longer."

"You can't blame a guy for trying. That car may become my new extracurricular activity."

"Shall we continue on? Over there is the irrigation pond. It used to be a small little decorative pond during the golf course days. My parents had it enlarged when we were kids."

"Did you swim and fish in it, too?" asked Nick.

"We didn't swim in it. It's fed by some very strong springs, making it hard to swim. And that was one rule we obeyed! We did fish there sometimes with fishing poles we made with a stick, string, and a bent nail, but we never caught anything. But, we did ice skate on it when it froze each winter. We would have skating parties and light a small fire to warm up. No comments on playing with fire, please. We had parental approval! I remember one winter we were planning a big skating party with lots of friends from school, and it snowed about a foot the night before. We were so upset. There was no way we could shovel that much snow off the whole pond. So Dad hooked up his snowplow to a tractor, drove onto the pond and cleared the ice! It was so cool to watch! My mother had her heart in her throat the whole time, worrying the ice wouldn't hold the tractor, but it did. He was my hero that day!"

"Grandpa was a pretty amazing guy. I would much rather have a skating party than a birthday party any day!" said Meg. "Were you a pretty good skater, Mom?"

"I'll have you know I was a very good skater. I could do figure eights, skate backwards, waltz, and jump a couple of barrels in my day."

"Mom, we're learning new things about you all the time."

"Okay, my turn for speculation--could the Revenue Man have been sunk in the pond?" asked Lucas."

"I'm not sure how deep the original pond was back then. I know they didn't find anything suspicious when they made it deeper and enlarged it. In drought years, we would pump a lot of water out of there to irrigate the fields, practically to the bottom, and we never saw a skeleton with cement shoes."

"So, it is a possibility. And you wouldn't object to Nick diving in there in a wetsuit and scuba gear to explore the depths?"

"Hey, why me? On second thought, I'll do it, but soon, before the weather gets much colder."

"If you do, I'm going with you," said Meghan.

"Oh, my devoted wife! We'll make it a romantic adventure."

"I think we should exhaust a few other possibilities first," countered Dan. "Let's head for the woods."

The woods bordered the edges of our property on the entire south side. They were about eight hundred feet deep before running into the railroad tracks, which was where our property ended. The woods continued on the other side of the tracks, but that was another farmer's property. The area was always overgrown, but since I had last been here, the plant life had really flourished. Trees of various kinds, sizes and shapes, mostly maples and oaks, were surrounded by Boston ferns, lady slippers, jack-in-the-pulpits, laurel and other plants with names I didn't know. At that time of year, they were all the different colors available in nature. It was awe-inspiring! Downed logs and tree stumps were frequently seen and whole ecosystems were growing inside their rotting carcasses.

"This isn't the woods. It's the forest primeval! I've never seen a wooded area so dense," said Emily. "And the ferns and flowers are magnificent."

"I'm glad we came before all the wildflowers die in the late fall. I used to love to explore here. It was always so quiet and peaceful. I never felt scared or feared getting lost."

"It looks like it would be really easy to get lost. You only have to go in about five feet, and you are totally invisible to anyone passing by," said Meghan. "And look at these ferns! I pay good money to buy these from a greenhouse, and here they grow wild. Amazing and beautiful."

"Is there any poison ivy around here?" asked Dan.

"Yes, there is. I'm not sure if the leaves stop being toxic with the change of seasons, so look out for 'three leaves and shiny, everyone,'" I answered.

"I definitely think old Roy is buried in these woods somewhere. This would be a perfect place to get rid of a body," pondered Nick.

"That's what we thought as kids. It was our favorite place to hunt for him and to play Cowboys and Indians. But we never found anything. Once in a while, we found some arrowheads. There was an Indian settlement at one time on the other side of the tracks. The owners found hundreds of Indian relics over there."

"And what Boundary Rule did you say was, 'Do not go into the woods?'"

"Boundary Rule 1, but we figured since we had permission to play detective, our investigations overrode the 'No Woods' rule. Rationalizing, I know, but we were determined, if dumb kids, remember? Plus the woods weren't quite as dense then, and there used to be a few clearings here and there. Any suggestions as to how we go about finding an eighty-some-odd-year-old grave?"

"Let's also look for evidence of a still or old barrels, or whatever they used to make the liquor," suggested Dan. "Didn't you say they made some whisky themselves and bought some from bootleggers, too? This seems the most likely place to make the booze, and probably to bury a body."

We split into groups of two, but always kept an eye out for each other. It really would be easy to get lost. I thought I located where we had found one of the hobo rest areas near the edge of the woods. The soil looked charred, and we found part of a rusted out tin can, but no still or grave. We explored the wooded area for a couple of hours from one edge of our property to the other, and finally gave up as we all met by the railroad tracks.

"It looks like any evidence that was here has been consumed by nature over the years. What Boundary Rule covered the railroad tracks, Lily?" asked Dan sarcastically.

"Actually, 'Do not go near or play on or cross the railroad tracks' was Rule 1a, part of the Woods Rule. You see if we didn't play in the woods, we couldn't get to the tracks to go near or play on or cross them."

"But you did, didn't you?"

"Well, a few times, especially when we were playing Cowboys and Indians. We would sneak over the tracks to the hilly area in the woods where the Indian settlement had been. I found an old grinding stone, and Tony found a spear point over there one time"

"So you not only broke the rule, you trespassed? What would your parents have said if you got caught?"

"I would have been grounded till menopause! But you sure make it sound much more serious than we thought it was at the time. We used to put coins on the track and wait for the train to flatten them like any other red-blooded American kid in those days. And . . ."

I suddenly decided that I probably shouldn't tell the next story. I didn't want my husband and my kids knowing I was a criminal—a lawbreaker who was lucky not to have ended up in reform school. We hadn't planned on getting in trouble, and it was a totally harmless adventure. Well, not really. It was theft . . . and dangerous. And we shouldn't have done it. But it was probably also the best time I ever had as a kid!

"What were you going to say, Mom?" asked Meghan.

"Oh, nothing, Meg. It wasn't important."

"Don't hold out on us now. I love hearing all your stories. I wish I had known about you being a delinquent when I was younger so I could have reminded you of your misspent youth whenever I got into trouble."

"Yes, come on Lil, I can tell this is going to be a great story," Dan said, trying to encourage me. "We'll still love you, whatever you did."

So, my family convinced me to tell them about my greatest adventure, the story of how my brothers Tony and Dom, Jack the kid who lived next door, my sweet dachshund Bonnie Boots, and I "borrowed" a railroad handcar and rode the rails! I was about ten, so Tony and Jack were probably eleven. Dom was eight, and Bonnie was my age since my Aunt Michelina, my Godmother, had given her to me when I was a baby. Bonnie followed me everywhere, so of course she was part of this adventure.

We were playing Cowboys and Indians near here when we came across the handcar on the tracks. It was the kind you see in the silent movies with a small wooden platform on metal wheels that fit on the rails. In the center of the platform was this seesaw-like piece of wood with handles. To get it to move, one guy pushed down on one side of the seesaw thingy, making the other side go up so another guy could then push down that side, over and over, and somehow that made the wheels turn. The railroad workers used them to go short distances to check track or carry supplies to fix rails and ties. We figured they must have left the railcar here while they went to lunch or something. I think it was my idea to take it for a ride, but Tony always bragged it was his, at least when adults weren't around.

It certainly wasn't Dom's! He kept whining that we could get hurt or get in trouble. Having no patience, I told him to go back home through the woods by himself and threatened him within an inch of his life if he told on us. Tony took a different approach. He used his considerable powers of persuasion to convince Dom that we needed him to come with us to take care of Bonnie Boots, who might be afraid. He asked Dom to sit on one side of the handcar and hold Bonnie tight to protect her. You can see why Uncle Tony became a lawyer. Bonnie was a brave soul and would have been just fine, but Tony's approach worked. Dom climbed on with Bonnie, and I learned a little about diplomacy that day.

It was not easy to get that thing moving! First we tried Tony on one side of the seesaw and Jack on the other. Then Jack and me on the same side. No dice! Finally Tony and I sat on the handles of the wooden part that moved up and down and rode it like a seesaw. Jack pushed a little from the back at the same time, and we finally got the thing moving, slowly at first, allowing Jack to jump on the back. Dom kept trying to tell us Bonnie was scared, but she seemed fine; he was just being a wimp. We got it moving a little faster, and a little faster, just like "The Little Engine That Could." We were yelling and screaming with delight. We thought we were very cool!

Near the end of our property, we went around a bend and suddenly we were going down a hill which wasn't really very steep, but seemed like a mountain riding on that handcar. We got moving pretty fast; fast enough that Bonnie's ears were blowing in the wind! And of course we had no idea where, or if there was a brake. Dom started crying, Bonnie started howling, and the seesaw was moving us up and down, instead of our controlling it. I have to admit, I was getting kind of scared myself. What if this thing jumped off the tracks or ran into something on the track—like a train! We could be killed! We were just contemplating jumping off, which was also a scary proposition, when the land dipped, slowing us down very quickly, and then we leveled off. At which point Jack finally found the brake, and we were able to stop, to everyone's relief.

Relief was short-lived however, because as we climbed down from the handcar, who did we see coming toward us but the railroad crew returning from lunch. Busted! The looks on their faces ranged from astonishment, to anger, to suppressed laughter. One person looked totally enraged, and fortunately or unfortunately, depending on your perspective, that was my Uncle Andrew, the head of the railroad crew. He rushed up to us and grabbed Tony and me by the arms. He would have grabbed Jack and Dom and even Bonnie Boots if he'd had enough arms. He proceeded to yell at all of us to the tune of: "What are you crazy kids doing; you could have been killed; is that any way to take care of your little brother and that poor dog; that handcar is railroad property; I ought to call the police and charge you with theft, etc., etc."

My family has a history of confusing fear and anger, so I knew he was mostly scared that we might have been hurt, and eventually he ran out of bluster, and hugged each of us in turn, even Bonnie. Once he was calmer, he asked, "What am I going to do with you?" Then he proceeded to answer his own question, "I'm taking you to your father right now."

Dun, dun, dun, dunnn! So we were fortunate he didn't call the cops, but unfortunately, and probably worse, we had to tell my father what we did. The fear/anger thing was an affliction my father shared, so Dad's first reaction was to spank Tony, Dom, and me pretty hard. My little buns were rather sore! Then he proceeded to yell in similar fashion and with similar words as my uncle. When he calmed down, he was practically in tears because he feared his little bambini could have been hurt. Jack and Bonnie Boots got off easy; Bonnie because she was a dog, and Jack because my dad would never touch someone else's kid. But Dad did make Jack confess to his parents with him overseeing the confession. In addition to the spanking, we had to stay in the yard—a perimeter from the house to the garage to the barn to the greenhouse for two whole weeks! That's a very limited space for a gang of cowboys! We did our penance, but amongst ourselves, we thought it was one of the greatest adventures of our lives!

I shared this story while we ate our picnic lunch, and everyone laughed so hard, I thought we would all end up with indigestion. It was so much fun to relive those adventures. I was beginning to realize that my childhood hadn't been so awful. There were times it certainly was difficult for a kid, but there were lots of special moments also, many of which my parents made possible. I was a normal kid with a hundred acre playground, when we had time to enjoy it. There were lots of good times, and it wasn't all work. How could I complain about never having a birthday party when I got to have skating parties on my own pond with delicious cupcakes, s'mores and hot chocolate lovingly prepared by my sweet mom, and the ice cleared with a tractor by my dad!

I had adventures that most kids at that time could only dream of, even if we did break the rules sometimes. Experimenting and pushing the boundaries are part of growing up to be a confident and independent person. All kids do it in some form or other, and my disobedient acts were legal, most of the time, and not self-destructive or hurtful to others. What I was starting to understand was that it was when I reached junior high and high school, the time when kids experience independent activities that lead to emancipation from family and movement to adulthood, that I had to work on the farm more and more. As a result, I missed out on lots of activities, which at the time, seemed very important to me and were actually part of that emancipation process. So I hated the farm and everything related to it. Maybe I experienced alternative activities that led to adulthood, certainly a strong work ethic, but I just didn't appreciate them, and they definitely weren't as much fun! I never hated my family like lots of kids said they did, just the work and the things I missed out on. These realizations eased my troubled soul somewhat. I was beginning to feel relieved and less tense. We hadn't found the Revenue Man, but I'd found out some important things about myself.

We took a different field road back to the house, and along the way I shared some memories. Just looking at an area, or remembering where something had been planted brought back events I hadn't thought about since I was a kid. Now, they seemed like stories to be treasured as part of family lore.

"Over there was where a glider landed one time. The air had suddenly gone still and the pilot lost the wind, so he had to land. The only clear place was the field where we had just planted squash and cucumbers. The pilot landed safely, but the field where the glider had slid was pretty messed up. He was very apologetic and offered to pay for the damage, but my parents wouldn't let him. He offered my dad a ride some time as compensation, but fat chance of that—my father was totally afraid of flying, and never got on a plane in his lifetime.

People would often stop by the farm to ask for planting advice. Three monks from the nearby Trappist Monastery came once each year, and my dad gave them seeds and stuff. I remember the first time I saw them. I was mesmerized! I had never seen men in long robes, which I thought were dresses, and I was confused when they smiled but wouldn't answer me when I spoke to them. (My mother later explained that Trappist monks take a vow of silence, and only one monk is allowed to speak when it is necessary to talk to the public.) I was especially fascinated by the black mastiff they brought with them. I had never seen such a huge dog before! I thought it was a pony, the shortest, ugliest pony I'd ever seen! A wild rabbit ran by, and the huge animal let out a loud, deep bark, and I was so startled that I almost fell over on my butt! One monk suppressed a chuckle at my reaction, and he gestured to me to pet the beast. The dog was really very friendly and proceeded to use his large tongue to lap my face! One big slurp, and I felt like I'd received a bath in smelly dog drool! But despite that, I instantly fell in love with him. Every year when they came, I would look for that dog. I was really disappointed they never brought him again.

At last we arrived back at the house, contented and satisfied after our fun day. We didn't find any evidence of the Revenue Man, but we did have a plan for another adventure when we would dig up the Model A at Thanksgiving. So we had learned a little more about the farm, discovered a few surprises, but most important, I had learned more about myself.

CHAPTER TWELVE
THE PROPOSAL

Since Lucas and Emily were leaving early the next morning, and since it seemed we had been eating all day, we decided to go out for a very light dinner, maybe just hors d'oeuvres or dessert. At one point I excused myself to go to the ladies room, and when I returned, I saw that my entire family was talking animatedly and gesturing excitedly. As I walked up to the table, I asked what was going on, and suddenly everyone stopped talking, arms moved to laps, and heads were bowed a little sheepishly.

"Oh, is this some kind of intervention? I don't drink, smoke, or do drugs, and I am now a grownup, not a mischievous child. I do sometimes say bad words, and I have put on a few pounds of late. Is that what this is all about? Is this a fat intervention? It's okay; lay it on me. I can take it."

"Lily, you are as beautiful as the day I married you," said Dan.

"Okay, flattery; now I'm really worried. I'm still cute, but not as beautiful as the day we were married. What do you all want from me?"

"Lil, the kids and I have been talking, and we have a proposal for you."

"A proposal . . . o—kay."

Meghan spoke first, "Mom, we've all been here a few days now and have learned a lot about this place and its history and about you. We know you've decided to sell the farm and rid yourself of childhood demons, and we understand that, but…we would like you to reconsider."

Next was Lucas' turn, "Mom, we've listened to all your wonderful stories, and we look around and see all the potential in this place that we know is hard for you to see. The house could be a wonderful bed and breakfast. The garage would make a perfect antique store, and we certainly have the inventory for it. And you love antiques."

Nick chimed in, "I'm looking for a job, and I told you I wanted something different and creative. I would love to redesign the house as a bed and breakfast, and then I could run it, too, while rehabbing the other buildings. Meghan could eventually build the barn into a community theatre. She'd have her own theatre and theatre company."

Dan took a turn, "Eventually we could get a florist or gardener to use the greenhouse. We could keep a small piece of property to plant fruits and vegetables for the bed and breakfast, in which you of course would never have to work! "

Finally, Emily added, "Lucas and I can't be here all the time, but he can use his skills to handle all the legal aspects, and I will donate all my mom's muffin and bread recipes."

I just sat there stunned. Was I hearing that my family wanted to keep the property and repurpose its use? I had never, ever, ever even considered the possibility of keeping the farm, as a farm or as anything else. My plan was to sell the property and leave as quickly as possible. And I certainly didn't realize my family, including my dear husband, was thinking otherwise. We had a lovely home in Colorado. Would we stay there and let the kids keep and run this place? We had planned to retire and travel and enjoy our hobbies and be able to sit and drink that second cup of coffee each morning instead of having to run out the door to work. Most of all, Dan and I would have choices. For the first time in our lives we would have choices of what we wanted to do each day without a lot of have-to's or should's. We would not be tied down to a job or anything that kept us from spontaneity and enjoying life. And the sale of the farm would also give us the money to do all that, as well as to leave a significant inheritance to our kids. All this was happening so fast, I couldn't think clearly. I think I was suffering from shock!

"Uh, how long was I in the bathroom?" I asked. "Did you think of all this in the time I was gone? It sounds like you have it all planned out. I need to digest all this a little and get up to speed. First question, where would the money come from?"

Lucas responded, "You could still sell off most of the land as a farm, or you would probably get more if you sold it as house lots, and then you could keep the buildings. I know the economy is slow right now, but this is a beautiful area, and I'm sure you can get top dollar. A whole lot more money than will fit in your coffee can, Mom. The people who want to live in the 'burbs' would have the money for prime real estate. I can do the research on price, number of possible lots, time frame, etc. Then Nick and I can develop a business plan for the bed and breakfast and all other components. As a professor, I get several vacations, and I can come help with building or whatever on my breaks."

"Since Meg and I are staying around for a while, we can get started on the antique store right away since just about everything needed to open it is already there. Maybe we'll be able to park that Model A out in front! With the sale of a lot or two or three, we should have the money to renovate the house into a bed and breakfast. When we sell a few more lots, we can start on the community theatre. We'll do one thing at a time as the money comes in, so we don't have to make major expenditures out of our pockets," contributed Nick.

Meghan's turn was next, "Mom, we're hoping you and Dad will want to move here, too. Then we'll all live closer to each other and be together more often. Dad, or contractors can build you a beautiful house, and we are hoping you will want to run the antique store. Don't tell me that hasn't always been a dream of yours! You said you want to travel, right? You still can. Think of all the antiques you can bring back from your trips! And Dad can do all the website, reservations and advertising stuff as well as help with building and maintenance."

"Lily, we obviously don't have this all planned yet, and by the look on your face, I can see you are understandably overwhelmed. We all just started talking and the whole idea just started to come together. But ultimately, it is your decision and yours alone. You own this place, and we all know you have mixed feelings about it. You also just retired from your life's work and were looking forward to slowing down, not starting a whirlwind of a business venture and a whole new occupation.

We'll all understand if you don't want to take on any of this, and that will be perfectly okay with all of us. But please take some time before you answer, and consider our proposal."

I sat there quietly for a few moments, trying to take in everything I was hearing. My mind was whirling with all the ideas I'd heard, and with a vast array of emotions. On the one hand there were all the questions and fears. Did I want to do any of this? Would I enjoy it or feel tied down? What about our retirement plans and the kids' inheritance? What about the money? Could we handle such a large business investment? I know Lucas said we didn't have to invest our own savings, but my old fears about money rose to the surface, and I was having trouble breathing. And the biggest concern was my hatred of the farm. Yes, I was feeling better about the place and my childhood, but was I ready and able to let all the negative memories go and try to find happiness here?

On the other hand, the timeline could be adjusted according to land sales, so we shouldn't have financial problems. We each had skills that were necessary and could contribute to the project, and it would be a family venture. Yes, I had been looking forward to slowing down and having more free time, but I would probably go crazy with all that free time since I was never one to sit and do nothing. I really was feeling a lot more positive about the farm and my life here; nostalgia was a good thing after all! I had been planning all along to give most of the money from the sale of the farm to my kids as an inheritance. But why not give it to them now when they could enjoy it and use it to build their lives and fuel their passions? My kids' desires were the finally selling point for me. Everyone was looking at me, trying to discern some clue as to what I was thinking. Finally, I looked up at them and smiled.

"Let's order coffee and dessert. We have a lot of planning to do!"

They all clapped and cheered, and everyone started talking at once. Dan and I made eye contact, and he nodded, indicating that he agreed that I had done a good thing. I was hoping and praying it wasn't something I would regret.

We talked on and on into the night, tossing out various ideas, making decisions, developing a schedule and assigning initial responsibilities.

We decided to use the six weeks between then and Thanksgiving to do research and complete tasks that would help us to decide the feasibility of this whole project and provide the information we needed to make informed decisions. When we were all here for Thanksgiving, we would reconvene and based on the information we gathered, make a final decision whether to go forward with this venture or to just sell the property.

Lucas, the math genius was put in charge of all research related to financial and legal aspects, particularly regarding the land division into lots, estimated sale prices, sales agents, as well as business projections for each component of the plan. At Dan's suggestion, Lucas would also set us up as a corporation with myself as the Chairman of the Board, and the Board being everyone else. All this researching and juggling would be mind-boggling for me, but Lucas found it a refreshing exercise and would have it completed in no time.

Whether we decided to go with the plan or not, Dan's first job was to sell his web design business. He already had several interested parties, so hopefully the sale wouldn't take too long. The housing market was picking up in Denver, and I was confident we could sell the house if we went forward with the plan. If so, we would list it with a realtor after Thanksgiving. At some point, we would have to return to Denver for a few weeks to handle the paperwork and arrange for movers. We were both aware that closing out our lives there and moving here was going to be difficult both physically and emotionally, especially leaving all our friends and our lovely home. The chance of the closings and financial paperwork on the house and Dan's business occurring at near the same time and with a smooth transition, we knew, was practically impossible. We would just have to deal with situations as they arose. At some point, Nick and Meghan would have to sell their house and move their things also.

Nick decided he would like to get started on designing the bed and breakfast. As an architectural engineer, he was sure he could draw up plans for the house that reflected the time period of the inn. We wanted a homey atmosphere, but also modern conveniences for our guests. As someone who thinks that indoor plumbing, especially the shower is the greatest invention of all time, I insisted on nice bathrooms. Once we had some capital flowing, Nick and Dan, and probably some hired contractors would start rehabbing in the upstairs and ell apartments, while we were living in the third. Eventually we would complete the rest of the house, with living quarters for Nick and Meg, since Nick would be running the bed and breakfast. Dan and I would have to buy or build another house for us to live in.

Since getting some capital was the key to getting everything rolling, Meghan and I were responsible for cleaning out the greenhouse and make it appealing for a floral/gardening shop. Lucas would research whether we should lease or sell the building, or own the business ourselves, run by a managing florist/gardener.

We also needed to tackle the vegetable stand. We decided that the stand would be a better place to remodel as the antique store, since it was a large rectangular space with lots of windows and without bays like the garage, and best of all, it was right on the main road to help draw in customers. A lot of the counters in the stand could be used for the store, and there was also plenty of parking. We would continue to use the garage for storage. Since we had to sell all the antiques whether we kept the property or not, we decided to go ahead with the antique store right away. Meghan totally understood that the community theatre was way down on the timeline, so she was happy to help with the antiques, another of her interests, as she developed her ideas for the theatre.

Emily's job was to collect all of her mom's and any other recipes that would be distinguish us as a bed and breakfast with excellent cuisine. She would also search for antique and vintage tablecloths and cups, saucers and dishes for the breakfast area. Emily would also check out hotel supply companies regarding linens and mattresses.

If we decided at Thanksgiving that the project wasn't feasible, we would go back to the original plan to sell the place, as a farm or as lots, depending on Lucas' research. We could sell the antiques as a business, or individually as originally planned. And any greenhouse contract wouldn't begin until after the Thanksgiving date. If things didn't work out, all we would have lost at that point is time, and we had lots of that. But if they did work out, we were looking forward to an amazing adventure!

At 3:00 a.m., Lucas and Emily decided they'd better get some rest and leave a little later in the morning than they originally planned. We all finally went to bed exhausted, but I was too excited and wound up to fall asleep easily. This had been an emotional, but fulfilling day. I think we were all itching to get started on this project!

CHAPTER THIRTEEN
THE GREENHOUSE
AND VEGETABLE STAND

M eghan and I were ready and raring to get to work at 9:30 the next morning! We had already had breakfast, said goodbye to Lucas and Emily, cleaned up the kitchen, and then headed out to the greenhouse. The dimensions of the building were one hundred feet by forty feet, so it was a decent size for a floral or gardening business. Depending on the needs of the business, additional land could be made available for outdoor plants and gardening needs.

My father and brothers had built this greenhouse. The sides were cinder blocks for the first three feet, and then large windows were added all around the rectangle to a height where the roof started. All the glass sashes, which comprised the roof, could be opened for fresh air in warm weather, and there was a heating system for cold weather. The concrete floor was banked well for effective drainage. Dad had also installed a sprinkler system with several zones, as well as hoses for hand watering.

We found that the building was mostly empty. Three rows of long benches built to hold boxes or potted plants were still there but could easily be removed if necessary. There were a few old crates of terra cotta pots and trowels and other tools. I also found an old sickle and a scythe that were in great condition and just needed a little cleaning. We added those to the sale pile. The only real work here was washing the windows. I remembered seeing a power washer with a long hose in my dad's workshop. Meghan and I grabbed the washer, a ladder, a little detergent, a bucket, and a hose, and set to work on the outside windows. We took turns washing and hosing off the soapsuds. The windows did not have to be perfect or without streaks since this was after all, a greenhouse, so the work progressed fairly quickly. We finished the outside windows in a couple of hours.

The inside windows were quite a different story, however. Maybe using detergent was not the best idea. As we cleaned the window sashes that made up the roof, suds and water kept dripping down on us until we were soaked. We each grabbed a baseball cap, but they didn't help much. We were starting to get frustrated and our arms were starting to ache when Nick walked in to tell us to come in the house for a late lunch. A big glob of suds fell from the top sash right onto his head, and then slid down over his face! Meghan and I both started laughing. Then Nick took the suds from his face and threw them at Meg. So she got more suds from a bucket and threw them back at him. He retaliated by hurling suds at her and then at me for laughing. This continued on for a bit until Dan walked in to see what was going on, and we all threw suds at him. At that point, we all just lost it. A good laugh was the break we needed from work!

The guys helped us finish up the top and side windows, since they were now practically as wet as Meghan and I were. We were done in no time with all of us working together. Then Dan put the washer away. Meghan and I changed while Nick prepared our lunch. I just love teamwork!

It was almost 2:30 when we finished lunch, so we decided we would all check out the vegetable stand to see what needed to be done, but wait to start the actual work until the next day. I was very pleased that there were no vegetable carcasses that had rotted in there and that the place was mostly dusty. The stand was a big rectangle about seventy-five feet by sixty feet. It was one huge room except for a ten by twelve foot area walled off in a back corner as a small kitchenette which had a sink, shelves, a small frig, and a table and four chairs as well as the world's smallest bathroom. Once we added a coffeemaker and microwave, it would be a great room for coffee and lunch breaks, small storage, and our office. The building originally had horizontal doors about half way up the front side that could be lowered for business each day, giving the place an open air feel. But as the stand stayed open for longer seasons, Dad replaced the doors with three big picture windows that would be perfect for displays and let in a lot of light! Right now they drastically needed cleaning.

The rest of the area was filled with counters holding heavy wooden bushel boxes, which used to hold the various vegetables for sale. There were stacks of empty bushel baskets, some with covers, some apple boxes, and a few tomato baskets with handles. Some of these could be used for storage; some would be great to display pieces on or in, and some we could sell. Old boxes and baskets were very popular right now. The counters could be reconfigured or used as is. There was no ceiling, just rafters, which exposed the roof. I used to love listening to rain falling on that roof. Balanced on the rafters were several wooden planks and two-by-fours that would be perfect for building shelves. All we needed to buy were some shelving brackets, and the paint, and we could start the remodeling!

On the front side, the roof extended beyond the building for about twelve feet and came to rest on simple wooden columns, creating what was called a porte cochere, which is a fancy word for a drive through. It had been previously used for cars to drive under as they came to the stand to keep people from getting wet when it rained. We decided it would be a perfect place to put antiques outside in good weather. The last place we examined was a small lean-to on the back of the building that my father had added on as a place to store baskets of vegetables until we needed them in the stand. We opened the door and were delighted to see the old railway luggage wagon Dad had used to display pumpkins and other fall produce. I loved this old wagon! We decided to keep it for now to attract people to the store, and it would be a great way to display pieces. The stand would be perfect for an antique store, and we were anxious to get it open for business.

Meghan and I spent the rest of the afternoon planning the antique shop—paint colors, shelving placement, sales counter, and basic decor.

I decided I wanted the outside to be barn red, with cream and black accents. We selected a café au lait color for the walls. We wanted a number of different table sizes and display pieces to put various items on that could easily be reconfigured to give a totally different look. These would be stained or painted a dark or neutral color to accent what was displayed and not the table or box itself. We talked about what items to sell first, and advertising, which would be Dan's job. We drew up diagrams, made lists, and totally enjoyed every minute of our time! Meghan and I worked well together. We couldn't agree on a name, so we decided to get everyone's input for the shop's name and a date for the grand opening.

That evening at dinner, we shared everything with Dan and Nick, and they were very impressed with all we had accomplished. They agreed to start building the shelves, counter and other display pieces in the morning.

"Great, while you are doing that, Meghan and I will go buy the paint, stain and shelf brackets. Then we're going antique shopping!"

"Excuse me, Lil, but did you just say antique shopping?" queried Dan. "Don't we already have a garage full to bursting with antiques?"

"Well, yes, but we need a few different kinds of items that we don't have to round out the inventory, you know, to try to appeal to everyone's taste."

"I don't know much about antiques, but what else could there possibly be?" asked Nick.

"Well, we need some pictures, glassware and pottery, mostly small items. We figured we would hit the flea markets and a few antique stores to check out the competition. We should be back by lunchtime, and we'll even bring you a nice lunch, albeit a late lunch."

Dan and Nick kept teasing us about just trying to avoid all the work and wanting to spend money, but it was all in good fun. They were as excited about this project as Meg and I were.

"So, how are you feeling about all of this, Lily? Any regrets?"

"Absolutely none! I'm finding it's so much more fun to be redesigning and repurposing this place than it was to work on getting rid of it. I feel inspired. I think this was the right thing to do."

"I'm so glad to hear you say that. Me, too," agreed Dan.

"Me three!"

"Me four! I can't wait to dig up that model A and find the Revenue Man," said Nick.

"The Revenue Man has been waiting a long time to be found, and I guess he will have to wait a little while longer, but believe me, I haven't forgotten him."

CHAPTER FOURTEEN
THE RENOVATION

After a rainy evening, the next morning dawned bright and clear, another beautiful fall day. While the guys started working in the stand/soon to be antique store, Meghan and I took off to go shopping. First we went to Home Depot and picked out all our paint and stain colors, which was a much easier job than I expected since we already knew what we wanted. Next we looked for shelving brackets. We wanted something rustic looking, and nothing seemed to quite fit the bill. When we explained to the clerk what we were looking for, she suggested we try a building salvage store nearby. So we paid for our things and headed off.

Jim's Architectural Antiques was absolutely amazing! We chose some lovely wrought iron filigree brackets that were perfect for our shelves, as well as antique cornices big enough to be brackets or to set items on. Best of all we found a wooden workbench that with a little sanding and staining would be a perfect sales counter. I also saw a gorgeous wrought iron gate that I fell in love with and had to buy! He also had some embossed tin tiles from an old ceiling that were in perfect shape. We decided to buy several of those. Then I found a hand-carved oak hearth. I wasn't sure if I would sell it or keep it to display items on, but I was leaning toward the latter.

As we were talking to the owner, he and I realized that we went to high school together, but Jim Duchamp was a few years older. He had even worked for my father in the fields one summer. As a result of our shared history, Jim's prices got even better. I told him of our plans, and he said he would be tearing down an old house in a month or so that had three beautiful hearths, if we were interested. I told him if we found the old fireplaces when we tore down the ugly paneling, we might be back. Jim even offered to deliver the bigger items to the farm the next day. We left very pleased with our purchases and feeling like we'd found some great deals.

"You know, it's already 11:30. Let's grab some subs at that pizza and sub place we like and have lunch with the guys before we head to the antique stores and flea market," I suggested. "We can drop off the shelf brackets, the cornices and the paint. That will leave more room for this afternoon's purchases."

"I could really use a latte. Maybe we should add a Starbuck's franchise to our plans," joked Meg.

"That's not a bad idea; not a bad idea at all."

The flea market was mostly full of things even the fleas wouldn't want. It always amazes me what people will sell, but even more what other people will buy! However we did find several nice pictures: a couple of antique landscapes, two vintage watercolors of flowers and a couple of WWII posters. The latter were in excellent shape. I loved them! Meghan found a charming teapot and a big old coffeepot. We also found a beautiful set of old china in fabulous condition. And the prices were great.

We then headed to several antique stores along one street in a nearby town, locally known as Antique Row. We got a few ideas for decorating, but their retail prices kept us from buying much. We did get a couple of lovely pitchers and glassware that were on clearance. The owner informed us she was going out of business soon and offered a fantastic deal on an old phonograph, the kind with the big metal cone on the end like in the RCA Victor logo, as well as a couple of early radios. We scooped up all of them, gave her our cell phone number for when she was ready to sell off more of her inventory and loaded up the car with our treasures.

We got home about 5:30, absolutely exhausted! Dan, the darling man, was making minestrone soup for dinner. He informed us that Nick was in the garage, trying to start the old tractor. A few minutes later, we heard the sound of the tractor motor turning over and catching. We all went outside to see Nick driving up to the house on that orange spider tractor looking quite pleased with himself.

"I got it running! This thing is a hoot to drive. It's so open; I feel that I'm driving a big tall go-kart. Meghan, you want a ride?" Nick asked enthusiastically.

Meghan jumped on, and off they went around the yard. It did my heart good to see that funny-looking tractor moving again. I started to show Dan what we had bought when Meg and Nick returned. Dan absolutely loved the phonograph and thought we should consider keeping it for the Bed and Breakfast. They complimented our other finds, too, but not being as fluent in antiques as Meg and I, they were not as impressed by the deals we had gotten.

"Actually, the best items arrive tomorrow," said Meghan. We went to this fantastic place called Jim's Architectural Antiques. The owner went to school with Mom, so he gave us some great deals, and even offered to deliver them tomorrow for free. I think he has the hots for her. You better watch out, Dad!"

"Oh, Meghan, he does not. It's just the way people are in small towns. If you ever knew someone or the family, even remotely, you have a history, so you automatically trust him or her. You are sort of connected forever. His connection was working for Grandpa, not me."

"Sure, Mom, keep telling yourself that!"

"Well, Lil, sugar daddy or not, it doesn't seem like you had enough money in your Eight O'clock coffee can to any way near cover today's purchases. I know we have to use some of our own money to get started, but remember what we said about sales covering the project," Dan reminded me.

"I know, and believe me, I am keeping good records. I don't want to go into debt, especially if we end up having to sell. Meg and I also decided we should open the store shortly after Thanksgiving with a Grand Opening Holiday Sale. Even if we don't continue with the whole project, we do have to sell all of this stuff, and we will have an attractive place to do it. We could cut a tree in the woods, decorate it with my mother's vintage and Grammy's antique ornaments, hang a few fresh garlands that I think I still know how to make, and we are ready to go! What do you think?"

"I think that sounds like a great idea, especially when you see everything we were able to get done today. Come take a look," said Dan.

When we walked into the stand/store, Meghan's and my mouths dropped open in awe. Dan and Nick had accomplished so much work in one day! They had cut the vegetable counters to make several sizes and heights for displays. They also made some display blocks out of the old boxes, and even hung the shelves and cornices. I was so impressed that my eyes filled with tears of gratitude.

"See how much we can get done without you girls hanging around bothering us," quipped Nick. "How do you like it?"

"It's perfect!" I said, "Absolutely perfect."

"I totally agree. I love it!" agreed Meghan. "It's going to be even better than I imagined."

"Tomorrow we have a lot of sanding to do, if you ladies would like to help. We found two electric sanders in your father's workshop that we can use. I also found a few hand sanding blocks and plenty of sandpaper. I swear that everything we'll ever need in the way of nails, nuts, bolts, hinges—just about anything you can think of is in that workshop. We shouldn't have to buy much at all. I'm also thinking we should sand and eventually stain the floor to give it the classy, finished look of a nice store rather than a vegetable stand."

"That would look great. I move that from now on we call this place the Antique Store, and that it shall never again be known as the Vegetable Stand. All in favor say 'Aye!'"

"Aye!" they all yelled in agreement. "Dan and Nick, thank you so much for everything you've done. The place looks wonderful."

"I'm really glad you like it," said Dan. "Now I have to get back to the kitchen before my soup boils over!"

Early the next morning found the four of us sanding away on the counters and boxes, taking turns using the power and hand sanders. We wore our trusty breath masks so as not to inhale the serious sawdust we were creating. Jim Duchamp pulled into the yard in a small delivery truck about 10:00. We went out to meet him and help unload our purchases. Jim took one look at us and started laughing.

"Are you turning this place into an antique store or a hospital?" he asked. "What's with all the masks?"

"We're performing surgery on this place, Jim! Actually we are sanding counters and stuff. You've met Meghan, and let me introduce my husband, Dan, and Meghan's husband, Nick."

"Nice to meet you both. I brought all your purchases. These ladies drive a hard bargain, but I think you'll like what they bought."

We unloaded the hearth, workbench and other items. Nick and Dan were in awe of the workbench. They agreed it would make a great sales counter. We showed Jim the inside of the store, and then Dan and I gave him a tour of the other buildings, too, sharing our plans. He had some great ideas for the bed and breakfast, and started making a list of things we might need that he had or would try to find, in addition to the hearths he had already told me about. He loved the barn and said he would keep an eye out for theater stuff. He also promised to contact a friend, actually someone we went to high school with, whose daughter might be interested in the greenhouse.

Jim stopped short when he saw the tractor. "Is that an Allis-Chalmers Model G tractor?"

"It sure is; it's a 1952 that my father bought the year I was born. Nick drained the old oil and gas and put in new fluids, and got it running like new."

"I've been looking for one of these for a long time. They're getting pretty rare. They are so sought after now, that at auction they run anywhere from $4,000 to $10,000, depending on condition."

"You certainly know much more about it than I do."

"I have a big garden behind my place, and I need something like this to work it. Are you interested in selling it?"

"Well, Nick might be a little disappointed that his toy is leaving so soon, but yes, we are selling it," I told him.

"Would you take $8,000 for it?"

I was so shocked, I almost choked!

"Since you were so fair with us at your shop, how about I take $8,000 if you find any of the old planting and other equipment to go with it, and $7,500 if you we don't have them anymore. Does that seem fair?"

"That sounds more than fair!"

Jim and Dan checked the rest of the garage and barn and found a cultivator and some planting buckets. Jim also found a few old tools he wanted, so he wrote us a check for $8,000 on the spot. We helped him load the tractor on the truck and away he drove.

"Are you feeling sad about selling that tractor that your Dad kept because of you?" asked Dan.

"I don't feel sentimental at all with $8,000 in my coffee can! That covers all the purchases so far and gives us a little nest egg. But I think Nick is looking a little teary-eyed. We better get on that Model A project real soon."

"Jim is a great guy! I'm so glad you reconnected with him. He'll be a valuable resource as we progress, especially for the bed and breakfast and theatre. He said he has an industrial sander and a floor sander we can borrow, so after lunch, I'll run over to his place to get them. He also said he has lots of used track and industrial lighting that might look great in here or on the drive through. I'd kind of like to see the rest of his shop, too."

"Why don't you take Nick with you. He deserves a break, and maybe you two will see some things with your expert eyes that we missed and could use. Meghan and I will keep sanding now that we get the power sanders all to ourselves for a while!"

By the time Dan and Nick returned around 4:00, my arms were sore from all the back and forth motion of sanding on top of the up and down motion of cleaning the greenhouse windows. I would soon be in the best shape I had been in my life! The boxes and blocks were as smooth as clear ice and looked fantastic! I couldn't wait to stain them. The men came in all excited.

"We borrowed the industrial sander for the counters and the floor sander. It's also industrial strength, so it will smooth out this floor in no time. We also got a heater to install in the rafters."

"A heater?" I remarked. "I didn't realize we were in the market for one."

"Well, darling wife, you have to remember the stand was built primarily as a summer building. I checked that there is insulation in the walls, but the open rafters, while charming, do nothing to keep heat in in the winter. Jim had this unit from an old store that will throw off enough heat to keep this place cozy without having to install big furnaces or the like."

"Dan, that is absolutely brilliant! I hadn't even thought about heating this place. I was only thinking of the décor and antiques."

"I guess that's why you need to keep me around, kid—to think of all the other stuff. And because you love me! Come see the great lighting we got. You know, Lily, Jim is an asset and a good person! I think I've met my first friend here in Massachusetts."

We walked out to the car to find it full of lights. For the outside lights, Nick had found some big lights shaped like bells that were attached to a curved arm, which would allow them to be hung out a foot or so from the building, offering more light and style. I absolutely loved them! The shape was beautiful and felt warm, not stark. They made me think of a village country store. Nick had also picked some lights to highlight the sign on the store that were smaller, but compatible with the bigger bells lights.

For the inside, Dan had chosen some lovely pendant lights with delicate glass shades that looked old-fashioned but provided the bright light of modern fixtures. Meghan and I thought they were perfect and that the guys had done a great job.

"Jim also threw in this tracking light for free. We'll be able to move the lights around, allowing us to highlight different objects or areas as needed. He said it had been sitting around for a while, and we would be doing him a favor to take it off his hands."

"What a nice guy! I still think it's because he has a crush on Mom."

"If there is any reason for his generosity, Meg, it's his interest in the Model A in the field," said Nick. "We were telling him how we were going to dig it up over Thanksgiving, and he offered to bring his small backhoe and truck with a winch to help us. If it hasn't totally rotted away, he might be interested in buying it—that is, if you want to sell it, Mom."

"Gee, I don't know, Nick. We already sold the tractor. Could you bear to lose the Model A, too? What would he do with it anyway?"

"Oh sure, I just like the idea of finding it and seeing it. But I would have no problem with your selling it. Jim would give it a good home."

"First we have to dig the up the Model A, which won't be until Thanksgiving. We have lots of other things to do first," reminded Dan.

"Yeah, and one of them is to decide on a name for this place! Let's work on that tonight, okay?" I asked.

"Sounds great! Nick and I will carefully put all this lighting in the garage for now, and maybe tinker with the pick-up truck while you ladies prepare us a fine dinner as a reward for our excellent purchases!" said Dan.

Never one to be outdone, Meghan responded, "Talk about macho comments! Hey, we worked really hard while you were gone, you know, and my arms are about to fall off. So, we are going to relax with hot showers and then order Chinese. We'll call you when it arrives."

CHAPTER FIFTEEN
NAMING THE STORE

We never had any difficulty coming up with names for our children or the numerous pets we had over the years, but deciding on a name for the antique store proved to be a difficult task. We started pondering this dilemma as we ate our Chinese food. Everything was absolutely delicious; it could rival anything in Chinatown. We now had another great restaurant to add to the limited repertoire available in this area.

As everyone threw out possible names, I found myself being quite critical about the suggestions.

Dan: "How about Liliana's Antiques.'"

Me: "Too sweet."

Meg: "Roadside Antiques."

Me: "Too boring."

Nick: "Martelli's Retro."

Me: "Too Italian and too much like a used car dealership."

Dan: "Ye Old Antique Shoppe"

Me: "Too quaint."

Meg: "Spring Valley Antiques"

Me: "Too rustic and where is Spring Valley?"

Dan: "Lucas called in with 'Antique and Vintage Collectables.'"

Me: "Too obvious."

Meg: "Emily suggested, 'Old-fashioned Treasures.'"

Me: "Too cliché."

Nick: "How about 'Revenue Man Revisited!'"

Me: "Too hilarious and not relevant!"

Meg: "Special Treasures."

Me: "Too simple."

Nick: "Old Stuff Revisited."

Me: "Too cutesy."

Dan: "The World's Very Best Antiques."

Me: "Too long and too sanctimonious."

"Well, what are you thinking, Liliana? You must have some thoughts for a name."

"I've been tossing this around in my head for a while, and I want something that fits the store, but it should complement the bed and breakfast, and possibly the greenhouse and eventually the community theatre. It's almost as if we have to name everything at once! So, I'm thinking of something that relates to all of us, fits for all our ventures, and has kind of a nice ring to it—how about Delaney's Antiques?"

"Well I certainly like the sound of it, but this is your family's legacy, Lily," commented Dan.

"I have been a Delaney longer than I was ever a Martelli, and you and the kids are now my family and my legacy. We are all in some way Delaneys, including Nick and Emily. And Martelli's sounds too much like a mobster or an Italian dessert!"

"I think it's a great idea, Mom!" said Meghan. "Delaney's Antiques, Delaney's Bed and Breakfast, Delaney's Community Theatre. Hopefully the flower shop will concur or choose something similar."

"So is this going to be Delaney's Compound, like the Kennedy Compound or something?" kidded Nick. "Let's try it out—Let's stay overnight at Delaney's; I got tickets to a show at Delaney's; Did you get that antique lamp at Delaney's; Let's have coffee at Delaney's. It works, and I like it!"

"Oh Nick, we can always count on you for comic relief! Thank God, Meghan married you! What do you think, Dan?"

"I think it's wonderful. Thank you, Lily."

"Hey, don't think this makes you the boss or anything! I'm still in charge. So, if we are all agreed, I'm going to call Emily and Lucas and tell them the good news while you three design a sign for Meghan to paint!"

The next morning at breakfast, we divided up our tasks for the day. Dan wanted to sand the floor, but he and Nick would finish the sanding on the counters and move everything outside first. While they were doing that, Meghan was going to take measurements for the sign. Then while Dan was working on the floor, Nick and Meghan were going to the lumberyard to buy the wood for the sign and its border.

"What about you, Lil? What are your plans?"

"While I was talking to Lucas last night, Jim called on call waiting and said he talked to that florist friend of his, and I'm meeting her this morning for coffee. Her name is Hillary Bowers. He also recommended an electrician, so first I'm going to call Andy's Electric and schedule a time to have him install all these lights. Jim said Andy could hook up the heater, too. If we like him, we may want to hire him for other buildings in the 'Compound.' After I meet with Hillary, I thought I would go look at window coverings. I want something simple, but tasteful. Something that is understated and fits with the antiques. I haven't decided yet if we should have valances or blinds or shutters."

"I have no idea what might look good, so I'll leave the window coverings to your good taste, my dear wife," said Dan. "The electrician could come as soon as the day after tomorrow. Once I finish sanding the floor, I'll cover it with drop cloths until we finish the painting. Then we can stain and seal it, so the electrical can fit in during any of those steps."

"Dad, I'm going to get a ladder and tape measure from the workshop. Is it okay to enter your hallowed space?" asked Meghan.

"Just as long as you put everything back where you found it when you are finished."

"Aah, the sounds of my childhood!" I remarked.

Everyone headed out of the house, and I called the electrician. Andy himself answered. I told him what we needed, and he said he had a cancellation and could come the day after tomorrow to put up our lights. That done, I took off to meet Hillary.

I took our car since Meg and Nick would need the pickup truck that Dan and Nick had repaired. Hillary had given me directions to a coffee shop called "The Daily Grind," and I pulled up in front right on time.

The coffee shop had exposed brick walls, covered with shelves of coffees, teas, teapots, coffeemakers, and various sizes of cups. In the back was a floor-to-ceiling bookcase containing everything from Shakespeare to modern bestsellers, as well as newspapers and magazines for customers to browse and enjoy while they sipped. The coffee smelled great, and the pastries looked so good I wish I hadn't eaten breakfast! As I walked in, a woman about thirty or so walked up to me.

"You must be Liliana Delaney. Hi, I'm Hillary Bowers."

"Hello, Hillary, I'm so excited to meet you! Let's get some coffee and visit."

We ordered and then chose a quiet corner table. It was great to find a new coffee place with designer coffees, and my latte was exceptional. If Hillary wanted to butter me up, she's chosen the perfect place. We chatted for a while about the area before getting down to business. She had lived here her whole life and appreciated its strong points while being able to laugh at its drawbacks. Hillary was warm, confident and friendly, and I liked her sense of humor. We hit it off right away.

"I don't know how much Jim has already told you, but I'll give you an overview. I recently inherited my parents' farm. It used to be Martelli Farms."

"I remember shopping there with my mom. You always had the best sweet corn. She was very sad when your parents retired," shared Hillary.

"Well, my initial plan was to sell the farm, but now my family and I have decided to keep it and renovate the buildings. The vegetable stand will become an antique store, and that project is already under way. The house will be made into a bed and breakfast. Down the line, when we have sold several house lots, we will convert the barn into a community theatre for my daughter to run. The garage will be for storage, but we also have a greenhouse, with real glass, no plastic. It gets plenty of good sunlight and ventilation, as well as heat in the cold months, and it would be perfect for a florist or gardener, or both. Jim said you might be interested."

"I'm very interested. I have been a floral designer for ten years, and I would love to have my own shop. I would do flowers for all occasions, but also carry plants, vases, pots, and so on. I brought my portfolio to give you an idea of my work," explained Hillary.

I thumbed through the photos in her album, and I was very pleased with what I saw. She was an exceptional designer. I wish we could have used her for Meghan's wedding.

"This is very impressive. I love your designs!"

"Thank you. Are you thinking of selling or renting the greenhouse?"

"That would be up to the florist. We are open to either. We also would leave some land on either side of the greenhouse for spring and summer gardening materials, plant beds and such. We are totally open to your making changes in the building for a shop area, removal of the workbenches or whatever else is needed to make it into a floral shop," I said.

"At this point, I can't afford to buy the place. I would rather rent the greenhouse from you, fix up the inside and start out just doing flowers, but eventually the business could be expanded into a full flower and garden shop. Would that work for you?"

"I think that would be just fine. Everything we're doing is a work in progress. My husband is a website designer so he can help with your website and advertising if you like. And we can all lend a hand getting the building ready. We will be finalizing our decision about whether to sell or renovate the property over Thanksgiving weekend. Will that work for you?" I offered.

"That sounds great! Is it okay if I stop by to visit a few times to look at the greenhouse so I can start planning?"

"Of course. I'd like you to meet my family and see what we are doing. Stop by anytime."

"Do you have names for your businesses yet?"

"Well, we have decided to call the store 'Delaney's Antiques.' And then maybe Delaney's Inn or Bed and Breakfast and Delaney's Community Theatre. We have a theme going," I admitted.

"Then how about I call my business 'Delaney's Floral and Garden.' It would keep with the theme, and Bowers Floral and Garden sounds much too dreary and reminds one of a funeral home."

I really liked this woman! I was confident she would work out and not only because Jim recommended her. Her portfolio was a selling point, but mostly I liked her personality She was good people, you could just tell, and I knew my family would like her, too. We decided on a rental price and then said goodbye with a plan for Hillary to visit in a couple of days. I was just getting into my car to leave when Nick and Meghan pulled in next to me in the truck. Meghan rolled down her window.

"Hey Mom, we saw your car so we stopped. Looks like you found a new coffee place and went without me," teased Meghan.

"Actually, Hillary Bowers suggested we meet here. You are going to love her! And this place. Do you want to go in?"

"I'm going to head back to the compound and start building the sign. Meghan, why don't you join your mom, and I'll see you both later."

"Are you sure I can't convince you to join us? They have great pastries, and you could bring some back for Dad."

"Pastries? Okay, you twisted my arm. I'll get coffee and pastries and take them back for Dad and me. I'm sure he could use a break."

After a coffee and pastry lunch—unhealthy, but very satisfying—Meghan and I continued on to the fabric store. If I found something I liked and decided on valances, I could make them myself and save a lot of money. I had to think of my coffee can!

Meghan and I headed to the drapery fabric, and we had only checked out two aisles when we found exactly what we wanted. It was a barn red and tan modified check, made of a rough weave, durable fabric to give it that homespun look. The cloth was rustic, and would look great with the café au lait paint we had chosen. Best of all: it was on sale! We decided to make ruffled valances to put above each window in the store. It would give a homey, old-fashioned feel to the place and pull everything together. I figured out the yardage we would need and had it cut while my daughter chose the curtain rods.

Meghan needed to stop by the paint store again to get paint and brushes for the sign. Since the store was close to the cemetery, I decided to visit my parents' graves again while she shopped.

"Hi Mom and Dad, I'm back. I hope you are both doing well. How could you not be doing well—you're in heaven, right! The flowers still look great! I wish you could see the beautiful fall trees, or maybe you can. I used to ask the nuns at school about that, but they never conclusively agreed on whether you were watching what was going on down here. I hope so!

"Well, our plans have changed quite drastically, and I hope you will be pleased about them. You see, I don't think we are going to sell the farm after all, at least not all of it. Dan and the kids and I are planning a totally new venture. We are researching right now and will make a definite decision by Thanksgiving on whether it is feasible or not. Are you ready for this?

"We are going to turn the house into a bed and breakfast. The vegetable stand is already being converted into an antique store, and we can practically fill it up with all the pieces we found on the property. I know you never liked antiques, Mom. You always said old things make us look poor, but it would really surprise you to learn that some of that old stuff is worth a lot of money now!

"I also talked to a really nice lady today who wants to open a floral shop in the greenhouse. And when we have everything else going, we are going to make a community theatre out of the barn for Meghan to run. As for the land, Lucas is researching whether we would do better to sell it in one lump sum or to sell it as house lots. Either way, we'll keep a few acres for a garden for the bed and breakfast, and to build a house for Dan and me.

"Just telling you all this makes me very nervous all over again. I just hope we can pull it all off! I know; I know I said I was retiring, but this project is giving me renewed energy and a chance to give something to my kids, as well as to spend more time with them. I hope you like the idea, and that you're pleased some of the land will stay in the family. If you hate it, make the ground rumble or something, okay?

Otherwise, I'm taking no response as a yes . . . No earthquakes, huh? Great!

"Oh, one more thing. I hope you won't mind if we call the businesses Delaney's. Martelli's is associated with the farm . . . and sounds kind of gangsterish, no offense Dad, and Delaney's seems a better fit. If you could make a flower bloom or something, I'd interpret that as your giving us your blessing. If it dies, I guess you hate the idea . . . Nothing, huh? Well, I guess the jury is still out on that one. Think about it, okay? And put in a good word for us with the powers that be up there, if you can. Well, got to go. Thanks, Mom and Dad for listening. I always feel better after I talk to you. Love you, and I'll be back soon!"

When we arrived home, a young calico kitten was waiting by the door when I got out of the car. It started mewing and carrying on. I bent to pet her, and she purred and then started wrapping herself around my legs. What a pretty little thing she was! She had no collar or identifying marks. I wondered where she lived since there were no nearby houses. I hoped someone hadn't just dropped her off to fend for herself, which happened often when we were kids. As I walked toward the house she followed me.

"Are you hungry little one? Come on, I'll find you something to eat, okay? Look Meg, I have a new mini-friend."

"Oh, she's adorable! I wonder where she came from. She seems kind of young to be out on her own."

I opened the door to the house, and she ran in and jumped on the couch as if she belonged there.

"Don't get too comfortable, kitty. I'm going to give you some food, and then out you go to your own home."

When I opened the door the next morning, she was there again as if waiting for me. She came running in and jumped on the couch again, and while I got her some food, she promptly fell asleep.

"Listen here, Girlfriend, I don't know what to make of you. Do you belong to someone else who lives around here? I'm beginning to suspect my parents sent you instead of a blooming flower. Could that be the reason you showed up? Well, just in case, I better keep you around, so you can stay here for now. If someone comes to claim you, I'll know I was being a little crazy. And if they don't, I guess you can live with us. In the meantime, I think I'll call you Grace, just in case you are kind of a miracle message or something from Mom and Dad, okay?"

CHAPTER SIXTEEN
COUNTDOWN TO THANKSGIVING

The days began to get shorter and the weather cooler, but we were so busy we hardly noticed. Dan finished sanding the floor, and we covered it with drop cloths while we painted and the lights and heater were installed. Andy the electrician came and put up all the lights, adding a dramatic difference to the interior and exterior, and it was nice to have that heater on cold mornings! He did great work at a reasonable price and was very interested when Dan shared our plans. He offered to help Nick with his designs for the bed and breakfast by working with him on a lighting plan.

Hillary came as promised, bearing coffee and pastries from The Daily Grind. We all went to the greenhouse, including Grace, to discuss possibilities. I could tell that everyone liked Hillary right away, and the coffee and scones were appreciated, but not a factor in that! Hillary said she would like to set up the front of the greenhouse as the retail showroom, and then use the back area for designing floral arrangements. She would need a good-size cooler and was checking out the possibility of a used one. Nick and Dan offered to help her fix up some of the extra boxes and counters from the vegetable stand for her showroom and work area. She already had some shelving to use. Hillary said she would like to use some of the old planter benches to grow flowers for spring pots and Memorial Day arrangements and to meet the spring garden demand. She obviously had been making plans, showing us her commitment and impressing us with her ideas. She decided she would like to start renovating in January since she had a commitment to the florist where she currently worked until December 21st.

We had developed a schedule of working on the antique store in the mornings and on our own individual projects in the afternoon. In this manner, we painted the inside of the building, including the rafters and the inside of the roof. It made the whole place look larger and much brighter. We stained and sealed the counters, boxes, blocks and finally the floor, and the only words to describe the place were classy, but comfortable. The old vegetable stand had turned into a showroom! People walking in would feel at home and like being there, but they would also realize we sold quality products--just what I had hoped for. We had the caretaker paint the outside barn red with cream and black trim, since he already had scaffolding and ladders, and we had enough other things to do.

Our afternoon projects were activities for the store as well as to prepare for the Thanksgiving meeting to determine once and for all whether we were going through with this venture or selling the whole place outright. More and more I found myself hoping we could make it all work. Meghan's afternoons were filled with painting the sign for the front of the antique store, painting the old roofing slates and windows we'd found, and developing plans for the theatre. Nick worked on designs for the bed and breakfast, with input from Jim and Andy as to costs and decor. Dan spent his time on the website design, advertising materials and managing the responses to his ads to sell his Denver website business. And I made and hung curtains in the store, planned layouts for the showroom, and chose which antiques we would put in the store first, cleaning them up so as to present them in their best light!

As for Grace, no one had ever claimed her, so she was still with us. She followed me wherever I went, and I found myself falling in love with her. She was a frisky little thing who loved to play with anything she could find, even if it was something you were using, but she also loved to cuddle and lay in my lap and fall asleep! She took to sleeping at the foot of our bed near my feet at night. She liked all of us and seemed happy being a member of our family, but I was her favorite. And that was okay with me! I didn't tell my family that she might be a miracle, but I secretly believed she was a gift from my parents telling me all was okay... or maybe to keep an eye on me.

Suddenly, it was a few days before Thanksgiving, and Lucas and Emily were scheduled to arrive Tuesday. On Monday, Dan and I made a trip to the grocery store to stock up on provisions for the weekend. Dan was a great cook and always prepared the turkey, so I left him to pick one out while I got all the veggies and things needed for pies. We would have plenty of leftovers, but I got ingredients for several other meals, and then some. Italians feel they must at all times have on hand the fixings for a seven course meal, just in case someone gets hungry in the middle of the night or whenever. I did my parents proud!

We had decided to have our big meeting about the plans for the farm on Wednesday. We were all ready with our reports, and I think we all wanted this to work, if it was financially feasible. The facts and figures Lucas had researched would be the primary determinant of that. After the meeting, our anxiety would be dispelled and with decisions made, we could enjoy the holiday and weekend. I hoped. But whatever happened, we had food. Food to celebrate, or food to help us drown our sorrows—we were stocked up!

While we were shopping, Jim brought over a backhoe and some other tools, and he and Nick drove them to the Model A site. The guys hadn't forgotten their plan to dig up the old car; they had just been waiting for Lucas to arrive. There had been many a discussion about the hows and whys, and they were quite excited. They set Friday morning, promptly at 10:00 to begin the excavation. I have to say I was looking forward to this adventure myself!

The idea of scuba diving in the pond to search for the remains of the Revenue Man would have to be postponed and hopefully forgotten. The weather was getting much too cold, and I really doubted that was where he ended up. I suddenly realized that we'd all been so busy with the antique store that I hadn't thought about poor Roy Abernathy for days. So I made him a silent promise that we would get back on task and keep looking as soon as things quieted down a little.

A light snow was falling when Lucas and Emily pulled into the yard Tuesday afternoon. The prediction was just for a few inches of the light, fluffy stuff, but this was New England, and predictions were never too reliable. We all hugged excitedly, happy to be together again! We helped them carry their things into the house, all of us talking at once, as usual. We were all tense with anticipation of our meeting, which manifest itself in a heightened sense of levity. I wasn't sure if we could hold out until tomorrow! Thanksgiving was barely on our minds with everything else we wanted to talk about.

Emily had made several different kinds of muffins and breads from her mother and grandmother's recipes, so we all sat down to coffee and a taste-testing of the various treats. Emily cut each pastry into bite-size pieces so we could sample several, but I have to admit I had more than one bite of most of them. They were heavenly! Blueberry muffins were always my favorite, but the crescent rolls with orange frosting and the chocolate chip banana bread were to die for, too. The scones made my mouth and tummy happy. And today's sampling were only a few of the recipes she had brought from her family. The Daily Grind might have some competition from our little restaurant. Bless that darling girl for distracting us!

The guys shared the plans for the Model A, and of course, Lucas was pumped, and then we went on a tour of the antique store. Lucas and Emily could not believe it was the same place, and I have to admit, I was pretty pleased with it myself. Whatever happened with the rest of the plan, we could use the antique store to sell all the things we had found and if necessary, sell the store, too. So many things hung in the balance; so many decisions to be made.

The wait was driving me crazy; I was about to break out in hives. Finally about 6:00 p.m., I exclaimed, "Okay, I can't stand this any longer. I don't need to know the particulars yet, but I just need to know if this is a go or not. Are we building Delaney's, or do we just sell the place outright?"

Everyone looked at Lucas since he was the financial planner, and his research would determine the fate of the whole project. He stared back at all of us with a deadpan look, not revealing anything. "Lucas, I swear I will scream and lock you in the cellar until you tell me!" I hissed.

"And we'll all help her!" shouted Nick.

"Okay, okay, if you can't delay gratification until tomorrow, I guess I can give you a little hint," quipped Lucas. "I've checked and rechecked all the facts and figures, and it will be a ton of work, but the project is a go!"

We all cheered and screamed, and we maybe did a little jumping up and down. I took a deep breath as if I had been holding it for hours. We were going to do it! I was even more pleased than I expected to be. Actually, I was ecstatic!

"I don't want to go into any more detail tonight because it is kind of complicated, but I have handouts for everyone to look at and discuss in the morning meeting," explained Lucas.

"He wanted to do a power point presentation, too, but I nixed that," said Emily. The dear nerd did make everything very easy for us common folk to understand, though."

"I'm so happy! Let's open a couple of bottles of wine and celebrate!" I exclaimed.

CHAPTER SEVENTEEN
FAMILY MEETING

Everyone was too hyped up to eat breakfast before the meeting, so we made a huge pot of coffee, and served Emily's pastries while we sat around the big kitchen table and talked. Grace watched from a counter nearby. Lucas went first, and his "handouts" were actually whole packets of materials, but I must say his research was informative and understandable. He first shared what the profit would be if we sold the land outright as opposed to dividing it into lots and selling it. He had even talked to a few developers about buying the land and building houses on it. It seemed that the best option would be the sell it as lots. Even with the expenses for taxes, a surveyor, and a realtor (so we didn't have to handle the sales and paperwork), we could do better financially selling the property as individual lots. Lucas is amazing! With the help of Google maps, he'd plotted out several possible lot configurations and suggested costs based on one and two acre lots. He had provided us with excellent information to make decisions.

The next part of his presentation was the estimated costs for renovating the bed and breakfast, community theatre, paving the driveway and parking areas, and building a house for Dan and me. He also included a timeline with dates for the building of each of these and the bed and breakfast opening, based on projected land sales. He even projected initial income for each project—the antique store, bed and breakfast and community theatre, until each component was up to speed. The income projections were sobering, but manageable, and the land sales would more than cover everything. As Lucas put it, even if everything went bust, none of us would be using our own money, so we would just be back to where we were before all this started, minus the land, but we would not be in debt.

Maybe not in debt, but certainly disheartened. We were all so invested in this project, we would be devastated if it failed. The dreams of Meghan's theatre, Nick's bed and breakfast, my antique store, and all Dan's hard work for all of it would be for nothing. But the worst part would be my losing everything my family had bequeathed to me. This project had to succeed; I couldn't lose everything Mom and Dad had worked so hard for all those years! I was determined to make things work for them and for my kids' futures.

"Thanks for the comprehensive information, Lucas. We really appreciate all the time and expertise you put into this, and you gave us just what we need to make decisions. So, I think we take a vote. All in favor of selling the land as lots, say aye," I directed.

"Aye!"

"It's unanimous. Okay then. All in favor of the antique store, say aye."

"It's already built and the grand opening is scheduled in two weeks," said Dan.

"True, but this is a formality. All in favor?"

"Aye!"

"Unanimous." All in favor of the bed and breakfast?"

"Aye!"

"Unanimous again. I'm beginning to see a pattern here! And the community theatre."

"Aye!

"Fantastically unanimous! All in favor of using Lucas' projections and timelines as our guideline for the project, say aye."

"Aye!"

"Ladies and Gentlemen, we are all in unanimous agreement. Now, let's share our designs for each building. You've seen the antique store. Now that we have agreed to that project, the Delaney's Antiques sign will go up, along with the grand opening signs and dates.

"Dan, since you have been working with Hillary on the plan for the greenhouse, why don't you share that next."

"You bet. Hillary Bowers is going to rent the greenhouse for a flower shop. She will use the front half of the greenhouse as a retail store, and the back for her cooler, design tables, plantings and storage. In the spring, she will add outside plants, soil, fertilizer, etc. for gardeners, so we have to leave some land available for display. She is not interested in being a grower at this point, but I think we should still leave some land available for planting as Lucas showed in his diagrams, in case the situation changes in the future. Do you all agree?"

"I think as Chairman of the Board that I'm supposed to conduct the vote."

"Oh, sorry Lily, I mean Madame Chairman or Chairperson, you go for it!"

"Ahem, Ladies and Gentlemen of the Board, do you agree on renting the greenhouse as a floral shop to Hillary Bowers."

"Aye!"

"The ayes have it; continue please, Dan."

"Hillary is super nice and has great ideas. She will stop by this weekend to meet Lucas and Emily, and to get the verdict. She'll be really happy to know we are going forward with this because she wants to open in late January or early February. Nick and I will be helping her remodel the retail area, using some of the old counters from the stand, I mean antique store. I think that's everything. Lucas, I was wondering if you could help draw up the contracts."

"The plan sounds great, Dad, and I will be happy to do the contracts. I can probably crank them out this weekend."

"Of course, you can, whiz kid," kidded Meghan.

"Is it okay if I go next?" asked Nick. "I've been sharing my ideas with Lucas so he could do the projections of cost and so forth, but this is the first time anyone, including Meg, has seen my designs."

Nick gave a brief introduction and then handed each of us some diagrams for the various areas of the house. We took a few minutes to study them before responding, while Nick nervously awaited our comments. He had decided on Victorian style since it fit well with the structure of the house and barn and our antiques. He had taken the kitchen of the downstairs apartment where we were staying now and redesigned it as the entrance, lobby and sitting area of the bed and breakfast. The room was quite large, a typical old farm kitchen and perfect for this purpose. As a guest entered, there would be a couple of comfortable couches, chairs and a coffee table to the right, facing a fireplace, which we assumed was where the stove was located now. Perpendicular to the fireplace, the current old wooden cabinet with glass doors on top, and the counter would be refinished and set up as a coffee bar. If guests looked straight ahead when entering, they would see the front desk, a high, long desk typical of those used in hotels for check-in. He had even drawn hand-carved accents on it. To the right of the desk, sort of behind the fireplace area, where several floor to ceiling windows were located would be a few tables with period chairs for playing games, visiting over coffee or working on a computer. The windows would have elegant Victorian style valances and blinds to maximize light and pull all the areas together. The room would make just the statement we wanted—class, comfort and a warm welcome.

Nick proposed that the old living room, two of the bedrooms and the bathroom be converted to the living space for Meghan and him. He had redesigned the living room to have a small kitchen that opened to the living area. They would also update the bathroom and bedrooms. It looked comfortable and spacious, and best of all, Meghan really liked it.

The upstairs apartment would be converted into four guest rooms, each with a luxurious modern bath as I'd requested. The rooms would each be decorated Victorian style, but slightly different in furniture and décor, and with various size beds to accommodate the needs of the guests. All would have TV, Wifi, and DVR's, but all these modern conveniences would be in a wardrobe cabinet so as not to spoil the effect.

The large kitchen in the ell part of the house would be the breakfast room, and Nick proposed it be a breakfast and lunch restaurant open to the public also. He included the old bar we had found, refurbished of course, for a serving counter, and square tables, each with four chairs, which could easily be reconfigured for various size groups. We discussed whether the décor here should be strict Victorian or more speakeasy, given the history of the place. The latter was definitely the favorite choice, and I felt we could decorate so that it blended with the Victorian décor in the rest of the bed and breakfast, so we voted on "The Speakeasy" for the name of the breakfast and lunch restaurant. I was certain that Nick could make it work. The ell living room, also large, would be basically divided in half with a kitchen and storage area on one half. The other half would be a hall leading to guest rooms, and the restrooms. This placement would be a buffer for sound, so as not to bother the people in the three additional guest rooms converted from the ell part of the house.

Nick's plan also included rebuilding the wrap-around porch. He knew how much I loved that porch, or piazza as my grandmother called it, and had asked to see old photos. He designed it just like the original. It added so much to the house—beauty, elegance, and style. It returned the house to the Victorian time period when the additions had been added, and the place had been operated as an inn. He had even drawn wicker rockers and tables and hanging planters. The guests would like it, and I couldn't wait to sit out there and rock in those chairs with a nice cup of coffee! Everyone loved the design. What Lucas was to numbers, Nick was to style. It seemed we all had a vision of what we thought the place should look like, and Nick had captured all of our ideas into his plans. We were thrilled!

"All in favor?"

"Aye! Aye!"

Meghan was next. Surprisingly, my usually loquacious and often sarcastic daughter was a little nervous. I thought maybe she hadn't had time to work out all her plans with everything else on her docket, but then I realized that this was her baby, a project that had become very important to her and dear to her heart, and she was worried we might not like or care about it. It's hard to open up about your passion to others who may not share it and let them critique you. But she didn't need to be concerned. We respected her and trusted her knowledge base, and we would give her our wholehearted support.

With Nick's help with the scale, her design converted the old, dilapidated barn into a two hundred seat black box theatre. The black box effect helped cover up the building's flaws and used its best features to advantage. Theatre-goers would enter a central lobby with restrooms off to each side. They would proceed into the theatre itself through the left, center, or side entrance doors, depending on which of the three areas of the auditorium they held seats. All the second floor haylofts would be removed, and then one long balcony would be rebuilt above the back third of the auditorium, using the existing beams, and allowing for seating and a central projection room for lights and sound. The half loft above would be used for additional lighting and sound speakers.

The stage was rectangular, elevated about thirty-six inches off the floor. The proscenium arch was bordered with a carved wooden design to give it definition and add a little character to the place. The first floor and the balcony would be slightly inclined to allow rows of seats to be on different levels for better viewing. The whole place would be carpeted, and Meghan has chosen comfortable, stylish seating with sufficient legroom for the audience's comfort.

The cellar below would be rebuilt with insulated walls and floors. The larger room, previously the washroom, would be made into the green room and ladies and men's dressing rooms. One of the storerooms would be for costume storage and the other for prop storage. Each storage room would have a garage door opening directly to the drive-in section to allow easy access and movement of their contents. A solid wall would be built, closing off the old drive-in opening to the washroom, thus providing the fourth wall of the green room.

For the exterior, Meghan had designed an old-fashioned marquee with Delaney's on the top and space for the name of the show. Big bell-shaped lights, similar to those on the antique store, would run across the entire front entrance. The shape of the building might still be that of a barn, but the sign and lights would definitely prove it was a theatre!

Meghan was the one who knew theatre and knew better than anyone if her design would work, so we had little to add. But we were totally impressed with her ideas. She was so relieved, and then excited. The theatre would be expensive and would take a while to build, so it would be the final component of our project. Meghan had also consulted with

Lucas about costs, and she felt good about the choices she'd made. There was no venue like this in the area, and Meghan had the talent and determination to make it work. We never doubted her for a minute! The vote on the theatre was also unanimous.

Emily shared more recipes that sounded mouthwateringly delicious. She also had a lead on several places nearby to get linens and laundry service. And she found a place online that specialized in original and reproductions of different designs of china dishes and cups. Best of all, they were quite reasonable! As busy as she was at the hospital, Emily had taken the time to contribute to the venture, and I loved her for it.

By the time we had finished our discussion, we were exhausted and exhilarated—and very hungry for a real meal. Lucas, as usual, wanted to go to the Clam Shack for seafood, so we all threw on coats and took off! On the way, Dan asked me how I was feeling about everything.

"Happy. Very, very happy! I'm feeling like this is what we were meant to do. What a grand retirement we'll have, my darling husband. Do you agree?"

"I totally agree. We could never be the type of old fogies who sit around all day, watching TV or napping. We needed a change from our previous long terms jobs and to try new exciting projects that incorporate our passions, and this seems perfect. We get to do fun things we love, be with our kids, and still travel. I'm feeling very happy, too, Lil."

"This is going to be a very blessed Thanksgiving, Dan. We have lots to be thankful for, and lots to look forward to."

CHAPTER EIGHTEEN
RECOVERING THE MODEL A FORD

O ur Thanksgiving was very traditional with watching the Thanksgiving Day parades on TV, overeating a massive turkey dinner, watching football, eating leftovers, playing board games and eating some more. By mid-afternoon, I felt bloated and suggested we go for a walk. The men wanted to watch more football, so we three woman bundled up and headed out. Fortunately the snow prediction had been correct, and the two inches of fluff had already melted thanks to a bright, cheery sun, so we didn't even need boots. It was a lovely day! My heart was full of love for my family and excitement about our future. It was just my stomach that was uncomfortable. We decided to walk down to the pond and back. As we passed the old strawberry field, an old memory surfaced that I had totally forgotten.

"This is the field that my best friend Janene and I set on fire when we were about eight or nine. We were playing Indians. We conducted a very solemn blood brother ceremony."

"Wait a minute, Mom, what did you say? Blood brothers?" asked Meghan.

"Well, yes. I suppose it was actually blood sisters, but we weren't so politically correct back then."

"How do you become blood brothers or sisters?" asked Emily.

"First, we made a tiny cut in each of our index fingers with the jackknife I had borrowed from my brother when he wasn't looking.

Then we said some words that sounded kind of Indian to us and put our index fingers together to mix our blood."

"You mixed your blood!" exclaimed Meghan in astonishment. "Are you the same mother who lectured Lucas and me over and over again about never touching any one else's blood, never ever? I just see blood, and I panic and hold up the hex sign because of all those lectures, and you mixed blood in a blood brother ceremony?"

"Well, we didn't have HIV or Aids to worry about when I was a kid, which is why I was so strict about it with you and Lucas. I'm sorry if I made you so paranoid about blood, but it was done with the best of intentions, and I still think it was good advice."

"And you stole a knife!"

"Borrowed, not stole, and it was a very dull knife, which I returned, cleaned! Do you want to hear the rest of this story or not?" I asked.

"By all means, please continue."

My friend and I decided to see if you really could start a fire by rubbing two dry sticks together—one held vertically by one hand, while the other is held horizontally and rubbed across the center of the first stick. That was how they always showed it being done in Cowboy and Indian TV shows. And it does work! And it worked very quickly. We were so thrilled when the fire started! We were sure we were now official Indians. But then the wind blew, sparks flew, and the nearby brush and plants started to catch on fire. It was fall, and the field held some dry brush that had blown in, and the leaves of the strawberry plants were dead and dried out enough to burn quickly.

"A neighbor saw the smoke and flames and called the Fire Department. My dad was a volunteer firefighter; imagine his surprise when he found out the fire was in his own field! The Fire Department arrived quickly—in a small town they didn't have far to go—and put the fire out in no time, since it had pretty much run out of fuel when it reached the end of the strawberry field. Oh boy, we were in big trouble, not only with the firefighters, but worse, with my dad.

"Luckily there wasn't any serious damage, and burning a field like that is good for fire prevention, if it is a controlled burn. It's also supposed to make the soil more fertile the next year. So they did not press charges against my friend and me. However, every Saturday for a year, we had to go to the firehouse and wash all the trucks, which was not easy for two little kids, but we dutifully served our time. They made us scrub those trucks until we could see our faces in the shine!"

"Mom, you really were a holy terror as a child! I can't believe you didn't end up in the Juvenile Detention Center."

"They used to be called Reform Schools, and come on, I wasn't really that bad. The fire was an accident and didn't really do any damage, and I had consequences for that for a whole year of Saturdays. Plus, I have never rubbed sticks together again. I don't even light the gas grill. I had consequences for lots of the crazy things I did, at least the serious ones that were discovered. Why, most of the time I was a poster child for a great kid! I got excellent grades. I listened to teachers and behaved in class; I was a model student, and teachers loved me. I respected my elders, sold whist tickets for the church, magazines for the school, and cookies for the Girl Scouts. I was a Rah Rah, active in lots of school and civic activities. I even went to Girls' State! The only detentions I ever served were for talking too much in high school. All of those experiences, good and mischievous, made me the excellent mother I am today, and you, daughter, are lucky to have me!"

"You know what, Mom, I am very lucky to have you. I would never want any other mother. Maybe I'm just jealous of all the fun you had."

"Well, we certainly did have fun."

By this time we were getting chilled and were glad we were almost back to the house. My full stomach felt better, and I was ready for some dessert. When we got inside, we saw that the guys had the same idea. All the pies were sitting on the counter uncovered, with one or two slices removed from each. At least they had put the ice cream back in the freezer and put on a pot of coffee. While we ladies sat in the kitchen eating our pie, the football game ended, and the guys decided to join us. When they asked about our walk, Meghan and Emily spilled the beans about my latest story, and the teasing began again.

"That's it. I'm not sharing any more of my life stories with any of you!"

"She tried to convince us she was a model child and a great citizen," said Emily.

"Well, she certainly turned out okay, I think," said Dan. I love you, Hon, no matter what they say."

"Thank you, Dan. Now, who's up for a rip, roaring game of Pictionary?"

The day of the Model A excavation was chilly, so I made hot chocolate and coffee to take with us. I offered to prepare turkey sandwiches for a picnic lunch, but Dan assured me we would be finished by then. I doubted it, but it might be good to take a break and return to the house to warm up. Jim arrived right on time with several more shovels, ladders and a screen.

"Are you planning to sift the dirt? Is this turning into an archaeology dig?" I asked.

"We'll sift the soil for car parts that might have rusted and fallen off," responded Jim.

"And just in case the Revenue Man's skeleton is down there," Nick added.

"I'm sure he isn't there, Nick, but I won't burst your bubble. Then again, who knows what else got thrown down there."

"I have a question," said Meghan. "If we are selling this land as lots, how will we explain that big hole to buyers?"

"Good question, Meg. Jim and I already discussed this. We are going to level that slope somewhat and use the dirt we move to fill the hole," replied Dan.

And the adventure began! First we took turns using the shovels to dig some of the soil around the edges of the car so Jim wouldn't get too close with the backhoe. Once Jim started digging with the scoop of that machine, progress unearthing the car moved quickly. We sifted the dirt he brought up, and found a few very rusted, mostly unrecognizable car parts. The guys were so excited you might think we had found the tomb of a lost pharaoh—complete with treasure.

After a couple of hours, the Model A was exposed down to the running boards, and we took a break to have coffee and check out the car. We could still distinguish some of the green paint on the body and the black running boards, although there was lots of rust all over both. The convertible cloth top had mostly rotted away, but it looked like it had been tan colored. Nick and Lucas used brooms to brush off some of the sandy soil until Dan was able to pry up the partially rusted hood of the car and check the engine. It still had a lot of sand covering the spaces, and lots of parts had rusted. One headlight had a crack but the grill and bumper were in better shape because they were chrome. The tires had been old-fashioned wide whitewalls and were now flat and falling apart, and the fenders were pocked with rust. Nick had done research on the Internet and identified the vehicle as a 1928 Model A Town Car.

"The town car was Ford's bigger, more expensive model. This baby could do up to sixty-five miles per hour, and when new cost about $1200. It was a pretty classy car back then. Look, it even has a rumble seat in the back!"

The rumble seat was quite cool. Since it had been closed all these years, we had to get the dirt out of the crack and pry the rusted handle to open it. The seat was rotting, but still intact from not being totally exposed to the outside dirt.

"Let's check out the inside," said Lucas.

We got the doors open and more sandy soil poured out, but we could see the seats had been leather, so they were in a little better shape than the top, but definitely had deteriorated more than the rumble seat. The front floorboard was mostly rusted away, and you could see the frame beneath, also rusted. The clutch and gearshift were in pretty bad shape also. Since the car had only been buried about nine or ten feet down, the only things crushed were the tires. The wheels practically rested on the ground!

Dan and Jim tried to get a look at the state of the frame to be sure it wasn't so rusted out that it would fall apart when they tried to move it. For all we knew, the whole thing was barely holding together. They decided to go for it, and everyone got back to digging and sifting. In another hour, the rest of the car was exposed, and Jim and Dan checked the sturdiness of the frame again.

"I have two questions, if I may," I said. "One, how do you plan to get this thing out of there, and two, what are you going to do with it when you do?"

"Are you serious, Mom? This car is an amazing piece of history," exclaimed Lucas. "I can't believe Grandpa ever put it down there!"

"He put it down there because it no longer worked, was falling apart, and they needed to fill the hole for a field. People didn't collect or make rat rods of these old cars back then. This thing is a little too far gone for restoration, or even for a parts car. So, I ask again, what do we do with it if we get it out?"

"We can put it in front of the antique store to draw in customers," offered Nick.

"I want the place to look like an antique store, not a junk yard," I responded.

"I would love to have it," said Jim. "If we can get it out in one piece, I'll give you $2,000 for it, because I can fix it up some, and it will be the perfect statement to draw people into my salvage place. Who could see this and not want to stop and check it out. I really want it!"

"Jim, are you serious?" asked Dan.

"Totally serious."

"You can't pay $2,000 when you did the majority of the work to get it out! How about $1,000?" I negotiated.

"$1500 and not a penny less! Plus I get to come over tomorrow and help you all move everything into the store for the opening."

"Jim, you are the kindest man on the planet! The car is yours, if we can get it out."

"As to how we are going to get her out of there, we'll try lifting it. We'll attach the cables from the winch on my truck to the strongest parts of the car frame and lift it out, ever so carefully. I think it will work, and if it falls apart, we've still had a hell of a good time!"

"Well now," I said, "I say we break for lunch, and then come back and get that sucker out of there!"

We walked back to the house in good spirits, and everyone pitched in to get lunch on the table. Leftovers, to me, are the best part of Thanksgiving, and we ate heartily after all that digging. The air had warmed up some, but the warm house felt good after being outside all morning.

We hurried back down to the car as soon as we were finished eating, toting a few brooms to remove more dirt. While Jim and Dan placed the cables, the rest of us swept out any dirt we could get to from the interior and the engine. Finally it was time to try to get the Model A out of the hole. Jim raised the hoist very slowly as we all held our breaths. The chassis creaked and groaned loudly at first, and I was sure it was going to crumble to pieces, but the car held together. We heard a few breaking sounds and some small pieces of metal fell off and into the hole, but the old girl continued to rise! At last, she was slightly suspended above the hole. Jim had Nick jump in the truck and move the truck forward, barely coasting, until the car was over solid ground. Then Jim carefully lowered the car, and she still did not fall apart! We removed the cables and really checked her out. She must have been a real beauty in her day. It was kind of sad to see her so deteriorated, but there was still something noble and majestic about her. Cleaned and shored up, she would look great in front of Jim's store—if he could get her there. We were all elated!

I noticed Nick wasn't with us any longer. I looked in the hole, which now seemed huge, and saw him exploring the bottom and sides.

"Did you find anything else, Nick?"

"A few more small car parts, I think, and the rims of a few broken wheels. This looks like a bucket of some sort, and maybe pieces of a broken plow. They must have thrown all this trash in as landfill, too. But no bones—animal or human. You were right, the Revenue Man was not buried here."

"Sorry, Nick. Are you sad the car is leaving here, too?"

"Nah, I was mostly interested in the challenge of digging it up and seeing how the old girl had fared all these years. Just don't sell the golf cart, okay? I'm kind of attached to that thing. I'm even thinking of painting it."

"Nick, you are a trip! The golf cart is yours until its dying day!"

"Thanks, Mom!"

Jim called his son Jack to bring over a bigger truck with a ramp. Jack was the spitting image of Jim, physically and personality-wise. He instantly fell in love with the Model A, and agreed it was the perfect attraction for the front of their business. He was really sorry he had a previous commitment and missed our adventure.

We helped load Jim's backhoe, screen and tools, and collected all our tools and brooms and headed back to the house. Beer and wine was served to all, and we celebrated bringing a rusty old car back to life! Jack fit right in, and he and Nick hit it off. We were all making new friends. Overall, it had been a fun and productive day, and my coffee can was $1500 richer!

CHAPTER NINETEEN
THE GRAND OPENING

We had all agreed that Saturday of Thanksgiving week would be used to move items, including the old stoves from the apartments and items from the garage, to the antique store in preparation for the Grand Opening. I had picked an assortment of items that I thought offered an eclectic and desirable mix to start the store, and had others ready to bring in when some of those sold. I had decided to set up the store like rooms in a house; all kitchen items would be in a kitchen area, living room stuff in a living area, and so on. I thought this arrangement would help people see the potential of the antiques to fit into their own settings. And of course there was a miscellaneous area for things that didn't fit anywhere else.

Jim and Jack showed up bright and early. We made our plans as we shared coffee and another batch of Emily's scrumptious muffins. The guys planned to tackle the old stove in the upstairs apartment first because of its weight and the difficulty in getting it through doors. Sexist or not, I was not going to try to help with that heavy thing! After some measuring, they decided to take the stove down the wide interior stairs, straight out the front door to a piano moving dolly that Jim had brought, and then wheel it to the store. Thank God we had met Jim! He had the equipment needed and was very kind to share it with us. While they accomplished that, Meghan, Lucas and Emily helped me finish cleaning and moving some of the antiques from the garage, hauling them in the golf cart trailer. Once one stove and the chrome table and chairs were in the kitchen area, the rest would be easy.

Nick and Dan had removed the siding near the mysterious attic doors we had found in the ell part of the house so they could use the doorway to carry out the blanket chest and desk and whatever else was still in the attic. All those things were taken to the garage for refurbishing.

I used Meghan's artistic eye and Emily's good taste to decide where to place or hang various things. We decided Lucas' best skill was driving, though he did offer some good suggestions for places to hang the pictures, so that became his job. It was actually exciting; sort of like moving into a new place and deciding how to decorate. It was important to me that the store be pleasing to the eye. I wanted people to be able to easily look from antique to antique and most importantly, I did not want to overcrowd the place with too many items. I had been to so many antique shops where there was so much stuff that it was too difficult to look at everything. It practically hurt one's eyes and definitely messed with the brain! I wanted each of my antiques to stand out and present itself in its best light, so someone would fall in love with it, and want to buy a special piece of history.

Emily and Meghan worked so well together in organizing and setting up items that I decided to go into the back room and set up the office. Lucas and Emily had bought us a Keurig coffeemaker and a wide variety of coffees as a grand opening present, and I set that up first, along with the microwave we had bought. I would use the table as a desk for now and set up my laptop. We could also store small items in the back room.We had a sink as well as a vacuum and feather duster, but I put all that stuff behind a curtain on the far side of the room, opposite the teeny-tiny bathroom. I wanted this to be a comfortable area for us to take a break or do paperwork, not a cluttered janitor closet

We called it quits around 4:30, with most of the antiques in place. We had accomplished a great deal. Emily and Lucas were leaving Sunday morning, and we wanted to spend their last evening with us enjoying each other's company, not working.

We had a lovely Italian dinner since even I was getting sick of turkey. We talked a little business, but mostly made plans for our Christmas together.

On Monday morning, Meghan and I headed to the woods again. We wanted to cut down a Christmas tree and gather greens for wreaths and garlands for the store. Our woods had enough of a variety of plants to create some gorgeous greenery. Much to Nick's chagrin, we took the golf cart and trailer so we could load everything to bring back. He cautioned Meghan about driving his baby and not to get it dirty but soon got over it. He and Dan were going to begin rehabbing the ell apartment that day. What man, or woman, can stay upset about anything when he gets a chance to break down walls with a big sledgehammer? I was kind of looking forward to engaging in a little of that action myself.

It didn't take us long to get enough boughs for garlands and wreathes, including pretty berries and colorful plants to decorate them, but finding the perfect Christmas tree was another story. It had to be tall, but narrow so as not to take up too much space in the store. And the branches couldn't be too full or the antique ornaments we had to sell wouldn't show up. Finally we found a tree that was as close to perfect as nature intended it to be. It had a slight bare spot on one side, but we could place that in the back towards the wall, and the tree would be fantastic. We located another evergreen that we would return for in a few weeks' time for the family tree. Meghan tied an old headband she found in her pocket around a branch to make it easy to find when we were ready for it.

We returned to find the guys covered with dust and plaster. When they removed their facemasks, they looked like raccoons with big smiles. They had torn down the walls between the bedrooms where the new guest rooms would be in this section. Meg and I got a chance to knock down a few pieces of plaster walls, too. I had to agree, it was kind of fun to wield a sledgehammer with all your might and whack away at a wall, making a huge hole, but it was also very, very messy.

We decided to contact someone about getting a big dumpster for all the rubbish and maybe do something about a ventilation system. It was amazing how much bigger the place looked. We found a few old newspapers that were once used as insulation in the walls, but not much else. The papers were too old and disintegrated to salvage or even read. We didn't find anything else; no evidence of bootlegging and definitely no bones.

After lunch, Meghan and I got the tree stand, ornaments and lights from a storage closet and started decorating the tree. There was a large collection of ornaments from my grandmother and my parents, and most of them were quite old. We decided to price them as we selected and hung them, so it took us most of the afternoon to decorate the tree. Meghan made a few small Victorian fans from scrapbook paper, and ribbon bows. She added a few feathers to make the tree look old-fashioned and absolutely beautiful. It was a little difficult to let go of some of the family ornaments, but I did have a houseful of my own waiting for me. So we chose a few of our favorites to keep for ourselves and Lucas and Emily and put the rest on the tree to sell.

I decided I wanted three big wreaths, one for each of the front windows, so the next day we made those, or Meghan did most of the work. I was able to put the greens on, but it was Meghan who added the decorations that made them unique and beautiful. We intertwined fir branches with laurel and some other wild plants, and then she added berries and red and yellow vine plants to the wreaths. We decided to wrap the two columns of the drive-through with garland, as well as put some greenery in the store, which meant another trip to the woods for more plants. The place was starting to look and smell like Christmas!

Early the next morning, we went plant picking again, and Meghan saw a live ring necked pheasant for the first time. We had lots of those beautiful birds around here when I was growing up. We would see them all the time, never realizing how special they were. We would often find their tail feathers on the ground and pretend they were old-fashioned quill pens. But then back to work, and we gathered even more greenery this trip.

"Mom, you know those big old bottles that were your grandmother's that we found? What would you think about gathering some of these plants and making some terrariums in them? It would be kind of a unique way to sell them."

"Meghan, that is a great idea! Can I help?"

"Of course! It's actually kind of fun. That'll be our next project after everything else is ready for the opening."

Once I remembered how I made garland as a kid, it didn't take us long to make all we needed. Nick and Dan hung them from the columns, wrapping them around from top to bottom. We put up the wreaths, and the two-sided sandwich board signs Meghan had made, announcing the Grand Opening in three days! Dan had put ads in all the local papers and flyers in all the stores in all the neighboring towns.

I spent a good part of the next two days baking cookies and breads from Emily's recipes. I thought it would be nice to offer coffee, hot cider, and sweets to customers, as well as to tell them about the bed and breakfast and restaurant where we would feature theses scrumptious pastries. Meghan made several terrariums, and they were lovely! I was sure they would sell. We were so busy I didn't even have time to be nervous!

But the morning of the opening, all that changed. First I couldn't decide what to wear. I never got upset about what to wear, and there I was throwing clothes all over our bedroom. Then I spilled the coffee all over the floor while filling the big pot in the store and had to mop up a big mess. Luckily the water didn't damage Dan's newly stained floor. I kept moving around the store straightening things, and changing the places of some items only to change them back a few minutes later. By the time we opened at 9:00, I was taking lots of deep breaths and meditating. When no customers had arrived by 10:00, I was panicking and regretting this whole venture. What if no one came? What if nothing sold? What if all this work was for nothing?

Finally at about 10:15, two cars rolled in. They were filled with seven middle-aged ladies who had talked about the store at their weekly church quilting meeting and decided to all come together and check it out. We offered them food and drink, and they exclaimed over the cookies and the antiques. Two of Meghan's terrariums were snapped up immediately. One lady bought a butter churn, and another bought the mantle clock Dan had repaired. Sarah, one of the ladies who introduced herself, texted her daughter on the spot, and included a picture of the chrome table and chairs. Her daughter loved them and asked me to hold him for her until her husband could pick them up later that afternoon. Everyone in the group bought something, and no one even quibbled about price. They promised to call everyone they knew and send them to the store over the weekend. They were the ideal first customers! By the time they left, I was over my jitters, which was great since the customer traffic was steady throughout the rest of the day. Some were just lookers, but most found something to purchase. By mid-afternoon, Meghan had to gather Dan and Nick, and the three of them started choosing and cleaning up more of the antiques in the garage to fill in the store spaces where items had sold, while I kept selling and raking in the money!

Sarah's husband arrived at 4:00 and loaded up the tables and chairs with Nick's help. He was really interested in one of the old stoves, too, so he took pictures to show his wife and promised to let me know if they wanted it.

We closed at 6:00, and spent another hour restocking. By then we were exhausted but happy. And my coffee can was full! I grabbed a handful of bills and sent Nick to get pizza to celebrate. What a day! We were just as busy the rest of the grand opening weekend. We didn't sell as much as the first day on either of those days, but we did darn well. At this rate, I was going to have to start buying inventory to keep the place full.

Jim and Jack came by on Sunday to see how we were doing, and I'm sure for the cookies and pumpkin bread. Jim brought a beautiful embossed metal antique cash register to see if I wanted it for the store, and I scooped it up immediately. It fit in perfectly with our décor.

They were surprised how much stuff we had sold. Jim told me that he was starting a salvage job on an old estate that included the contents of the house and a carriage house, and asked if we wanted to stop by to see if there was anything we could use. We had decided that Monday would be the day the store was closed each week, so Meghan and I planned to check out the house the next day. It was helpful that Jim and I were both in the antique business, but what he sold was so different than what I did, we could help each other out with locating things. And I loved the thrill of the hunt!

Meg and I met Jim at the house he was salvaging about 9:00 the next morning. The house had at one time been gorgeous—about the same age as our farmhouse, but obviously much more elegant! It was a manor house compared to ours. Jim showed us the fireplace mantles he had mentioned previously. They were all made of beautifully hand-carved wood, and one large one had marble accents. The large mantle I definitely wanted for the lobby of the bed and breakfast, and a smaller one for the tavern, since Nick and Dan had uncovered the fireplace there. I decided to put a hold on the third one until Dan could see it. I thought it would be perfect in the house we built.

Jim gave us free rein to check out both the house and carriage house and pick out whatever we wanted. We found a number of items in the house, including hand-embroidered linens, a very old music box that worked, a brass bed, some small tables, several nice chairs, and beautiful antique Christmas ornaments to replenish our quickly diminishing supply. We decided it might be a good idea to keep some of the larger ones to eventually put on a tree in the bed and breakfast.

In the carriage house, we selected several lanterns and carriage lamps, more old tools, an antique kid's wagon, and my favorite—a pedal car that was in great shape! I have fond memories of the red racer pedal car we had as kids, and I loved them. I was tempted to keep this one for display only, but I always hated when I went into a store and fell in love with an item and then learned it was only there to draw in customers. I would sell it, but hopefully not too quickly.

Meghan was knowledgeable of the value of various antiques, but more importantly, she had an excellent eye. Her artistic nature resulted in her seeing potential in even the most obscure remnants of the past, and she knew how to refurbish them to make them beautiful and desirable. She was a real asset to the business, and I couldn't have asked for a better person to help me choose items. She often saw value in things that I would have passed over. We enjoyed working together, and we made a great team.

Jim again gave us great deals, and we were very pleased with ourselves as we loaded up the pick-up truck with most of our purchases. He would kindly store the mantles until we were ready for them. All in all, it was a good morning's work! We hit The Daily Grind for a latte to reward ourselves for a job well done and then headed home with the items we'd purchased. I couldn't wait to show them to Dan and Nick.

CHAPTER TWENTY
SURVEYORS AND DEVELOPERS

The following week, the surveyor came to measure the property lines and lay out the lots. Based on Lucas' projections, Dan and Nick had already designed a rough plan for one and two acres lots, and a small park near the pond. Dan showed the surveyor the plan and the dimensions of the land we wanted to keep for our own enterprises, and then spent the day with him, mapping out the lots. There would be room for about sixty houses. Surveying is not a quick job, and by evening, they were about halfway finished and planned to resume in the morning.

At dinner, Dan told us the surveyor had mentioned having a couple of developer friends who might be interested in buying all the lots.

"I explained we wanted to sell each lot individually in order to get top dollar, and he said that was great, but selling to one of these developers meant we might get slightly less, but it also meant we did not have to pay for the roads, the park, water hook-ups, etc., and we didn't have to wait for the money. I said I didn't like cookie cutter houses, and he said both of these guys were custom builders who worked with each client to make sure the houses weren't all alike. And because they would be charging more for custom building, they would pay us more also."

"Wow, that sounds like something we should at least explore. I would love to avoid all those expenses and even more so the hassles,"

I responded. "If it worked out, we could be done with the land part of this and just concentrate on our own business ventures."

"That's what I thought, too. It won't hurt to talk to them. Why don't I schedule one developer to come by Friday morning and the other on Saturday afternoon? Do you think you can free yourself up from the store for a while to meet them?" Dan asked.

"I'm not sure I'll understand much of what they're talking about."

"Mom, just study the spreadsheets Lucas gave you of what you could make per lot and the expenses for roads, water, realtor, etc. and you'll be able to compare it to what they are offering."

"Meghan, I never knew you were so business-minded."

"I'm not, but I am married to someone who knows this stuff. Lucas based his estimates on typical housing developers, not custom builders. You might as well explore all avenues. Lucas certainly would."

"I think Nick should be with you to talk to them instead of me. He's an architectural engineer, and they all speak the same language. I totally trust the two of you to help us make the right decisions," I said.

"I'll be happy to meet with each of the developers, if that's okay with you, Dad. I think between the two of us we can ask all the right questions, and then we can both discuss our findings with Lucas. Also, I could totally use a break from working on the restaurant," offered Nick.

"That's an excellent idea! Let's look over Lucas' initial research so we have the facts and figures in our minds. It's so great to have such varied talent in this family!"

Friday morning, Carl Fielding of Fielding Custom Developers arrived at 9:00. He was dressed in khakis and a long-sleeved cardigan, but he looked like a builder disguised in business casual clothing. His strong body probably would be more comfortable in jeans, a flannel shirt and a hard hat. He definitely had the look of a man who worked hard with his hands for a living. After introductions, Carl, Nick and Dan set out to view the property while Meghan and I stayed in the store. It seemed like they were gone a very long time, but finally close to noon, they returned with big smiles on all their faces. They shook hands and said goodbye to Fielding.

Meghan and I were dying to hear what was said. Nick and Dan came into the store and told us that Fielding was very interested in buying the land. He liked the plans we had drawn up and suggested a few modifications. He thought being located on Route 9 made this property very desirable for people commuting to work in Worcester or other surrounding towns. He was going to put together an offer and bring it by early next week for us to consider. They hadn't discussed prices, but they did let him know we were meeting with at least one other developer. Dan and Nick felt good about Fielding's ideas and felt positive about the meeting, but everything depended on those financial figures.

Saturday afternoon was a repeat of Friday morning; only this time the developers were Chris and Cathy Paulson of Paulson and Paulson Custom Builders. Cathy did the designing, and Chris did the building. I liked the idea of working with a company that considered both aspects of development. They seemed very personable, but I reminded myself that was their job. However, I always put a lot of stock in first impressions. Armed with hot coffee against the increasingly cold weather, they headed out to view the property with Dan and Nick. They were also gone a long time, which I hoped was a good sign. Everyone came back, again with smiling faces. While the men talked a little longer, Cathy came in for more coffee and to check out the shop. She bought one of Meghan's terrariums, the prettiest one I thought, some antique Christmas ornaments, and the pedal car. We had a long discussion of our mutual love of pedal cars. I hated to see the car go so soon, but I had to admit the woman had good taste! If she was just trying to butter us up, she was spending a lot of money to do so! She said they had loved the property and were interested in keeping a couple of lots for themselves to build a home near the pond for their own family. So they must have really liked the place, and I really liked her! But business is business, so we would have to objectively compare the offers.

In the meantime, Nick contacted Lucas, and together they checked out the reputation and experience of each builder. Fielding Custom Builders had been in business about fifteen years, and had a solid reputation and work record. Paulson and Paulson had only been in business eight years, but Chris had run his own construction company for several years before that. They also had glowing recommendations and good financials. That was reassuring!

Carl Fielding brought his offer by the following Monday morning. I hoped his quick response was a good sign! We went over the report and visited a while over coffee and told him we would get back to him by the end of the week. I was glad the store was closed on Monday so I could study the proposal without interruptions. In a nutshell, Fielding's offer was somewhat less than what we would make selling the lots individually and building the roads and park ourselves, but it would give us the cash immediately to develop our projects, and we would not have to deal with selling, building and so forth. We would have to decide if it was worth it to us to take less money, in order to gain time and avoid tedious tasks.

Chris and Cathy Paulson came by early that same afternoon with their proposal. We reviewed it with as critical an eye as we did Fielding's. The Paulson's offer was very similar, except for two things. First, they were proposing about $1200 more per lot, which was very positive, but what might clinch the deal was their offer to build a custom home for Dan and me, and all we would have to pay for was the materials. The cost of building a house was considerable, and though the amount was not listed per se, if computed, it added serious money to the deal!

We faxed both proposals to Lucas, who said he would check them over and get back to us tomorrow or the next day. Never a patient person, I wasn't sure I could wait until tomorrow or the next day! I was learning that making money was very exciting, and, I was really getting the hang of it. To keep myself busy, I went to the garage and cleaned up some more antiques. It was time to put out those signs we'd found, some more clocks and old toys. I also added a few items I thought people might buy for Christmas gifts. I tried to help Meghan make more terrariums, but I wasn't very good at it. My first try looked like a weed patch. Meghan was complimentary, but then she took it to "finish," which meant she practically started over.

I decided to go to the house instead and cook to take my mind off things. I made my homemade lasagna and a lovely salad. I always add

Italian sausage and real ricotta to my lasagna, and of course, Mom's perfect homemade tomato sauce. I did use store bought salad dressing since I wasn't great at making it. My dad always made the salad dressing in our house. He would get out the imported olive oil that came in the beautiful gallon cans he bought at the Italian store in Worcester and pour it over the greens. He added vinegar, sometimes a little garlic or Parmesan and then tossed the salad. No measuring, no premixing, and it came out perfect every time. I could never replicate it, but I remembered it as the best I'd ever eaten.

When everyone came in for dinner, they remarked how great the house smelled. There was nothing like Italian food to make the mouth water and give the house a feeling of home. We all ate a lot, and we ate well. It was delicious! Nick said if they lived with us much longer, he was going to start putting on weight. I doubted it; he was a tall beanpole with a very fast metabolism and probably always would be.

We discussed the proposals as we put the leftovers away and did the dishes. We were just about finished with our tasks when the phone rang. It was Lucas—about twelve hours earlier than our earliest expectation. Dan answered and did the talking, or at least tried to as we all crowded around the phone, yelling out our questions. When we finally let Lucas speak, he said he had looked over the offers very carefully, checked everything out, and was changing his original suggestion that we sell the lots individually. He felt that both offers were good, but Paulson's was too good to pass up. We would be getting almost as much as if we sold the lots individually, and we would not have to do any of the work since they would take over everything.

Plus, we would have the money to develop the bed and breakfast and then the theatre, instead of having to wait and do a little here and a little there as money dribbled in. Lucas felt that if we invested some of the money we received for the land, we would more than make up for the difference of what we would get if we sold the lots ourselves. It was a win-win all the way around! We were all whooping and jumping up and down! Despite my age, I was still good at whooping and jumping up and down when excited and happy, and I was very excited and very happy! We told Lucas we would keep him posted, and decided to call

Chris and Cathy. They said they had been waiting by the phone, hoping to hear from us. Then it was their turn to whoop and jump up and down! They promised to stop by the next day to talk some more and make plans to get our lawyers working on this.

Dan and I stayed up talking late into the night. So many things were happening so fast that it was blowing our minds! We felt very blessed. Dan had also received an excellent offer for his web design business. Our Denver lawyers were currently drawing up the paperwork, and Dan would need to return to Denver sometime soon to sign the final papers. Our realtor had informed us that she had several interested people looking at our house, but so far no contract. We talked about reducing our already reasonable price, but she had suggested we wait a little longer. So, we planned to stay here through Christmas, since the holiday promised to be a busy time for the store, and to have Christmas here with the kids. Then shortly after the New Year, we would fly to Denver to finalize the sale of Dan's business and to pack up the house. We would hire movers to move most everything, but we would drive back our other car, possibly with a small trailer of stuff we needed now, like some of our kitchen things and the rest of our winter clothes. We hadn't originally planned on being away so long, so we hadn't packed many warm things suitable for New England winters.

If the house didn't sell soon, we might have to make another trip to Denver eventually to close on that sale. It was going to be sad leaving our home that we loved dearly and which had so many family memories. We would need to say goodbye to so many wonderful friends we had known for years. Hopefully they would come visit when the bed and breakfast was finished. When I was little, I could never understand how you could feel multiple emotions at once, but I sure was feeling them now! Exhausted, I finally fell into a deep sleep.

CHAPTER TWENTY-ONE
CHRISTMAS IN DENVER

A few days later, all of our travel plans changed. The realtor called to tell us there was a contract on the Denver house. The buyers had a pre-approved loan and wanted to close as soon as possible, so they offered above the asking price on the condition that they could move in by December 30. December 30! I almost choked! How could we ever move everything by then and run the antique store? As we were discussing the possibilities, Meghan happened to mention that she and Lucas had been talking about how it would be nice to spend one last Christmas in the Denver house where they grew up. That little comment touched the old heartstrings, and suddenly I wanted that last Christmas, too, and I would move mountains and part seas to make it happen. But what could we do about the store? Meghan and Nick could stay here until the 23rd or 24th, but they couldn't run everything by themselves, especially with all the Christmas sales. We couldn't close it for a week or more just after we opened. I kept trying all different scenarios in my mind, but nothing seemed feasible.

Later that afternoon, Jim stopped by to say hello, and Dan told him the news about the house contract, and the desire to spend Christmas in Denver. He suggested we call Hillary Bowers to see if she could help out with the store, and he and Jack could fill in, too, if needed. When they told me, I thought it was too much to ask of anyone, especially around the holidays, but Jim's response was, "That's what friends are for!" We hadn't known this man for long, but he made me feel like he had been my best friend for many years, and for the first time since we got here, I felt I was a member of this close-knit community.

I called Hillary, and she was very willing to help out. She finished at the florist on the 21st of December, and could start here on the 22st. I felt bad she wouldn't have a break, but she said her Christmas plans had changed, and she was staying home, so this would work out fine. She would also take good care of Grace, who would not be pleased about my leaving her behind. We decided to close the shop at noon on Christmas Eve and not reopen until December 27. Hillary, with help from Jim, would run the store until December 31, when we returned. It looked like everything might work out after all, and suddenly I wanted it to with my whole heart!

Then began a whirlwind of phone calls, internet, and faxes to sign the contract, contact the travel agent, confirm with Lucas and Emily, call a moving company, get lots of inventory ready for the store, etc., etc., etc. One of my good friends in Denver wanted to have a going away party for us. Would we even have time to attend? Organizing all of this was probably harder than any work we had done so far. We decided that Dan and I would leave on December 18 to start getting the house ready for Christmas and moving, and for the closing on Dan's business, which he moved up to December 22. I kept making lists, and amending lists and rewriting lists to try to remember everything we needed to get done. Sometimes I listed things that only took a minute, or things I had almost finished, just so I could cross them off the list and feel I had accomplished something. Crossing off things became very comforting! There were also lists of everything that needed to be done for the antique store, but Nick and Meghan handled most of that, including orienting Hillary and getting all the stock ready for the store.

Finally, December 18th arrived. I gave a sigh of relief when we boarded the airplane, and promptly fell asleep. I awoke just as we were landing. Our best friends, Kay and Sam Barrett were waiting for us just past security and after lots of hugs and luggage pick up, they drove us home. I was a little nervous to see the house after being gone so long. This had been our home for many years, and we had abandoned it. Now we were deserting it forever. Kay had thoughtfully gone to our house before heading to the airport and turned on the lights to make us feel at home. She had had her cleaning people go through the place so everything was sparkling and dust-free. And she had coffee and breakfast in the refrigerator. Oh, I would certainly miss these dear friends. It felt good to be home, even if it was only for a short while.

The next day we started packing up over twenty years of family stuff, and it was much more difficult emotionally than it was physically. Finding the kids' grade school pictures, report cards, trophies, and gifts to us brought back so many memories. I finally set up one big box labeled Lucas and another labeled Meghan, and put most of their childhood things in there (except those I couldn't give up) for each of them to sort when they packed up their old rooms after Christmas. I got most of our clothes, jewelry and other bedroom stuff packed, as well as the linen closet. We would have our furniture and anything we didn't need right away moved to Massachusetts and then put in storage until the house was built. I then started on the bathrooms, leaving out only what was needed for our short stay. I felt I had made a pretty good dent in the upstairs rooms.

The next morning I started on the basement. Our basement was finished with Dan's man cave, a theatre room, and an extra bedroom, so it was nothing like my parents' scary cellar, but there were still tons of things to go through. It absolutely amazes me the stuff that collects over the years! I think we could probably measure a six-inch layer of stuff for each year we had lived in this house. Some things were definitely worth saving, but there were others that I wondered why we had kept in the first place. I guess there was more of my family in my genes than I realized. When Dan had finished packing the garage, he joined me.

"Dan, I think we have to bite the bullet and get rid of a lot of this stuff. All this old camping gear—it goes to Goodwill."

"What if the kids want it?"

"Dan, it's so old, even Goodwill may not want it. That Coleman stove is practically an antique. Those old comforters we kept just in case we wanted to use them again—gone. The same goes for that card table with the broken leg, your Dad's old movie projector, that god-awful chandelier we took down when we moved here. It is time to let go, Dan. We can do it!"

And we did. We tossed out or set aside so much stuff to donate that the basement now looked huge. We should have done this year's ago. We did keep Dan's dad's fishing gear, and the projector since it still worked and might sell in the store. Meghan's red wagon that my dad made was carefully put in the keep pile along with anything else we just couldn't part with. The rule of thumb was anything that hadn't been used in a year was chucked—with exceptions of course. The living room set in the basement was still decent, but we would take the leather set upstairs with us, so we gave the basement furniture to a neighbor whose son was moving into an apartment. Tools and stuff in Dan's workshop, miniscule compared to my dad's, we gave to the Barretts. Dan had enough in Massachusetts to last a lifetime. We brought our huge Christmas tree upstairs, along with decorations and garland. In a way, it seemed silly to go to all that work of decorating a house that we were selling in a few days, but it was a family tradition, and our last Christmas in this house, and family was family!

Kay and Sam came over the next day to help. The guys packed all the books after I weeded out the keepers, while Kay and I started on the kitchen. We packed everything we thought wouldn't be needed over Christmas. Kitchens are always the hardest to pack and unpack. There are so many things—dishes, glasses, cups, bowls, utensils, pots, food and much more. Some things don't really fit into any category, so I had always ended up with a junk drawer for those items. We threw away lots of things here, too. I was not going to pay movers to ship a half-used box of salt or can of cinnamon. I also didn't really need six pickle forks or three Tupperware pitchers. Kay took one and we donated the others. Where did all these things come from? Did they reproduce on their own or something? Goodwill and ARC were going to love us with all the stuff we were giving them.

The closing on Dan's business was at 11:00 on December 22nd. He was selling to one of his best web designers, which made Dan and the staff feel positive about the continuity. After the paperwork was complete, Dan took the entire staff out to lunch at our favorite Mexican restaurant. One thing we would definitely miss about Colorado was the Mexican food, which is practically non-existent in Massachusetts. Heck, I had only seen one Taco Bell, if you can call that Mexican, and it was near Boston. I wondered if this restaurant would ship; it was definitely a little far for takeout.

During lunch, everyone was complimenting and thanking Dan, and I could see he was starting to get emotional. He had started this business from scratch and built it into a very reputable web design company. He had loved his work, and he wanted to move on, but he would miss the business and especially the people he worked with. The staff gave him a joke gift of farmer's overalls, a plaid flannel shirt and a straw hat, and everyone roared, including Dan. But then they gave him his real gift—a set of Macgregor golf clubs and two-dozen monogrammed golf balls. Dan loved the clubs and was so moved by their generosity that his eyes welled up with tears. He had a hard time getting through his thank you speech. It was nice to see the man I loved so appreciated and honored by his coworkers. I swelled up with pride.

After the festivities, we decided to do a little Christmas and grocery shopping. With all the planning and preparation for this trip, we hadn't done much shopping at all. We decided to take some of the money from the sale of the business and give each of our kids and each of their spouses $10,000. We had never been able to do that before, and we felt excited and almost giddy about it. We wanted them to have some money that was theirs to do as they pleased now, and not have to wait for everything until we passed on. We also bought some other small gifts to have under the tree. Then we split up in the mall for a while to buy gifts for each other, which was kind of fun and mysterious.

At the grocery store, we bought a huge prime rib roast for Christmas dinner and all the veggies to go with it. I got bread and rolls and stuff for desserts, and any other food I thought we would need for a few days. I decided I would rather run back to the store if we needed something than to throw food out when we left, but I did buy a few special treats like chocolates and special coffee and hot cider with spices just for fun.

By the time we picked up the kids at the airport on Christmas Eve, we had everything packed that could be packed up to that point. It hadn't been very long since we had last seen them, but we were so excited when they arrived. We bustled everyone into the car and took off for home. On the ride, we mostly caught each other up on the news--the store was doing great selling gifts for Christmas; the lawyers hoped to have the land deal ready for signatures shortly after the New Year; Meghan and Nick had found someone to sublet their house for a year so they did not have to hurry to sell it; Lucas and Emily were pregnant; Nick had completed refinishing the old tavern bar; we closed on the house on the 28th . . .

Wait . . . what was that? Lucas and Emily were pregnant? Our first grandchild? Meghan and Nick's first nephew or niece? I think I started screaming! We were all overjoyed! I was practically crying! And then all the questions began. How far along was she? What was the due date? Was she feeling ok? Any morning sickness? Then Lucas reminded us that he had a part in all of this and needed some attention, too. We all hit him for being selfish. That evening we all pampered Emily as we decorated the tree to the point she told all of us to knock it off. She was a nurse and knew what she could or couldn't do, and she planned to enjoy this holiday like everyone else, except without wine.

Christmas Day was as special as it looked in a Norman Rockwell painting and just as perfect as we'd hoped it would be. We didn't talk much about what the future held; rather we shared memories of all the times we'd had in this house: happy, sad, funny, and triumphant. It was a real tribute to our family and this home. Next year when we gathered again, it would be in our new home, with a baby in our midst, and we would begin to make new memories. But for today, we were here together, and it was a special time.

The kids were very appreciative of their small presents and the unexpected money. Nick and Emily gave us socks as a joke, and a note explaining that our real gift was a cherry dining table they had gotten from Jim for a song and refinished for the new house. The pictures showed it was absolutely beautiful. Like my father, I loved cherry wood. Lucas and Emily gave us a gorgeous desk set for the check-in counter of the bed and breakfast, and an antique silver ink well to sit beside it. They were beautiful and would receive a place of honor on the desk. I gave Dan a pair of Oakley sunglasses and covers for his new golf clubs. He had been real mysterious about his gift for me, trying to make me guess, hinting how special it was. Finally he presented it to me. A small box with fancy wrapping--that looked promising. I opened it to find a tanzanite ring! The tanzanite was square cut, and it was enhanced by small diamonds on the shanks. I inhaled as if in shock when I saw it.

"Oh, it's beautiful! Thank you, Dan! I absolutely love it!"

"I love you, Lily. I wanted to get you something extra special, and tanzanite is beautiful and rare, just like you. I'm so glad you like it!"

"I really do! I love you, my dear husband."

We hugged and kissed until the kids suggested we get a room and other crass comments. It was a wonderful Christmas!

The next two days we all finished packing up, and said goodbye to friends and our lives in Denver. On the evening of the 27th, we drove the kids to the airport. Lucas and Emily were heading home. He was still on Christmas break, but she was due back at work the next day. Nick and Meghan were flying to Chicago to pack up some of their clothes and personal items, which they would drive back to Massachusetts in their other car. They planned to return to Massachusetts January 2nd. On the morning of December 28th at 10:00, we signed the closing papers, and the house officially belonged to a new family. Then we finish packing the rented trailer with the last of the items we were taking with us. The movers arrived at 1:00 and loaded up all the boxes and furniture. I had arranged for a cleaning service to come in and prepare the place for the new owners. At last, everything on my list was completed and crossed off with big bold strokes. We walked through the house one last time to make sure everything was gone, and to say goodbye. Then we climbed into the car and drove away.

"Are you sad, Lil?"

"A little. I'll miss our life here. But I'm excited about our new life, too. You?"

"Ditto. I'll always be happy as long as I'm with you. Love you, kid."

"Ditto."

CHAPTER TWENTY-TWO
BACK TO WORK

We pulled into the farmyard on December 31, early in the afternoon in the middle of a raging snowstorm. The temperature was five degrees. There were already four inches of powdery snow on the ground, and it was accumulating fast. Dan backed the trailer up to the door of the antique store to unload some items from the Denver house that we had decided to sell. I gave Hillary a big hug, and I was glad the see the heater we'd installed kept the place cozy warm. Grace stuck up her nose at me at first and decided to ignore me, but a minute later she jumped into my arms, licked my face and purred ever so loudly. I had really missed her, too!

Hillary said the store had been very busy before Christmas, but since then things had been slow and steady as expected. I looked around to see that she had sold a number of items. The man who bought the chrome table and chairs did come back, and he bought an old stove for his wife for Christmas. All the terrariums were gone, as were the lamps, signs, some dishes and the last of the glass butter churns. We got busy moving the new items into their spots to fill up the place again. Hillary admired a pair of antique wrought iron sconces, so I gave them to her, along with payment for running the store. We wouldn't have had such a spectacular Christmas without her help.

By the time we finished unloading the antiques, two more inches of snow had fallen, and it didn't look like it was stopping anytime soon. Dan suggested we close at 3:00, since it was New Year's Eve, and we sent Hillary on her way with words of caution about driving in this snow. While I checked the receipts and closed up the store, Dan unloaded more items into the garage and took our bags into the house. He looked like a snowman by the time he had finished! By 5:00, it was dark outside, the snow was eight or nine inches deep, and the forecast said it would slow down but continue through the night.

"It feels strange for just the two of us to be here," I said. "It's so quiet, and with the darkness and the snow outside, I feel closed off in our own little world."

"Well, let's take advantage of that. Hey, it's New Year's Eve! Let's have a nice dinner, then cuddle up in warm blankets and watch some old classic movies with a little wine and welcome in the New Year," suggested Dan.

"Who are you kidding, Dan! We're old fogies. We'll fall asleep by 10:00, especially after a long day of driving in a snowstorm."

But we did just as he suggested. I made some chicken noodle soup and warm bread for dinner—no fancy canapés for us. Then we got into our pajamas and put on warm socks, of course. I grabbed a couple of warm throws I'd brought from Denver while Dan chose some movies, and we opened a bottle of wine. We cuddled up with Grace by my side and watched "An Affair to Remember," one of my favorite Cary Grant movies. I don't know if it was the romance, the feeling of contentment snuggling with my darling husband, the wine, or all three together, but just as Cary Grant was discovering why Deborah Kerr didn't meet him at the Empire State Building, we started feeling kind of romantic. A few kisses turned into a deeper passion, and things progressed to other body parts. I will leave out any more details in order not to offend those who think older people dry up and can't experience romance and passionate sex, or those who may be uncomfortable picturing two middle-aged people making love. Suffice it to say that Grace took off to her cat bed, and that we didn't see the rest of the movie. And yes, we were in bed by 10:00, but not because we were tired.

ew Year's morning the sun was bright, and the snow had stopped,
but it was still very cold. I had forgotten how much colder the wet
cold of New England feels compared to equal temperatures, but the
drier cold in Denver. I was so glad we'd brought the rest of our winter
clothes. Despite several layers, the cold went right through me. Dan
and I were shoveling the steps and walkways, and discussing calling a
plowing service when Jim drove into the yard in a heavy dump truck
with a big snowplow on the front. Dan jumped into the truck with him
while I returned to the warm house. They had everything cleared in
less than an hour, and when they came inside to warm up, I had coffee
and coffeecake waiting for them. Jim's cheeks and nose were red and
rosy, and he could have passed for a beardless Santa. We visited for a
while about everything that had happened while we were gone and
about his holidays, and then he left to do some more plowing. He had
saved us a lot of backbreaking work. I suggested we find out if they
made snowplows for golf carts. Nick would love that!

Since it was a holiday, we would have to wait a day to call storage
places about our house contents. We would need a reliable place to
store our stuff for several months once the movers arrived. Since we
also couldn't call for a plowing service to be available on a regular
basis, and since the store was full and didn't need more inventory,
we decided to talk about plans for our new house. We didn't need
anything as big as we had in Denver, so I suggested a three bedroom
with a finished basement and a theater room. I loved the one we had
in Denver. Dan said we should have a ranch style house since we
were getting older and shouldn't have a house with too many stairs. I
wanted a big, beautiful kitchen with granite countertops and stainless
steel appliances and every cool kitchen gadget available. He suggested
the kitchen open to a large great room, which would serve as living
and family room, since we really didn't need both. We would have
a library/office, luxurious bathrooms, of course, and lots of closet
space. There would be gas fireplaces in our bedroom, the great room,
and the office. We wanted an oversized two-car garage as well as a
big deck on the back. I told Dan I would like the house surrounded
by lovely trees on an acre lot, and a vacant acre lot next to it, just in

case Meghan and Nick got tired of living at the bed and breakfast and wanted their own home. We agreed on everything about the house except the color, so we decided to leave that for a later decision.

After New Year's, everything seemed to happen very quickly. Nick and Meghan arrived back on January 2nd, despite a big snowstorm in Chicago. They had brought their household items like dishes, linens, and books, as well as all their clothes and a few pieces of furniture they did not want to trust to tenants. They were excited to be back, and we were excited to see them.

Two days later, the movers arrived. Dan met them at the storage locker we had succeeded in renting, and they unloaded all our belongings. They would stay in storage until the house was built.

The next week we met with our lawyer, the Paulsons, and their lawyer to sign the papers for the sale of the land. Everything was in order, but I found myself a little hesitant to sign the contract. It wasn't fear or doubt about the consequences; I think it was just the finality of the whole thing. All of my life, my family had owned and been surrounded by this huge, by New England standards, piece of land. Once I signed those papers, there would only be a few acres left. I suddenly felt claustrophobic, like I was being pigeonholed into a tiny space. I had to breathe deeply a few times and collect myself. Finally I took the pen in hand and signed. It was done. The farmland was sold to the Paulsons, and we were embarking on our own adventures. I was excited, but I also felt like crying.

I stopped by the cemetery later that afternoon. The flowers were dead due to the cold, so I removed them and replaced them with a spray of winter greenery.

"Well, Mom and Dad, it's done. I signed the papers this morning and eighty acres of the farm now belong to Paulson and Paulson. They'll be building custom homes on the property starting in the spring. They're really nice people; I know you'd like them. They like the place so much they're going to build their own home there, down near the pond.

"Still, I feel kind of weird about all of it. It's like my huge world just shrunk to the size of a postage-stamp. If I take my usual daily walk, I will be trespassing on someone else's property. I hope you are okay with what I did. We got a really good deal, and now we can move forward with our other plans. But it feels like a part of me, or rather of you is gone. Please let it be okay! You don't need to send me a sign this time. Grace is absolutely great, and I love her, even if she sometimes gets mad at me and pees on the floor. FYI, we don't need another pet just now. I just hope and pray I have your blessing.

"I better go. It's getting a lot colder. The weatherman says it is one of the coldest Januarys on record! I'll be back soon. Stay warm! I love you both."

The nicest thing about selling the whole place at once was that the money was available now for all our plans, but we decided to still do the bed and breakfast first and the theatre later. However, we could shorten the timeline before we had both up and running. Nick and Dan hired contractors to help with reconfiguring the rooms into guest rooms, the apartment, etc. With several workers, the walls went up quickly. While they were working on the building, Meghan and I ordered furniture, linens, dishes, pots and pans, ledgers, guestbook, everything that would be needed for the bed and breakfast. Thanks to Emily's research, we found bulk food suppliers and a laundry service. The two of us, in addition to running the antique store, handled anything that could be done before the opening. We figured, barring any unforeseen problems, we could open sometime this summer.

Dan and I met with Chris and Cathy Paulson and described our ideas for the house they would build us. They made several excellent suggestions and promised to start building as soon as the ground defrosted enough to dig the basement. They would start on the other lots only after our house was completed. We would be paying for materials, but Chris and Cathy would get everything needed at their prices, which would be a big savings for us. It was exciting to think we would be living in a brand new custom-designed house.

Hillary opened the flower shop at the end of January. She had the concrete floor painted, and it really made a big difference. The retail section was filled with beautiful plants and flowers, vases, and décor items. The lighting she chose showed everything to its advantage. The store was lovely. She had brought a lot of her customers with her and business was steady from day one. I would pop by often and bring her coffee since she was too busy to stop for a break, and she seemed very satisfied to be a new business owner. She felt she was now investing in herself and not just making money for other people. From experience, I can say there is something intoxicating about that.

CHAPTER TWENTY-THREE
GLITCHES

As the construction progressed, Nick was continually disappointed he didn't find the Revenue Man buried in one of the old walls or floors, but he was totally pleased with the progress being made. However, we all started feeling that things were going too well. Dan's business had sold; our Denver house had sold; the farmland had sold; the antique store was doing well, and the bed and breakfast was developing nicely. With any new venture, there are always glitches and setbacks, but we kept rolling along with no serious problems and in a timely manner. We all kept waiting and dreading that something seriously negative was going to happen. It was like we were jinxed, only in reverse. Finally in mid-February, our first problem reared its ugly head. The electrician discovered the wiring was too outdated to support everything we planned, and a borderline fire hazard, so we would have to redo the electrical throughout the entire house. The same day the plumber told us that many of the existing pipes were old and needed to be replaced, and a larger system added if we were going to put in the baths I wanted. Both would be expensive and add at least a month to the remodel. We were all positively elated! The electrician and plumber must have thought we were crazy, but we felt the curse of too much good luck was lifted, and we were actually relieved. We okayed the changes immediately and went out to dinner to celebrate.

The next day, we found out that was only the beginning of the problems. In order to do the complete rewiring and plumbing, they needed access to the entire house, including the area where we were living which meant we suddenly had no place to live. We were no longer relieved when we learned this. Problems have a way of compounding, and that was exactly what was happening. The saying goes that bad things come in threes—rewiring, plumbing, and moving—that was three and hopefully would be the last for a while, especially since each cost us considerable time and money. So we kept our chins up and started looking for a rental.

In this area, most people do not rent, they buy, and live in a house for a long, long, long time. You would be amazed how many houses around here have brass eagle plaques over the front door, indicating the mortgage has been paid off. Some of those eagles have lots of patina on them from hanging there for many years. Finding a rental proved to be very difficult. We checked the newspapers, Internet, realtors; we even drove around the area looking for rental signs with no results. We were checking into a couple of apartments as a last resort when Cathy Paulson stopped by, and I told her our dilemma. She said Chris had just finished remodeling a house they bought as a fixer-upper, and it wasn't on the market yet. She suggested we rent it until our house was built, and we agreed immediately without even looking at it. It was a four-bedroom so we would have lots of space, more than we had now. It was in the next town, meaning we would have to commute, but we didn't care. We'd have a roof over our head.

So, we prepared to move . . . again. Changing houses was becoming a hobby, or more like a bad habit. Some of the furniture went to the antique store as planned. Anything else that could be stored was put into the garage or barn, and we took a bare minimum of furniture with us. The rental house had lots of built-ins, so we didn't need to move dressers and such. The house was very spacious and comfortable, and we settled in for the next several months. Chris had done quality work on the remodel, and I felt confident he would build us an equally beautiful house. Everything was moved into the rental house on a Sunday, and Meghan and I used Monday to clean out the years of debris in my parents' house.

In the kitchen, we carefully packed my mother's china and stemware, which had been a wedding present, making it around seventy years old. The china was a complete set for twelve in a pattern I had never seen anywhere else. I wasn't sure how much I liked it, but it was a part of my life and a gift from my mother that I wanted to keep and pass down to my kids. I don't think my mother had used these dishes and glasses more than two or three times in her whole life. She kept them for "special occasions." They only came out of the china cabinet twice a year to be washed and dried and carefully put back. She would be nervous the whole time we were cleaning them. I broke one of the wine glasses one time while drying it, and she almost cried. I felt so bad, and tried to glue it back together, but it was too fragile. She cherished these dishes and glasses so much, that she put them away to protect them, but she never let herself really enjoy them. She used to do that with lots of things that were special to her. In her cedar chest we found wool blankets and hand-embroidered linens and a silver tray that had never been used. Maybe it all related to growing up poor. I don't know. Whenever I caught myself being compulsive about saving something, I would stop and use it instead. If it broke or wore out, so be it; at least I'd enjoyed it.

We donated a lot of the pots, pans and everyday dishes, except for a few things that would go into the antique store. The kitchen table and chairs were colonial reproductions, so they were donated along with most of the appliances. I kept all of my mother's cookbooks and her recipe box. It was strange to see her handwriting on the recipe cards. It was like a part of her lived on in her handwriting. I had already cleaned out the pantry of can goods, again to avoid botulism, so packing that took very little time. In the drawer of dishcloths and dishtowels, I found two Baby Ruth candy bars hidden amongst the towels. That made me laugh out loud! My mother loved chocolate. When we were little, she would hide candy bars so we kids wouldn't find them, and they would be her special treat once we had gone to bed. Baby Ruths were her favorite, but even chocolate chips would do. All her kids were grown, and my dad dead. She had lived in this house alone for eight years, but she still hid her candy bars. God, I loved that woman and her quirks! Unfortunately, I inherited her love of chocolate, but I didn't hoard it. My hips were proof of that.

In the living room we separated the books in the bookcase. Some of the older ones would go into the store. Unbeknownst to my parents, they had a few first editions. There were lots of children's books that Meghan sorted into ones to keep for Lucas and Emily, and perhaps for her and Nick, and others for the store. I kept a few important to me, including the Family Bible, which hadn't been updated for a long time. Soon we would add Nick and Emily's child. There was a set of encyclopedias that had become obsolete with the Internet that we decided to put into the store since some people bought them for collections. Then we moved on to a closet in the living room. It was only about one foot deep and had shelves from top to bottom. We had always kept games and puzzles there, as well as a box of toys, knitting paraphernalia, and family picture albums. How could I have forgotten about this closet? So many memories were recalled as we removed everything from the shelves. We decided to take the picture albums to the rental house to explore. Some of the games were vintage, but in excellent shape, so we decided to add them to the store pile, along with some of the puzzles. In the toy box, I found a Howdy Doody doll; what a funny-looking fellow he was! We found three kid's cowboy hats, two toys guns and holsters, and a child size guitar.

"Hey Mom, are these from your Cowboy and Indian days?"

"Aah yes, that they were. We got those for Christmas one year. Tony, Dom, and I asked for cowboy hats, and cap guns and holsters. My mother didn't think it was lady-like for a girl to have a gun. (She never considered perhaps no kid should have a gun!) As a result, the boys got guns, but Lily didn't get a cap gun and holster. No, no, I got a guitar, like I was freaking Dale Evans or something. I was so upset! I don't even want to look at those things; donate them."

"Are you kidding me; they're vintage and worth some money. They are going to the store," responded Meghan. "If they bother you so much, I'll hang them where you won't notice them."

"I guess you're right. Sorry, a little unresolved anger just reared its ugly head for a minute. I hated being treated differently because I was a girl. I remember I wanted to learn to play the trumpet, but my mother thought the way you had to purse the lips to play it was also unladylike, so I had to learn the clarinet instead. I liked the clarinet, but I wanted to play the trumpet!"

"Time to let it go, Mom. Take a deep breath and move on."

"You're right, Meg. It's silly to get all crazy about something that happened so long ago. What else did you find in the toy box?"

"Look, it's one of those old ballerina jewelry boxes. It's a little dirty on the outside but can be cleaned up. The gold leaf design on the top isn't even worn."

"It's a music box, too. Wind it up and open it. We can see if the ballerina still dances around."

Meghan opened the box. It was lined in pink satin, with one small compartment on the top and a larger one on the bottom. In the center of the top compartment was a pretty little plastic ballerina in a pink net tutu. She turned around and around to the music. It still worked perfectly. I had begged for this jewelry box for my birthday one year, and I treasured it as a little girl. It had a few pieces of junk jewelry in it, but also my Mickey Mouse watch, my baby ring and bracelet, and a locket from Italy my grandmother had given me for my first communion.

"Mom, I'm sure this would sell quickly in the store, but may I keep it? I would love to give it to my own little girl one day and tell her it was her grandmother's."

"Of course you can keep it, as long as you take the baby ring and bracelet, too. I'll give the locket to Lucas and Emily for their baby. I think I would like to keep the Mickey Mouse watch for myself. Maybe I'll take it to a jeweler and get it working again."

Since we had taken the living room furniture with us to the rental house, all that was left in that room was the threadbare Oriental rug. I hated to throw it away, but it was too far-gone for anyone to want it. At Dan's suggestion, we put it in the garage to lay the antiques on instead of putting everything directly on the bare concrete floor.

The bedrooms we had used didn't take very long to clean out since we had already moved all the clothes and beds to the rental. Once we moved into our own places and unpacked our own beds, we would discard the old mattresses and linens. Two of the bedframes were old ornate iron, and we would sell them. The one in my parents' room was solid cherry wood, so we would probably keep that for the guest room in our new house. We finished two of the bedrooms and decided to call it quits for the day. I would finish up my parents' room and the bathroom the next day while Meghan minded the antique store.

The next morning I started in the bathroom. Everything in the medicine cabinet went straight to the trash. Most of the medicine bottles had expired, and the rest looked like they had been there forever. Mercurochrome? Does that stuff even exist anymore? Out to the trash it all went! Make-up in the drawers joined the bottles. Since I had already cleaned out the linen closet, all that was left in the bathroom was a small chest of drawers, which held some half-used creams and lotions and an old hair dryer and curling iron, all of which helped fill up my trash bag very quickly. I did find a lovely vanity set with several jars, and a brush, comb and mirror on a tray. They were made of Bakelite, and each item had mother-of-pearl inlay in a flower pattern. The mirror was worn and some of the silver backing had worn off in spots, but they were still lovely. I could remember this set sitting on the vanity in my parents' room when I was little. I thought about keeping them, but decided to put them in the store pile. Someone else would probably appreciate them even more than I would.

I had saved my parents' bedroom for last because I knew I was liable to get emotional while clearing out the personal things. I started with my father's dresser, thinking it would be empty since he had been gone almost ten years. I was wrong. My mother had not thrown any of his clothes or other items away. His Fruit of the Loom t-shirts and underwear were folded neatly in the drawers as if they had just come from the laundry. It was rather embarrassing to see and then have to touch my father's undergarments. If he were here, he would have been mortified. I just grabbed them in a big pile and threw them in the trash. The other drawers held jeans, work trousers, work shirts, and sweaters.

All were in good shape so they went to the donation box. My father's type of clothing did not go out of style. In the bottom drawer, I found my dad's wallet. It was kind of curved from sitting in his back pocket all those years, and the leather was worn. It held his driver's license, a few grade school pictures of Lucas and Meghan, and over $200 in cash! All those years it had just sat there, and my mother had never opened it. I decided to keep it the same way, as a memento, but maybe minus the cash.

My mother's dresser was neat also, but removing her items was even more difficult since they were more recently used. Most of her underwear was pretty worn, and I quickly threw it in the trash, almost embarrassed for her. I felt sad my mother was so exposed. I didn't want anyone going through my undergarments this way. I decided I was going home and trash all my less than perfect underwear, and from this day on, I would buy nice underwear and replace it often! The rest of the clothes in the drawers would be donated. In her top drawer, I found scarves and a few pieces of costume jewelry. The older pieces I would keep or sell. Way in the back of the drawer I found a purple box, and the tears that had been close to the surface spilled over. Soon I was sobbing.

When I was in second grade, the teacher had each kid bring in an egg carton and a picture of something our mother liked. I brought a picture of violets because my mother loved flowers, especially violets. I painted the egg carton with the brightest purple poster paint, pasted the violets picture on the top, and stapled a purple bow in the top left corner. I gave this homemade jewelry box to my mother for Mother's Day that year. Even as a second grader I knew the box was pretty ugly and I wasn't totally comfortable giving it to her. I remembered how my mother, ever so graciously expounded on how beautiful the box was, and she promptly loaded her earrings into the egg compartments. Now when I opened it, I found several pairs of clip earrings still in the box. She had used this atrocious box for her lovely jewelry and kept it all these years. She treated it as if it were something special because I had given it to her. I don't think I had ever loved my mother more than I did at that moment. I wondered if I had ever been so selfless and kind to my kids.

On the top of the dresser was a polished wood jewelry box that she had received as a graduation present from the Lane Co. who made cedar chests. They used to give the small boxes to girls when they graduated from high school, and she kept and used it all those years. I had gotten one when I graduated, too, but I had no idea where it ended up. I put the box in the desk she kept in her room to sort through later.

Mom's Infant of Prague religious statue with its silk robes and rosary wrapped around it was also on the dresser. It was made of chalkware, so it scratched and broke easily. The face on this statue was practically gone from being dropped, and the whole thing was pretty scarred up. But what was I going to do with it? I didn't want it; it was too damaged to sell, but I was not sure it was okay to throw away a religious item like this. I finally decided to send it to my brother Tony. He could be the one to deal with it.

I asked Nick and Dan to move my parent's desk to the backroom of the antique store so Meghan and I could carefully sort each item and decide what we wanted to keep. It was a beautiful old piece made of cherry wood. It might just move to my new home.

My parents' closet was full of clothes—both my mother and father's. Why did she keep these all these years? I bagged all of them up for donation and then started on the stack of boxes in the corner. There were a few old hats and shoes, mostly outdated, so I trashed them. The old luggage and wooden ironing board we could sell. Under a pile of boxes, I found the cashbox we had used for the vegetable stand. The old metal box was dented and battered from all those years of use, but imagine my surprise when I opened it and found everything set up just as if we were opening the stand tomorrow. In the top compartment there were quarters, dimes, and nickels in their respective slots, and ten $1 bills with a flat rock holding them down, in case it got breezy. Lifting up the top compartment, I found two $10s, two $5s and twenty $1s secured with a rubber band in the bottom for making change. There were a couple of pencils and a pad to mark down purchases. My parents had not operated the vegetable stand for over fifteen years. This was like finding an historic artifact. Had my mother kept it as is for some reason, or did she just forget it was there? And what was I going to do with it? That decision would have to wait for later.

The last item to unpack was her cedar chest. I could just imagine what I would find in it. There were the wedding present blankets and linens and greeting cards. I swear my mother must have saved every Christmas, Valentine, Mother's Day and any other card my father or we kids had ever given her. Some of them were quite old. I was really moved that they had meant so much to her. I found our baby books, report cards, birth certificates, and first communion and confirmation certificates. I put all that stuff in a box to be sorted later. The cedar chest itself would be sold.

By the time I finished, I was physically and emotionally drained and went searching for my family for a late lunch. Dan and Nick had just brought the desk into the backroom of the antique store, and Meghan was heating the leftovers I'd brought for our lunch. After eating, I started cleaning out the desk. The cover opened down on hinges to form the desktop. In the cubbies were stamps, clips, rubber bands and all those things needed to do paperwork. The drawers were full of old tax statements and receipts, and any over seven years old were pitched. My mother's checking and savings accounts had been closed over a year ago, so the extra boxes of checks were shredded and thrown away. The only really interesting thing we found was a copy of my grandmother's will, leaving the farm and all her personal possessions to my father. In polite lawyer-speak, it said that since he had worked the farm and taken care of her in her final days, he was to get everything, and none of the other kids better complain. As far as I knew, that is just what happened.

Meghan and I decided to wait until Emily was here to sort the jewelry box. My mother hadn't owned a lot of valuable jewelry, but there were some lovely pieces we should all share. I knew I wanted to keep an onyx necklace and earring set that I had coveted since my father gave it to her. Mom had never worn it. As usual, she had been waiting for a special occasion. It was almost as if she didn't think she was good enough or important enough to wear something so special. I planned to wear it a lot!

With my parents' room cleaned out, everything on the property had finally been sorted, moved, prepped for sale, or tossed in the trash. It had taken months, but it was done. I intended to enjoy the next few months just running the store and enjoying the rental house. And I did not intend to clean out another room or closet or move anything except antiques for a very long time. When the new house was ready, we would be unpacking again, but after all this, that should be a breeze. And I definitely planned to hire a cleaning person.

Again I felt like a portion of my early life was gone . . . the land, the house, and all the items that had been present when I was a kid. It seemed having mixed feelings about things was becoming a way of life for me, but at least I wasn't angry about the farm any more.

CHAPTER TWENTY-FOUR
THE HIDDEN ROOM

It was a Monday morning, and I had decided to sleep in. It had been a month since we moved to the rental house, and lately everything had been running smoothly again. The electricians and plumbers were making excellent progress. Nick and Dan were getting everything ready to start putting up walls as soon as the rewiring and plumbing were completed. The antique store business had been steady. We had taken in some consignment pieces as well as our own pieces, and that was working out well. Jim kept finding us items also. So, I decided on this very cold Monday, with the store closed, I was going to snuggle under the covers for as long as I could and enjoy my day off.

Which lasted until about 8:30 when my cell phone rang, waking me from a deep sleep. Grace startled also. She jumped out of the bed and ran off. I was rather out of it and confused when I answered. It was Dan.

"Liliana, you and Meghan need to come to the house right away."

"Is everything all right? You and Nick aren't hurt, are you?" I interrupted.

"No, no. No one is hurt. We've just run into something we think you should see."

"Something good or something not so good?"

"Lily, just get over here as soon as you can, okay? And stop worrying!"

I quickly threw on jeans and a sweatshirt, brushed my teeth, and ran a brush through my hair. Meghan wasn't asleep when I checked her room, and I detected the delicious smell of fresh coffee, so I headed to the kitchen. She was sitting at the island painting some of the slates she had recovered from the garage. She painted lovely New England scenes, and she had already sold several.

"Meghan, Dad just called and said they found something important to show us. He wants us to get to the house right away. His call woke me up from a sound sleep, so I am still a little woozy. Dad said he and Nick were all right and not to worry. But I'm worrying anyway."

"Mom, let me get you a cup of coffee and a muffin to take with you, and we'll head out. I'll drive."

"That's probably a very good idea. I'll grab our coats."

We pretty much kept to the speed limit, but it seemed to take forever to get to the house. I rushed in the front door and called for Dan. He yelled back that they were in my parents' room. We carefully threaded our way through the debris of the kitchen and living room to get to the bedroom. The place was a disaster area, but I was so anxious to find out what was happening that I hardly noticed. Dan and Nick had been pulling up carpet in this room, only to find three layers of old linoleum, all in pretty bad shape. When they finally got to the wood floor below, they found something very unexpected: a trapdoor in the middle of the floor! A real trapdoor like you see in western movies. It was about forty by thirty-six inches and had an iron ring on one side as a handle and two big hinges on the opposite side.

"Lil, did you know there was a trapdoor here?"

"No, no one ever mentioned it, but considering all those layers of linoleum, maybe my family never knew. It must date back to colonial times when they built trapdoors to underground areas so that they had a place to hide if there was an Indian raid."

"Maybe it was used as a part of the Underground Railroad," suggested Meghan.

"What's under the door?" I asked.

"We haven't opened it yet, Mom," said Nick. "We felt you should have the honor."

"I can't believe you had the patience to wait; I wouldn't have. Let's open her up!"

At first the door was stuck in place, probably due to the dirt and grime that had settled in the cracks over the years. But the guys finally got it moving, with a crowbar and some groaning from the rusty hinges. Once the door was open, we all grabbed flashlights and knelt on the floor around it to look inside. It was pitch black and smelled rather dank and dusty. There was a wooden ladder attached to one side of the hole.

"I'm going down the ladder," I said.

Dan grabbed my arm to stop me.

"No, you're not! No one is going down there until we have better lighting and our own ladder. Who knows how old that thing is. The wood could be rotten and break as soon as anyone steps on it."

"Dan!"

"Patience, Liliana. It will only take a minute."

Nick got an industrial light strip to shine in the hole. Dan got an extension ladder. It hit bottom at a depth of about ten feet. At least we knew about how deep the hole was. I got breath masks for everyone. I could barely contain myself; I was so excited!

"I'm Chairman of the Board, and it's my house, so I'm going down first."

"Well, since you pulled rank, Lily, you go first, but please, please be careful!" admonished Dan.

I cautiously climbed onto the ladder while Nick held it steady and held on tightly to the sides. I felt like I was descending into the abyss; it was so dark! I remember spelunking in caves when I was in college, and at one point the guide had us all shut off our headlamps to experience complete darkness. This darkness reminded me of that—the total absence of light. The light strip Nick had set up mostly lit a small area around the ladder, so I couldn't see when I'd reached the bottom. I stepped down looking for another rung and instead found the dirt-packed floor, just like in the basement of the house. The light did not extend much beyond the ladder, so I had no idea of the dimensions of the space. I pulled the flashlight out of my pocket and started shining it around in a circle.

"Are you all right, Lily?" Dan called.

"I would be much better if you were down here with me. It is so dark, I can't see much of anything."

Dan climbed down the ladder and added his beam to mine. Now I could make out a stone wall behind me about three feet away. Dan yelled for Nick to lower the light strip to help us see better. When he did, we were able to make out other walls. We started near the wall behind the ladder and slowly paced along it to determine the dimensions of this space we were in, whatever it was. The wall behind the ladder was eight to ten feet long. A railroad lantern hung at each end of the wall, about six feet high. We decided it probably was not a good idea to try to light them. Who knew how long they had been here and what was in them. Then we reached a corner and followed a similar wall, about the same length and also made of old fieldstones, similar to the stone on stone walls of the cellar.

The second wall had some rough wooden shelving attached to it, and there were what looked like brown bottles, some full and some empty, probably about twelve of them on the shelves. At about six feet along that wall, I saw a glint of metal reflecting off my flashlight just in time to avoid bumping into something. We used our hands and lights to explore this metal contraption. There were a couple of large tarnished copper pots connected with some metal tubes and a big wooden barrel.

"Dan, it's a still! A real still! This is where they made the whisky during Prohibition. I can't believe we found it! For years I searched for this thing, and it's been hidden down here the whole time."

"Meghan and Nick, grab some more flashlights and come on down. You won't believe what we found," Dan yelled up to them.

When they joined us, their additional light made it easier to make out the apparatus. From what we could see, it didn't look very rusted or corroded.

"Is that really a still? Amazing!" said Nick.

"We'll probably have to take it apart to get it out of here and clean it up for the antique store," said Meghan. "I'm sure it will be a hot item."

"We can't sell it! It's a part of the history of the place," exclaimed Nick.

"So is everything in the antique store, Nick. What else would we do with it?"

"I think we should put it in the restaurant. What a conversation piece it would be! We could build a little display platform for it and put up some plaques with the historical information on it. And then the restaurant would really be like a speakeasy. I think it would be absolutely awesome!"

"I think it's a wonderful idea, Nick, if we can get it out of here, and if it is in good shape when we see it in decent light. We can put some of those bottles around it on a shelf. But I suppose we will first have to find out if it is legal to even have a still, even if it is not operational."

"Is that homemade whisky?" asked Meghan.

"More than likely, but no one is going to drink it to find out. That stuff would probably kill you!" said the ever-conscientious Dan. "I mean you, too, on that, Liliana."

"Me! I wouldn't touch the stuff. I'm not that crazy. Let's check out the rest of the place."

The second wall ended up being about ten feet long also before we hit the corner and turned to the third wall of the same length. The third wall was all stone with no other features except two more hanging lanterns. At the end of it, we turned to the fourth wall. Fourth wall—one, two, three, four—this was a room! I kept shining my light all over the walls looking for a door. There was none. We were in a totally enclosed, secret, hidden room! The only entrance and exit was through the trapdoor we had used. No wonder it was so dark in here. And how spooky, but at the same time, very awesome!

"How could this room have been here all this time, and my family never realized it? It must be visible from the cellar. I want to have a look. And you know what? Knowing now that we would be stuck down here in total darkness if someone shut that trapdoor is spooking me!" I emoted. "I've seen too many horror movies."

Just then I heard squeaks and the skittering of little clawed feet. It startled me and I dropped my flashlight, and of course, the light went out. I bent down to try to find it, moving my hand back and forth in the darkness. Suddenly my hand hit on a pile of something like long sticks or tubes that rattled against each other at my touch. I put my hand out again, feeling around to see what I'd found. I picked up one of the long objects and stood up, just as Dan shone his light near me. It was a bone! A big long bone, like a leg bone.

I screamed, and dropped it in the pile at my feet where it rattled against the other sticks, aka bones! I grabbed Dan's light from his hand and shone it down on the pile. It was a skeleton! I screamed again, louder and very shrill this time.

"Lily, what's wrong? Are you all right?"

Dan, Meghan and Nick rushed over to me, and with the increased light, we were able to see more details. There were some shreds of a suit jacket, pants and rotting shoes, but they were mostly in tatters from decay and rodents. It looked like a rat's nest had been made in an old fedora. All of the flesh from the body was gone. Most of the bones were disarticulated, but still in situ, so we were pretty certain the remains were of a human, especially because of the skull. We kept trying to make out more details, as much as our lights would allow. I finally located my flashlight; it had fallen into the chest cavity of the skeleton. I had to touch the skeleton to get it out. I reached very carefully under the rib cage and breastbone and gingerly lifted my flashlight out. I accidentally touched the hipbone while extracting the light, and I almost screamed again.

I slapped the light against my leg to try to get it working again, and as it turned on, it reflected off a shard of metal near the hipbone. I bent to pick it up and scraped the dirt off on my pants. It was gold-colored and a couple inches or so long and one and a half inches wide. It was rounded at the top, and rectangular at the bottom. I held it up close the light, and I thought I could make out an eagle, a big U and a big S, and after rubbing off more dirt, I could see the words Prohibition Agent.

"Oh my God, Dan, I think I've found the Revenue Man!"

As we shone our lights around some more, Dan noticed a piece of decaying leather sticking out of the ground. He picked it up to find a wallet. Opening it, he found a corroding driver's license for Roy Abernathy. There was also a moldy picture of a woman and two young children, a boy and girl. We had finally found him, and sadly, it looked like he had had a family.

We were all too shocked to speak. I realized I was crying. Poor Roy

Abernathy. A good, dedicated man trying to do his job, enforcing a stupid law because he loved and believed in his country, and this is how he ended up—in some dark, dank corner of a hidden room with his family never knowing what happened to him or being able to properly mourn him. He had gotten in the way of some illegal business, so he had been murdered and just discarded here. They didn't even bother to bury him properly! The things human beings do to each other just astound me! He deserved better than this. Much better.

I thought about all the times we had tried to find him when we were kids. But to us, it was just a game, a joke; something we did for fun, sort of like acting out a legend. I'm not sure we ever really understood that he was a real person who had been a victim of greed, and I hoped we had never been disrespectful to his memory.

"Gee Mom, the Revenue Man was here the whole time. Just think, your whole childhood, you were sleeping above a decaying corpse!"

"Thanks for reminding me of that, Nick!"

I felt like we should cover him or something, but we had nothing with us to do so, and we didn't want to disturb the crime scene any more than we already had. The crime scene; that's exactly what it was. We went to the antique store, and Meghan made coffee while Dan called the Police. I had always thought I would feel triumphant if we ever found the Revenue Man, but all I felt was sad and numb. We were all rather somber.

"The Police Officer I spoke to said that even though it was a very old case, they would be calling in the FBI since it … he was a federal officer. A local detective will be here in a little while to meet with us and check out the scene. He said we might have to stop working on the building until this case is closed, and it's hard to know how long that will take. Nick, you may as well send the workers home for the day. Tell them we'll call them when we know more."

Detective Will Sanderson arrived shortly after, and I spent the better part of an hour telling him the background to all of this, as I knew it. I explained the history of the property, the vegetable stand historians, my dad's stories and what we found. He, Dan, and I then went down into the secret room again to show him the remains. The Detective was as awed as we were by the hidden room, the still, and the skeleton. He called in the local coroner to pronounce Roy Abernathy dead, as if there was any doubt, and then the County Crime Scene Unit. Even in this rural area, protocol was followed. He said the FBI would probably not arrive until tomorrow or the next day since this wasn't a high priority case, and we were not to enter the house until they had cleared it for our use again.

Detective Sanderson then asked to check out the cellar to see if he could find an entrance from there to the hidden room, or any other clues as to how all this happened. I really didn't think we would learn anything about the murder, but I wanted to see if we could enter or even locate that room from the cellar. He, Dan and I went back into the house and down into the basement.

"This must have been a creepy place to grow up, huh?" Sanderson asked.

"I always hated the basement, but it wasn't half as creepy as it is now, knowing there was a hidden room nearby with a dead body in it!" I retorted.

We shone our flashlights along the walls of the basement near where we suspected the room to be. All we saw were stones and more stones. Then just past the coal bin, I noticed that the wall jutted out a little farther than the previous section, almost on a slight curve. Other than that, the stone walls looked the same as the rest of the basement. We surmised that this section was one wall of the hidden room, a wall that had been built to close off a secret area from the rest of the cellar. It was probably built at the same time as the rest of the cellar, since the stone looked no different. If you didn't know the room was there, you would never have noticed that there was anything but a long basement wall. It was ingenious really, and I commended the early builders who had designed it. We searched and searched, and even tried to push in stones to open a secret entrance, like in the movies, but there were no doors. We hadn't learned anything to help with the investigation, but a mystery had been solved.

It was probably a good thing I hadn't known about that room when I was a kid; there would surely have been another boundary rule that

I would have broken. And I probably would have been traumatized by what I found; I'm glad I didn't know. Except that poor Roy would have found peace much sooner if I had.

We were allowed to open the antique store, so I kept busy while waiting for the FBI. The remains could not be removed until they investigated the scene, and even though Roy had laid there for eighty some odd years, I hated his having to lay there one day longer. Dan and Nick kept busy in my father's, now Dan's workshop, and Meghan worked in the back room of the store painting more slates. She could have worked in the garage, too, but she sensed I didn't want to be alone. I was jittery and found I was having a hard time keeping my mind off what we had found and on my work. About 1:00 p.m., a black SUV drove into the yard, and two men in dark suits got out and came into the store. They identified themselves as Special Agents of the FBI and showed me their badges. Dan had seen the car drive in, so he came to give me moral support.

They had Detective Sanderson's file of his findings, but I was asked to repeat the entire story again. They were stern-faced and showed little change in expression as I spoke, stopping me only to ask for clarification. There is something about talking to law enforcement people, especially stone-faced law enforcement people, that makes me immediately feel like a suspect and that I am guilty of something. My hands get sweaty. I have trouble making eye contact, and I over-explain things. This isn't only with the Police or FBI; it happens with security guards at the airport and even the campus police at the university where I used to work. Maybe it's because of all those rules I broke as a kid and never got caught. It's like they have unfinished business with me.

When I finished explaining, they said my report corroborated what was in the Detective's file and FBI records about Abernathy's disappearance. They then asked to see the remains. Meghan watched the store while Dan and I took them to the hidden room. They looked at the skeleton, took numerous pictures, and then called in their Crime Scene Unit to have what was left of the body removed for autopsy. The

Crime Scene techs carefully put the skeleton in a body bag and took it up the ladder, and then put the remains on a gurney. The FBI agents put the tatters of clothing and his badge and wallet in evidence bags. Finally, they loaded Roy into the ambulance, thanked us and left. The FBI agents also thanked us, and told us they would be in touch when the case was closed and the crime scene released, so we could get back to work on the house. And that was it. The Revenue Man was gone. He would finally be put to rest.

I stopped at the cemetery on the way home that evening. I needed to talk to my parents, whether they heard me or not.

"Hi, Mom and Dad, How are you doing?

"Lots of things have happened since I was here last. I'm not sure I told you that Emily and Lucas are pregnant. They are both doing well. They are very happy, and I am so excited. My first grandchild! You will be great grandparents again. I'm secretly hoping it's a girl so I can make her girly things, but we'll all be happy with either.

"The antique store is doing well. Now that the land is sold, we are making great progress on the bed and breakfast, or at least we were. Dad, did you ever know there was a trapdoor to a hidden room under your bedroom floor? I doubt you or your family ever knew. Well, anyway, Nick and Dan were pulling up carpet and found three layers— can you believe it?—three layers of linoleum. They pulled that up to get to the bare wood floor. And you will never guess what they found— in the middle of the floor was a trapdoor! We got it open and went down a ladder to find a totally hidden room, about ten feet square. You couldn't see it or get in there from the cellar. The only entrance and exit were through the trapdoor. And in the room we found the still from Prohibition days and some old bottles of homemade whisky. But sadly, we also found the remains of the Revenue Man.

"He really did exist. We found his badge and wallet, and his name was Roy Abernathy. He had a family, too. I feel bad they never knew what happened to him. I feel bad that anything happened to him! Whoever killed him just threw his body in a corner of that hidden room and let him rot all these years in that damp, dark place. And we never knew he was there. As Nick reminded me, we slept above a corpse all those years! Anyway, the Police and FBI came and investigated, and the case should be closed soon. I can't stop thinking about poor old Roy, though.

"I think we should fill that room with sand. It might have historical significance, and we probably should preserve it. Maybe it was used during Indian raids or even as part of the Underground Railroad; but none of that can be proven. It is also the place where a brave man died, and it was his horrible tomb for over eighty years. I wouldn't want people tromping around in there. Somehow it seems disrespectful to his memory. I want a plaque in the Speakeasy, that's the name of the restaurant we're building, to tell the story of the Revenue Man, but maybe the story should end with his body finally being found, without all the gory details. I don't want the hidden room becoming a tourist attraction. I think you'd agree. And if the rest of my family doesn't mind, I think we should name the bed and breakfast Abernathy's. It seems fitting, don't you think? He spent more time there than any of us did!

"Well, I guess I'd better go. But, I wanted to stop by and tell you the news. Take care, and I'll be back soon. Love you both!"

CHAPTER TWENTY-FIVE
CHRISTMAS IN NEW ENGLAND

It's been ten months or so since the discovery of the Revenue Man. The FBI kindly moved very quickly to close the case, and our first task once we were allowed back in the house, was to fill in and seal the hidden room. After that, renovations progressed at a quick pace. Rooms were built, with the lovely bathrooms I wanted. The Speakeasy was furnished with the antique bar from the tavern days, the brass rail looking as shiny as the day it was made. The copper still sits on a dais, polished and gleaming, and surrounded by the whisky bottles and plaques, one with a picture and the story of Roy Abernathy. The lobby looks welcoming and comfortable. Fireplaces were uncovered in the lobby, as well as Meghan and Nick's apartment and the tavern, so we did end up buying all of Jim's antique mantles. Once they were cleaned up and refinished, the beautiful hand-carved designs were more evident. They are magnificent!

We opened Abernathy's Bed and Breakfast in September on Labor Day weekend. All the rooms were full, thanks in part to Dan's excellent website and marketing. People's interests were peaked by the history of the place and the beauty of New England. We had to turn away guests during the October weekends when the fall leaves were at their peak. We are also completely booked over the Christmas holidays by people desiring a real New England Christmas. Some local people have even come to stay here for a romantic weekend away. With all this business,

Dan has been doing shifts in the bed and breakfast, and we convinced Nick to hire more restaurant and household staff, including desk people so he isn't tied to the place 100% of the time. That way Nick can help Meghan with the theatre development; something they both love. And the household staff loves the Godzilla Vac—go figure.

Hillary's flower store is constantly busy, and she also had to hire extra help. She provides flowers for the rooms and restaurant, which is an excellent situation for both of us since she then gets lots of customers from our guests, and we get the beauty of her work. She is enjoying her success. Sometimes when the antique store isn't busy, I go over to her shop and bask in the beauty of the flowers. On warm days, Hillary, Meghan and I often take a coffee break on the wrap-around porch. Nick furnished it with round white wicker tables and high-backed wicker rocking chairs, and it is a very welcoming place. We three ladies have become good friends.

Speaking of friends, Jim and Dan have become the best of buddies. They have so much in common and really enjoy each other. They go fishing and golfing, and Dan often accompanies Jim when he goes to bid an estate to salvage, which helps us get first pick of some great antiques. We finally met Jim's wife Karen, and it turns out she was also a few years ahead of me in high school. We have all become friends, and we often go out as a foursome—to the few places one can find to go out around here, or get together for dinner and cards or board games. Karen is an excellent seamstress, and Meghan has been talking to her about making costumes for her shows. It seems we were destined to all become friends. I still miss our Colorado friends, but it is nice we are developing relationships here, too. And several of my buddies from Denver are planning a ladies vacation in the spring. They will stay at the bed and breakfast for a few days, and then explore New England. They want me to join them, and I just might need to go on a buying trip with them!

Delaney's Antique Store continues to do quite well, and I'm having a ball! If you love antiques, running a store is like playing with your favorite toys rather than working. Of course you do need to be able to share those toys and let the treasures go and live in someone else's house. I have hired a lady named Amy Larson who has an extensive knowledge of antiques to help me run the place on a part-time basis. That way Dan and I can get away. We have a couple of "buying" trips planned for after New Year's. One to the southern US, and one to Paris! We plan to combine business and pleasure.

As soon as the bed and breakfast was finished, Meghan got the workmen started on the theatre, and the renovations are progressing nicely. The inclined floor has been laid, and the lofts have been converted to the balcony and projection room. Converting the cellar storerooms to prop and costume rooms has been the most difficult since they were so primitive, but these guys have done an amazing job. You'd never know it used to be a dank old basement. They are currently working on the stage. The carpenter who made the artistic carved wood surround for the proscenium arch is a genius! It fits well into the converted barn setting, yet it is quite elegant and draws the eye to the stage without taking away from what is happening there. The workmen hope to be entirely done by April, and we hope for a grand opening in June.

Meghan has already been researching local talent and getting them interested in Delaney's Theatre Company. She was surprised and thrilled to find so many talented actors, singers, and dancers in this area where there are so few venues to showcase their talent. Well, that will all change very soon! For her opening show, Meghan is considering "Man of La Mancha." To me, that seems very appropriate since we are now living "The Impossible Dream."

The Paulson's have been going great guns since the spring, building beautiful houses on the old farmland. Their excellent taste and style are making this into a lovely community. True to their word, they built our home first, and Dan and I absolutely love it! It has everything we asked for and more, thanks to Chris and Cathy. The rooms are spacious and elegant, yet comfortable. The kitchen has all the latest devices, and I feel like a queen, or at least the queen's cook. The great room makes me want to entertain and never leave it to go to bed, but our bedroom is so beautiful, I also find I just want to luxuriate in our bed and not get up in the morning. Of course, we had to get some brand new furniture to go with our brand new place! But antiques are still the predominant décor.

Grace loves the house, too, and has her own little nook. I can't imagine life without her. She still follows me wherever I go, and I really like having her around. People in the antique store are totally charmed by her, and several have even offered to buy her, but I could never give her up! I still consider her my miracle.

I recently received a letter from Beverly Abernathy Andrews, Roy Abernathy's daughter. She is in her late eighties and quite frail, so her granddaughter wrote while Beverly dictated.

Dear Mrs. Delaney,

The FBI was kind enough to give me your name and address. I am Roy Abernathy's daughter, and the last survivor of his immediate family. My granddaughter, Lucy is writing for me since I am in poor health, but my mind is still sharp, and I can remember very well when my father disappeared. My family was devastated. Not knowing what happened to him has had a tremendous effect on our lives. I believe my mother never recovered and died at an early age, never remarrying, even after he was declared dead because she always hoped my father would return. They had a great marriage and loved each other deeply. My brother became a somber person who always seemed weighed down by responsibility, having to take over as the man of the family at such a young age. He became an FBI agent, I'm sure, because of my father. We may not have known what happened to Dad, but we always believed he was a hero.

I married a good man and have two daughters and two sons who have blessed me with several grandchildren. I have lived a good life, but the loss of my father has always left an emptiness in my soul. I was quite young, only about six when he disappeared, but I do have lots of memories of him that I would like to share with you. He was a good man, a kind man, a family man. He was kind of nerdy, that's the currently popular term my granddaughter assures me says what I want to express. People called him responsible and dependable, and he loved his country deeply. Serving the United States, even to enforce the ridiculous Volstead Act, made him very proud. He was a church-going man who read his Bible every day. He also had a wonderful, if somewhat corny sense of humor. His jokes would make you groan. He loved to sneak up on us kids and toss us around, and he would play and read to us for hours.

I am enclosing a picture of my father taken shortly before his death. I want you to know all this about him so you will think of the remains you found as a human being who lived a vital and uncompromising life: a man who loved his God, his country and his family with all his heart. I also want to thank you for finding him and helping answer the questions that have plagued my mind all these years. My father would be proud that he died in the service of his country. Since he was a veteran and because he died serving his country, he could have been buried at Arlington National Cemetery, but we decided to lay him to rest next to my mother. They didn't have a lot of years together on earth, but now they will rest together for eternity. You have brought closure to my family, and again I thank you from the bottom of my heart.

My best wishes to you and your family,
Beverly Abernathy Andrews

The signature was kind of scrawled. Or maybe it was my tears that made it seem so. I wrote back and told her we had sealed the hidden room and had a plaque about her father in the restaurant, and how visitors are often moved by his story. I also told her I had framed the picture she had sent and added it to the wall with the plaque. I would probably never meet this lady or her family, just like I never met Roy, but I felt close to them.

This will be our first Christmas in the new house and in New England. If the weather continues to cooperate, we will have a white Christmas with the whole family here to celebrate. Whenever I can pry Meghan away from the theatre, we have been picking greens to decorate Delaney's, Abernathy's and our new house. I have also been lying in stores of everyone's favorite foods. We have a glorious tree to decorate when Lucas and Emily arrive, and I have been buying up presents for everyone, especially my darling new granddaughter, Caitlin Liliana Delaney. She is the most beautiful child ever born, or at least her parents and grandparents think so. I intend to hold and cuddle her the whole time she is here!

So much has happened in the last one and a half years, and I don't regret any of my decisions. If anything, I feel I have grown so much by coming here and meeting head on all my resentment and anger about this place and my childhood. I've opened myself up to the positive aspects of my life then and now, and I think I am the happiest and most content I have ever been. My family agrees. We have all grown closer through this project, especially Dan and I. So I am glad we returned to the scene of what my kids think was my misspent youth. I now believe I was very fortunate to grow up and have the childhood I did. I feel very blessed!

Photo by Janene Martellaro

Carmella Gates worked as a special education teacher, a regional educational consultant and a university professor before she retired to write over thirty "outstanding plays for kids eight to eighteen," available through her website classicacts.net. She continues to write and direct children's plays. Carmella holds a BA in History and Education from Framingham State College, and a Master's Degree from Boston College in Deaf-blindness. She grew up in Massachusetts and now lives with her husband in Parker, Colorado. Her daughter Meghan lives nearby.

Return to the Scene is her first novel. She is busy working on the second novel in the series, *Ghost Light*.

CPSIA information can be obtained at www.ICGtesting.com
Printed in the USA
LVOW07s0003010415

432796LV00002B/148/P